The City of the Discreet

# The City of the Discreet

*by*

## Pío Baroja

*Translated from the Spanish by*
Jacob Fassett Jnr.

Skomlin
House of Memory

# Skomlin
## House of Memory and Imagination
For more information visit *www.skomlin.com*

## A Skomlin Book
### Melbourne, Australia

First published in 1905.
First English version, London 1917
© Skomlin, 2017

ISBN: 978-0-6482521-3-9 *(paperback)*
ISBN: 978-0-6482521-4-6 *(eBook)*

 A catalogue record for this
book is available from the
National Library of Australia

The paper used in this publication meets the minimum requirements of ANSI/NISO Z39.48-1992 (R1997) (Permanence of Paper). The paper used in this book is from responsibly managed forests. Printed in the United States of America, the United Kingdom and Australia by Lightning Source, Inc.

# CHAPTER I

## A CONVERSATION ON THE TRAIN

QUENTIN awoke, opened his eyes, looked about him, and exclaimed between his yawns:

"We *must* be in Andalusia now."

The second-class coach was occupied by six persons. Opposite Quentin, a distinguished-looking Frenchman, corpulent, clean-shaven, and with a red ribbon in his buttonhole, was showing a magazine to a countryman in the garb of a wealthy cattle owner, and was graciously explaining the meanings of the illustrations to him.

The countryman listened to his explanations smiling mischievously, mumbling an occasional aside to himself in an undertone:

"What a simpleton."

Leaning against the shoulder of the Frenchman, dozed his wife—a faded woman with a freakish hat, ruddy cheeks, and large hands clutching a portfolio. The other persons were a bronze-coloured priest wrapped in a cloak, and two recently-married Andalusians who were whispering the sweetest of sweet nothings to each other.

"But haven't we reached Andalusia yet?" Quentin again inquired impatiently.

"Oh, yes!" replied the Frenchman. "The next station is Baeza."

"Baeza!—Impossible!"

"It *is*, never-the-less—It *is*," insisted the Frenchman, rolling his r's in the back of his throat. "I have been counting the stations."

Quentin arose, his hands thrust into his overcoat. The rain beat incessantly against the coach windows which were blurred by the moisture.

"I don't know my own country," he exclaimed aloud; and to see it better he opened the window and looked out.

The train was passing through a ruddy country spotted here and there with pools of rainwater. In the distance, small, low hills, shadowed by shrubs and thickets raised themselves into the cold, damp air.

"What weather!" he exclaimed in disgust, as he closed the window. "This is no land of mine!"

"Are you a Spaniard?" inquired the Frenchman.

"Yes, sir."

"I would have taken you for an Englishman."

"I have just left England, where I spent eight years."

"Are you from Andalusia?"

"From Cordova."

The Frenchman and his wife, who had awakened, studied Quentin. Surely his looks were not Spanish. Tall, stout, and clean-shaven, with a good complexion and brown hair, enveloped in a grey overcoat, and with a cap on his head; he looked like a young Englishman sent by his parents to tour the continent. He had a strong nose, thick lips, and the expression of a dignified and serious young man which a roguish, mischievous, and gipsy-like smile completely unmasked.

"My wife and I are going to Cordova," remarked the Frenchman as he pocketed his magazine.

Quentin bowed.

"It must be a most interesting city—is it not?"

"Indeed it is!"

"Charming women with silk dresses... on the balconies all day."

"No; not *all* day."

"And with cigarettes in their mouths, eh?"

"No."

"Ah! Don't Spanish women smoke?"

"Much less than French women."

"French women do not smoke, sir," said the woman somewhat indignantly.

"Oh! I've seen them in Paris!" exclaimed Quentin. "But you won't see any of them smoking in Cordova. You French people don't know us. You believe that all we Spaniards are toreadors, but it is not so."

"Ah! No, no! Pardon me!" replied the Frenchman, "we are very well acquainted with Spain. There are two Spains: one, which is that of the South, is Théophile Gautier's; the other, which is that of Hernani, is Victor Hugo's. But perhaps you don't know that Hernani is a Spanish city?"

"Yes, I know the place," said Quentin with aplomb, though never in his life had he heard any one mention the name of the tiny Basque village.

"A great city."

"Indeed it is."

Having made this remark, Quentin lit a cigarette, passed his hand along the blurred windowpane until he had made it transparent, and began to hum to himself as he contemplated the landscape. The humid, rainy weather had saddened the deserted fields. As far as one could see there were no hamlets, no villages—only here and there a dark farmhouse in the distance.

They passed abandoned stations, crossed huge olive groves with trees planted in rows in great squares on the ruddy hillsides. The train approached a broad and muddy river.

"The Guadalquivir?" inquired the Frenchman.

"I don't know," replied Quentin absently. Then, doubtless, this confession of ignorance seemed ill-advised, for he looked at the river as if he expected it to tell him its name, and added: "It is a tributary of the Guadalquivir."

"Ah! And what is its name?"

"I don't remember. I don't believe it has any."

The rain increased in violence. The country was slowly being converted into a mudhole. The older leaves of the wet olive trees shone a dark brown; the new ones glistened like metal. As the train slackened its speed, the rain seemed to grow more intense. One could hear the patter of the drops on the roof of the coach, and the water slid along the windows in broad gleaming bands.

At one of the stations, three husky young men climbed into the coach. Each wore a shawl, a broad-brimmed hat, a black sash, and a huge silver chain across his vest. They never ceased for an instant talking about mills, horses, women, gambling, and bulls.

"Those gentlemen," asked the Frenchman in an undertone, as he leaned over to Quentin, "What are they—toreadors?"

"No,—rich folk from hereabouts."

"Hidalgos, eh?"

"Pst! You shall see."

"They are talking a lot about gambling. One gambles a great deal in Andalusia, doesn't one?"

"Yes."

"I have heard some one say, that once a hidalgo was riding along on horseback, when he met a beggar. The horseman tossed him a silver coin, but the beggar, not wishing to accept it drew a pack of cards from among his rags and proposed a game to the hidalgo. He won the horse."

"Ha! Ha! Ha!" laughed Quentin boisterously.

"But isn't it true?" asked the Frenchman somewhat piqued.

"Perhaps—perhaps it is."

"What a simpleton!" murmured the countryman to himself.

"Isn't it true either, that all beggars have the right to use the 'Don'?"

"Yes, indeed, that's true enough," answered Quentin, smiling his gipsy smile.

The three husky youths in the shawls got off at the next station to Cordova. The sky cleared for an instant: up and down the platform walked men with broad-brimmed Andalusian hats, young women with flowers in their hair, old women with huge, red umbrellas....

"And those young men who just went by," asked the Frenchman, full of curiosity about everything, "each one carries his knife, eh?"

"Oh, yes!—Probably," said Quentin, unconsciously imitating his interlocutor's manner of speech.

"The knives they carry are very large?"

"The knives! Yes, very large."

"What might their dimensions be?"

"Two or three spans," asserted Quentin, to whom a span more or less mattered very little.

"And is it hard to manage that terrible weapon?"

"It has its difficulties."

"Do you know how?"

"Naturally. But the really difficult thing is to hit a mark with a knife at a distance of twenty or thirty metres."

"How do they do that?"

"Why, there's nothing much to it. You place the knife like this," and Quentin assumed that he had placed one in the palm of his hand, "and then you throw it with all your might. The knife flies like an arrow, and sticks wherever you wish."

"How horrible!"

"That is what we call 'painting a *jabeque* (a facial wound).'"

"A ca—a cha—a what?"

"*Jabeque.*"

"It is truly extraordinary," said the Frenchman, after attempting in vain to pronounce the guttural. "You have doubtless killed bulls also?"

"Oh! yes, indeed."

"But you are very young."

"Twenty-two."

"Didn't you tell me that you have been in England for eight years?"

"Yes."

"So you killed bulls when you were fourteen?"

"No... in my vacations."

"Ah! You came from England just for that?"

"Yes—for that, and to see my sweetheart."

The Frenchwoman smiled, and her husband said:

"Weren't you afraid?"

"Afraid of which?—The bulls, or my sweetheart?"

"Of both!" exclaimed the Frenchman, laughing heartily.

"What a simpleton!" reiterated the countryman, smiling, and looking at him as he would at a child.

"All you have to do with women and bulls to understand them," said Quentin, with the air of a consummate connoisseur, "is to know them. If the bull attacks you on the right, just step to the left, or *vice versa*."

"And if you don't have time to do that?" questioned the Frenchman rather anxiously.

"Then you may count yourself among the departed, and beg them to say a few masses for the salvation of your soul."

"It is frightful—And the ladies are very enthusiastic over a good toreador, eh?"

"Of course—on account of the profession."

"What do you mean by 'on account of the profession'?"

"Don't the ladies bully us?"

"That's true," said the countryman, smiling.

"And he who fights best," continued the Frenchman, "will have the doors of society opened to him?"

"Of course."

"What a strange country!"

"Pardon me," asked his wife, "but is it true that if a girl deceives her lover, he always kills her?"

"No, not always—sometimes—but he is not obliged to."

"And you—have you killed a sweetheart?" she inquired, consumed with curiosity.

"I!"—and Quentin hesitated as one loath to confess—"Not I."

"Ah!—Yes, yes!" insisted the Frenchwoman, "you have killed a sweetheart. One can see it in your face."

"My dear," said her husband, "do not press him: the Spaniards are too noble to talk about some things."

Quentin looked at the Frenchman and winked his eye confidentially, giving him to understand that he had divined the true cause of his reserve. Then he feigned a melancholy air to conceal the joy this farce afforded him. After that, he diverted himself by looking through the window.

"What a bore this weather is," he murmured.

He had always pictured his arrival at Cordova as taking place on a glorious day of golden sunshine, and instead, he was encountering despicable weather, damp, ugly, and sad.

"I suppose the same thing will happen to everything I have planned. Nothing turns out as you think it will. That, according to my schoolmate Harris, is an advantage. I'm not so sure. It is a matter for discussion."

This memory of his schoolmate made him think of Eton school.

"I wonder what they are doing there now?"

Absorbed in his memories, he continued to look out the window. As the train advanced, the country became more cultivated. Well-shaped horses with long tails were grazing in the pastures.

The travellers commenced to prepare their luggage for a quick descent from the train: Quentin put on his hat, stuffed his cap into his pocket, and placed his bag on the seat.

"Sir," said the Frenchman to him quickly, "I thank you for the information with which you have supplied me. I am Jules Matignon, professor of Spanish in Paris. I believe we shall see each other again in Cordova.'

"My name is Quentin García Roelas."

They shook hands, and waited for the train to stop: it was already slowing up as it neared the Cordova station.

They arrived; Quentin got off quickly, and crossed the platform, pursued by four or five porters. Confronting one of these who had a red handkerchief on his head, and handing him his bag and check, he ordered him to take them to his house.

"To the Calle de la Zapatería," he said. "To the store where they sell South American comestibles. Do you know where it is?"

"The house of Don *Rafaé?* Of course."

"Good."

This done, Quentin opened his umbrella, and began to make his way toward the centre of the city.

"It seems as though I hadn't crossed the Channel at all," he said to himself, "but were walking along one of those roads near the school. The same grey sky, the same mud, the same rain. Now I am about to see the parks and the river—"

But no—what he saw was the orange trees on the Victoria, laden with golden fruit glistening with raindrops.

"I'm beginning to be convinced that I am in Cordova," murmured Quentin, and he entered the Paseo del Gran Capitán, followed the Calle de Gondomar as far as Las Tendillas, whence, as easily as if he had passed through the streets but yesterday, he reached his house. He scarcely recognized it at first glance: the store no longer occupied two windows as before, but the whole front of the house. The doors were covered with zinc plates: only one of them having a window through which the interior could be seen full of sacks piled in rows.

Quentin mounted to the main floor and knocked several times: the door was opened to him, and he entered.

"Here I am!" he shouted, as he traversed a dark corridor. A door was heard to open, and the boy felt himself hugged and kissed again and again.

"Quentin!"

"Mother! But I can't see you in all this darkness."

"Come"—and his mother, with her arms about him, led him into a room. Bringing him to the light of a balcony window, she exclaimed: "How tall you are, my son! How tall, and how strong!"

"I've become a regular barbarian."

His mother embraced him again.

"Have you been well? But you will soon tell us all about it. Are you hungry? Do you want something to drink?—A cup of chocolate?"

"No, no—none of your chocolate. Something a bit more solid: ham, eggs…. I'm ferociously hungry."

"Good! I'll tell them to get your breakfast ready."

"Is everybody well?"

"Everybody. Come and see them."

They followed a narrow corridor and entered a room where two boys, aged fifteen and twelve respectively, had just finished dressing. Quentin embraced them none too effusively, and from the larger room they went into a bedroom, where a little girl between eight and nine years old was sleeping in a huge bed.

"Is that Dolores?" asked Quentin.

"Yes."

"The last time I saw her she was a tiny little thing. How pretty she is!"

The child awoke, and seeing a stranger before her, became frightened.

"But it's your brother Quentin, who has just arrived."

Her fears immediately allayed, she allowed herself to be kissed.

"Now we shall go and see your father."

"Very well," said Quentin reluctantly.

They left the bedroom, and at the end of the corridor, found themselves in a room in whose doorway swung a black screen with a glass panel.

"We'll wait a moment. He must have gone into the store," said his mother, as she seated herself upon the sofa.

Quentin absently examined the furnishings of the office: the large writing-desk full of little drawers; the safe with its gilt knobs; the books and letter-press lying upon a table near the window. Upon the wall opposite the screen hung two large, mud-coloured lithographs of Vesuvius in eruption. Between them was a large, hexagonal clock, and below it, a "perpetual" calendar of black cardboard, with three elliptic apertures set one above the other—the upper one for the date, the middle one for the month, and the lower one for the year.

Mother and son waited a moment, while the clock measured the time with a harsh *tick-tock*. Suddenly the screen opened, and a man entered the office. He was clean-shaven, elegantly dressed, with a full, pink face, and an aristocratic air.

"Here is Quentin," said his mother.

"Hello!" exclaimed the man, holding out his hand to the youth. "So you have arrived without notifying us in advance? How goes it in England?"

"Very well."

"I suppose you're quite a man now, ready to do something useful."

"I believe so," answered Quentin.

"I am glad—I am very glad to see you so changed."

At this point an elderly man entered the office. He was tall and thin, with a drooping grey moustache. He bowed low by way of a greeting, but Quentin's mother, nodding toward her son, said:

"Don't you know him, Palomares?"

"Whom, Doña Fuensanta?"

"This boy. It's Quentin."

"Quentin!" the old man fairly shouted. "So it is! My boy, how you have grown! You're a regular giant! Well, well! How do you like the English? They're a bad race, aren't they? They've done me many a bad turn! When did the boy come, Doña Fuensanta?"

"This very minute."

"Well—" said Quentin's father to Palomares.

"Come," announced his mother, "they have work to do."

"We shall have a little more time to talk later on at the table," said his father.

Mother and son left the office and made their way to the dining-room. Quentin sat at the table and ravenously devoured eggs, ham, rolls, a bit of cheese, and a plate of sweets.

"But you'll lose your appetite for dinner," warned his mother.

"*Ca!* I never lose my appetite. I could go right on eating," replied Quentin. Then, smacking his lips over the wine as he stuck his nose into the glass, he added: "What wine, mother! We didn't drink anythink like this at school."

"No?"

"I should say not!"

"Poor boy!"

Quentin, touched, cried:

"I was lonesome, oh, so lonesome over there for such a long time. And now... you won't love me as you do the others."—

"Yes, I shall—just the same. I've thought about you so much—" and the mother, again embracing her son, wept for a time upon his shoulder—overcome with emotion.

"Come, come, don't cry any more," said Quentin, and seizing her by her slender waist, he lifted her into the air as easily as if she had been a feather, and kissed her upon the cheek.

"What a brute! How strong you are!" she exclaimed, surprised and pleased.

Then they went over the house together. Some of the details demonstrated very clearly the economic stride the family had made the hall with its large mirrors, marble consoles, and French hearth, was luxuriously furnished: displayed in a cabinet in the dining-room, were a table-service of Sèvres porcelain, and dishes, tea-pots, and platters of repoussé silver.

"This table-service," said Quentin's mother, "we bought for a song from a ruined marquis. Every one of the dishes and platters had a crown and the marquis' initials painted on it—but between the three girls and me, we have rubbed them all off with pumice stone. It took us months."

After seeing the entire house, mother and son descended to the store. Here, the commercial ballast of the house was in evidence: heaped-up piles of sacks of all sorts separated by narrow aisles. The employés of the store came forward to greet Quentin; then he and his mother reclimbed the stairs and entered the house.

"Your room is all ready for you," said his mother. "We shall have dinner directly."

Quentin changed his clothes, washed, and presented himself in the dining-room, very much combed and brushed, and looking extremely handsome. His father, elegant in the whitest of collars, presided at the table: his mother distributed the food: the children were clean and tidy. A girl in a white apron served the meal.

Throughout the entire meal there existed a certain coldness, punctuated by long and vexatious moments of silence. Quentin was furious, and when the meal was finished, he arose immediately and went to his room.

"They have forgotten nothing here," he thought. "I don't believe I shall be able to stay in this house for any length of time."

His baggage had been brought to his room, so he devoted himself to unpacking his books, and to arranging them in a bookcase. It was still raining, and he had no desire to go out. It soon grew dark; for these were the shortest days of the year. He went down to the store, where he came upon Palomares, the old dependent of the house.

"How did you like England?" he was asked.

"Very much. It is a great country."

"But a bad race, eh?"

"*Ca,* man! Better than ours."

"Do you think so?"

"I certainly do."

"Maybe you're right. Have you seen the store?"

"Yes, this morning."

"We've made a great fight here, my boy. We have worked wonders—your mother most of all. When she's around, I can laugh at any other woman, no matter how clever she may be."

"Yes, she must be clever."

"Indeed she is! She is responsible for everything. When I used to go into the office upstairs, and turn the screws on the calendar, I thought 'Today we'll have the catastrophe'—but no, everything turned out well. I'm going upstairs for a while. Are you coming?"

"No."

Quentin seized an umbrella and took a stroll through the city. It was pouring rain; so, very much bored, he soon returned to the house.

His mother, Palomares, and all the children were playing Keno in the dining-room. They invited him to take part in the game, and although it did not impress him as particularly amusing, he had no choice but to accept. It was a source of much laughter and shouting when Quentin failed to understand the nicknames which Palomares gave to the numbers as he called them; for beside those that were common and already familiar to him, such as "the pretty little girl" for the 15, he had others that were more picturesque which he had to explain to Quentin. The 2, for example, was called "the little turkey-hen"; the 11, "the Catalonians' gallows"; the 6, "the clothier's rat"; the 22, "mother Irene's turkeys"; the 17, "the crooked *Maoliyo*." Among the nicknames, were some that were surprisingly fantastic; like the 10, which Palomares designated by calling "María Francisca, who goes to the theatre in dirty petticoats."

At the end of each game, Palomares took a tray with a glass of water on it, and said to the winner:

"You who have won behold your glass of water and your sugar-loaf: you who have lost," and he pointed to the loser, "go whence you came."

His fun was hailed with delight every time he went through the ceremony.

"Now tell us what you did in Chile," said one of the youngsters.

"No, no," said Quentin's mother. "You two boys must study now, and my little girl must go to bed."

They obeyed without a protest, and soon after, one could hear the buzzing of the two boys as they read their lesson aloud.

"Well," said Palomares, "I'm going to supper," and taking his cloak, he went out into the street.

Quentin's father came in, and they had supper. The evening meal had the same character as the dinner. As soon as they had finished dessert, Quentin arose and went to his room.

He climbed into bed, and amid the great confusion of images and recollections that crowded his brain, one idea always predominated: that he was not going to be able to live in that house.

# CHAPTER II

## O, ORIENTAL, ROMANTIC CITY!

ON the following day, Quentin awoke very early. An unusual sensation of heat and dryness penetrated his senses. He looked through the balcony window. The delicate, keen, somewhat lustreless light of morning glowed in the street. In the clear, pale sky, a few white clouds were drifting slowly.

Quentin dressed himself rapidly, left the house in which all were still sleeping, turned down the street, went through a narrow alley, crossed a plaza, followed a street, and then another and another, and soon found himself without knowledge as to his whereabouts.

"This is amusing," he murmured.

He was completely at sea. He did not even know on which side of the city he was.

This made him feel very gay; happily, and with a light heart, thinking of nothing in particular, but enjoying the soft, fresh air of the winter morning, he continued with real pleasure to lose himself in that labyrinth of alleys and passages—veritable crevices, shadow-filled....

The streets narrowed before him, and then widened until they formed little plazas: they were full of sinuous twists; they traced broken lines through the city. Water-spouts, terminating in wide-open dragon mouths, threatened each other from opposite eaves, and the two lines of tiled roofs, broken now and then by projecting bay-windows, and azoteas (flat roofs or terraces upon the house-tops), were so close together that the sky was reduced between them to a ribbon of blue—of a very pure blue.

When one narrow, white street came to an end, on either side there opened out others equally narrow, white, and silent.

Quentin never imagined that there could be so much solitude, so much light, so much mystery and silence. His eyes, accustomed to the filtered and opaque light of the North, were blinded by the reverberation of the walls. The air buzzed in his ears like a huge, sonorous sea-shell.

How different everything was! What a difference between this clear and limpid atmosphere, and that grey northern air: between the refulgent sun of Cordova, and the turbid light of the misty, blackened towns of England!

"This is a real sun," thought Quentin, "and not that thing in England that looks like a wafer stuck on brown paper."

In the plazoletas, white houses with green blinds, with their eaves shaded by tracings of blue paint, their intersecting angles twisted, and splashed with lime, sparkled and shone. And from the side of one of these sunbaked plazas, there started a narrow, damp, and sinuous alley, full of violet shadows.

Sometimes Quentin paused before sumptuous façades of old manorial houses. At the furthest end of the broad entrance, the wrought-iron flowers of the grating stood out against the brilliant clarity of a resplendent patio. That drowsy spot was surrounded by rows of arches, and jardinières were hung from the roofs of the corridors; while from a marble basin in the centre, a fountain of crystalline water plashed in the air.

In the houses of the rich, great plantain trees spread their enormous leaves, and cactus plants in green wooden pots, decorated the entrance. In some of the poorer houses, the patios could be seen overflowing with light at the end of very long and shadowy corridors.

The day was advancing: from time to time a figure wrapped in a cloak, or an old woman with a basket, or a girl with her hair down her back and an Andújar pitcher on her well-rounded hip, would pass quickly by, and suddenly, instantaneously, one or the other of them would disappear in the turn of an alley. An old woman was setting up a small table, on top of which, and upon some bits of paper, she was arranging coloured taffy.

Without realizing where he was going, Quentin came to the Mosque, and found himself before the wall facing an altar with a wooden shed, and a grating decorated with pots of flowers. On the altar was this sign:

*Si quieres que tu doior*
*se convierta en alegría,*
*no pasarás, pecador,*
*sin alabar a María.*

(If you wish your grief to be changed to joy, you will not pass by, O sinner, without first praising the Virgin Mary.)

Near the altar was an open gate, and through it, Quentin passed into the Patio de los Naranjos.

Above the archway of the entrance, the cathedral tower, broad, strong, and resplendent in the sun, raised itself toward heaven, standing out in clear and sharp silhouette in the pure and diaphanous morning air.

Now and then a woman crossed the patio. A prebendary, with cap and crimson mozetta, was walking slowly up and down in the sun, smoking, with his hands clasped behind his back. In the shelter of the Puerta del Perdón, two men were piling oranges. As Quentin neared the fountain, a little old man asked him solicitously:

"Do you wish to see the Mosque?"

"No, sir," replied Quentin pleasantly.

"The Alcázar?"

"No."

"The Tower?"

"No."

"Very well, Señorito, pardon me if I have molested you."

"Not at all."

When Quentin left the Patio de los Naranjos, he met the French couple of the train near the Triunfo column. M. Matignon hastened to greet him.

"Oh, what a town! What a town!" he cried. "Oh, my friend, what an extraordinary affair!"

"Why, what has happened to you?"

"A thousand things."

"Good or bad?"

"Both. Just fancy: last night as I was coming out of a house, and was about to enter my hotel, a man with a lantern in his hand, and a short pike, commenced to pursue me. I went into the hotel and locked myself in my room; but the man came into the hotel; I'm sure of it, I'm sure of it."

Quentin laughed, realizing that the man with the lantern and the short pike was a night watchman.

"Pay no attention to the man with the pike," said he. "If he sees you again and starts to follow you, look him straight in the eye, and say to him firmly: 'I have the key.' It is the magic word. As soon as he hears it, he will go away."

"Why?"

"Ah! That is a secret."

"How strange! One says to him, 'I have the key,' and he goes?"

"Yes."

"It is marvellous. Something else happened to me."

"What?"

"Last night we went to a café, and I left my stick upon a chair. When I went back after it, it was no longer there."

"Naturally! Some one carried it off."

"But that is not moral!" declared M. Matignon indignantly.

"No. We Spaniards have no morals," replied Quentin somewhat dejectedly.

"One cannot live without morality!"

"But we *do* live without it. With us, stealing a stick, or stabbing a friend are things of small importance."

"You cannot have order in that way."

"Of course not."

"Nor discipline."

"True."

"Nor society."

"Assuredly not: but here we live without those things."

M. Matignon shook his head sadly.

"Are you going to continue your walk?" he asked.

"Yes."

"We shall go with you if we won't be in your way."

"Come by all means."

Together the trio began to wander through that puzzling entanglement of alleys. The barrio, or district into which they penetrated (the vicinity of El Potro), was beginning to come to life. A few old women with sour-looking faces, some with mantles of Antequera baize, others with black mantillas, were on their way to mass, carrying folding chairs under their arms.

"Dueñas, eh?" said the Frenchman, pointing his finger at the old women. "But their ladies, where are they now?"

"Probably snoring at their ease," replied Quentin.

"But, do they snore?"

"Some of them, yes."

"Snore? What is that?" Madame Matignon inquired of her husband in French.

*"Ronfler,* my dear," said Matignon, *"ronfler."*

His wife made a disdainful little grimace.

When the gossips in the streets caught sight of the trio, they exchanged a jest or two from door to door. Servant girls were scrubbing the floors of the patios with mops, and singing gipsy songs; balcony windows flew open with a bang, as women came out to shake their rugs and carpets.

Grimy-looking men passed them, pushing carts and shouting: "Fish!" Vendors of medicinal herbs languidly cried their wares; and a muleteer, mounted upon the hindmost donkey of his herd, rode along singing to the tune of the tinkling bells on his decorated asses.

Once, behind a window-grating, they caught sight of a pallid, anæmic face with large, sad, black eyes, and a white flower stuck in the ebony hair.

"Oh! Oh!" cried Matignon, and immediately ran to the window.

The maiden, offended by his curiosity, pulled down the curtain, and went on embroidering or sewing, waiting for the handsome gallant, who perhaps never came.

"They are odalisques," declared the Frenchman rather spitefully.

In the doorways on some of the streets, they saw men working at turning lathes in the Moorish fashion, using a sort of bow, and helping themselves in their tasks with their feet.

Quentin, who was already tired of the walk and of the observations and comments of the Frenchman, announced his intention of leaving them.

"I would like to ask you a question first," said Matignon.

"Proceed."

"I wish to see an undertaking establishment." "An undairtaking estableeshment," the good man called it.

"There are none here," replied Quentin. "They are all far away; but if you should see a shop where they sell guitars, you may be pretty sure that that is where they make coffins, too."

"Can it be possible?"

"Yes. It's a Cordovese custom."

M. Matignon's mouth fell open in surprise.

"It is extraordinary!" he exclaimed when he had recovered from his astonishment, and he drew a memorandum book and a pencil from his pocket. "Where did this custom come from?"

"Oh! It is very ancient. The casket-makers here declared that they were loath to confine their efforts to sad things, so from the same wood out of which they make a coffin, they take a piece for a guitar."

"Admirable! Admirable! And they do not know that in France! What a philosophy is that of the casket-maker! O, Cordova, Cordova! How little thou art known in the world!"

Pío Baroja

At that moment, a tattered, bushy-haired vendor of sacred images crossed a very small plaza which contained a very large sign-post. Upon his white, matted hair he wore a greasy and dirty hat as large as a portico. His loose-fitting, long-sleeved cloak was worn wrong side to: the back across his breast, and the sleeves, knotted and bulky at the ends, falling down his back. Under his right arm he carried the saint, and in his belt was a cash-box with a slot for pennies.

"Pst! Silence!" said Quentin. "You are about to behold a most interesting spectacle."

"What is it?"

"Do you see that man?"

"Yes."

"I'll wager you cannot guess who he is?"

"No."

"The Bishop of Cordova!"

"The Bishop!"

"Yes, sir."

"But he hasn't the appearance of a bishop, nor even of a cleanly person."

"That doesn't matter. If you follow him cautiously, you will be able to see something very strange."

After he had said this, Quentin bowed to the couple, and walked rapidly away in the direction of his home.

# CHAPTER III

## INFANCY: SOMBRE VESTIBULE OF LIFE

ARCHÆOLOGISTS guard those curious, twice-written documents called palimpsests as carefully as though they were so much gold. They are parchments from which the first inscriptions were erased years and years ago, to be substituted by others. More recently, assiduous investigators have learned how to bring the erased characters to light, to decipher them, and to read them.

The idea of those strange documents came to Quentin's mind as he thought about his life.

Eight years of English school had apparently completely erased the memories of his early childhood. The uniformity of his school life, the continual sports, had dulled his memory. Night after night Quentin went to bed overcome with fatigue, with nothing to preoccupy his mind save his themes and his lessons; but his removal from the scholarly atmosphere, and his return to his home, had been sufficient to reawaken memories of his childhood—vaguely at first, but daily growing stronger, more distinct, and more detailed.

The erased inscription of the palimpsest was again becoming comprehensible: memories long dormant were crowding Quentin's mind: of these recollections, some were sad and gloomy; others, and these were very few, were gay; still others were not as yet very clear to him.

Quentin endeavoured to reconstruct his childhood. He remembered having passed it in a house on the Calle de Librerías, near the Calle de la Feria and the Cuesta de

Luján, and he went to see the place. It was on a corner of the street: a rose-coloured house with a silversmith's shop on the lower floor, two large and pretentious balconies on the main floor, and above them, two rectangular windows. On top of the roof, was a diminutive azotea surrounded by a rubble-stone wall.

"That is where I was as a child," said Quentin to himself.

He remembered vaguely that hedge-mustard used to grow between the slabs of the azotea, and that he had a white cat with which he used to play.

He peeped into the shop, and there came to his mind the picture of a man with white hair whom his mother tried to get him to kiss—something she never succeeded in doing.

"I must have been a little savage in those days," thought Quentin.

He strolled along the Calle de la Feria and recalled his escapades with the little boys of the vicinity of La Ribera and El Murallón where they used to play.

His memory did not flow smoothly. There were large gaps in it: persons, things, and places were blurred confusedly. His vivid recollections began in the Calle de la Zapatería, where his parents established their first shop. From there on, the incidents were linked together; they had an explanation, a conclusion.

Quentin was taken to school when he was very young—three or four years old—because he was in the way at the store. As a very small child he was distinguished as a dare-devil, a rowdy, and a swaggering boaster; and many times he returned from school with his trousers torn, or a black eye.

Once he had a fight with one of his schoolmates who came from a town called Cabra (Goat). For this reason, the others used to poke fun at him, calling him a "son of a goat," and making rude derivations from the name of his home town. Quentin was one of the most insulting, and one day the tormented lad answered him:

"You're a bigger son of a goat than I am, and your mother is living with a silversmith."

Quentin waited for his comrade to come out of school, and then punched his nose—only to be thrashed by his victim's older brother afterwards. This affair gave origin to a continual series of fights, and nearly every day Quentin was crippled by the beatings he received.

"Why, what's the matter with you?" his mother once asked.

"They told me at school that my mother was living with a silversmith."

"Who told you?"

"Everybody," replied Quentin with a frown.

"And what did you do?"

"Fought 'em all!"

His mother said nothing more, but she withdrew Quentin from that school and took him to another, which was presided over by a dominie, and attended by a couple of dozen children.

The dominie was a secularized monk by the name of Piñuela—an old fossil full of musty prejudices. He was a strong partisan of the ancient pedagogic principle, so much beloved by our ancestors, of "La letra con la sangre entra" (Learn by the sweat of thy brow).

Dominie Piñuela was a ridiculous and eccentric individual. His nose was large, coarse, and flaming red: his under lip hung down: his great eyes, turbid, and bulging from their sockets like two eggs, were always watery: he wore a long, tight-fitting frock coat, which was once

27

black, but now with the passage of time, covered with layers of dirt and grease and dandruff; narrow trousers, bagging loosely at the knees, and a black skull-cap.

Piñuela's only store of knowledge consisted of Latin, rhetoric, and writing. His system of instruction was based on the division of the class into two groups, Rome and Carthage, a book of translations, and a Latin Grammar. Besides these educational mediums, the secularized monk counted upon the aid of a ferrule, a whip, a long bamboo stick, and a small leather sack filled with bird-shot.

Piñuela taught writing by the Spanish method, with the letters ending in points. To do this one had to know how to cut and trim quill pens; and few there were who had the advantage of the Dominie in this art.

Besides this, Piñuela corrected the vicious pronunciation of his pupils; and in order to do so, he exaggerated his own by doubling his *z's* and *s's*. One of the selections of his readings began as follows: *Amanezzía; era la máss bella mañana de primafera* (Dawn was breaking; it was the most beautiful day of Spring): and all the children had to say "primafera" and "fida" unless they wished their lessons to be supplemented by a blow with the ferrule.

The Dominie walked constantly to and fro with his pen behind his ear. If he saw that a child was not studying, or had not pointed his letters sufficiently in his copy-book, according to the principles of Iturzaeta, he beat him with the stick, or threw the bag of shot at his head.

"Idling, eh?—Idling?" he would murmur, "I'll teach you to idle!"

For more serious occasions, the stupid Dominie had his whip; but nearly all of the parents warned him not to use it on their children—which for Piñuela was the plainest symptom of the decadence of the times.

At first Quentin felt the profoundest hate for the Dominie: he tormented him every time he could with unutterable joy; he broke his inkwells; he bored holes in his writing-desk; and Piñuela retaliated by boxing his ears. Between master and pupil there began to arise a certain ironical and joyous esteem by force of beatings from the one, and pranks from the other. They looked upon each other as faithful enemies; Quentin's mischief provoked laughter from Piñuela, and the Dominie's beatings wrested an ironical smile from Quentin.

Once the pupils saw Piñuela advancing with his pointer raised on high, and Quentin running, hiding behind tables, and throwing inkwells at the Dominie's head.

One day two old women were gossiping in the shop at home. They were two street vendors, one of whom was called Siete Tonos, on account of the seven different tones she used in crying her wares.

"They have hard luck with the little scamp. He's a wicked little devil," said one of them.

"Yes; he's not like his father," added the other.

"But El Pende isn't his father."

"Ah! Isn't he?"

"No."

Quentin waited for them to say more, but the clerk entered the store, and the gossips fell silent.

El Pende was the nickname of the man who passed for Quentin's father. The boy thought about the conversation of the two old gossips for a long time, and came to the conclusion that there had been something obscure about his birth. He was proud and haughty, and considered himself worthy of royal descent, so the idea of dishonour irritated him, and made him desperate.

29

One day his mother went to ask the Dominie how her son was behaving himself.

"How is he behaving himself?" cried Piñuela with ironic geniality. "Badly! Very badly! He's the worst boy in the class. A veritable dishonour to my school. He knows nothing about Latin, nor grammar, nor logic, nor anything. I'm sure that he doesn't even know how to decline *musa, musae.*"

"So you think he is no good at studying?"

"He is a rowdy, incapable of ever possessing the sublime language of Lacius."

His mother told her husband what Piñuela had said, and El Pende launched a sermon at Quentin.

"So this is the way you behave after the sacrifices we have made for you!"

Quentin did not reply to the charges they made against him, but when El Pende told him that if he continued his pranks he would throw him out of the house, the thought that was in Quentin's heart rushed to his lips.

"It makes no difference to me," he cried, "because you are not my father."

El Pende boxed the boy's ears; the mother wept; and that night Quentin left the house and roamed the fields half-starved, until Palomares, the clerk, found him and brought him to his parents.

The boy began to take notice of things, and made it plain to his mother that instead of studying Latin, he preferred to learn French and go to America, as a schoolmate of his—the son of a Swiss watch-maker—had done.

Accordingly they took him to the academy of a French *emigré*, a violent republican, who, at the same time that he taught his pupils to conjugate the verb *avoir*, spoke to them enthusiastically about Danton, Robespierre, and Hoche.

Perhaps this excited Quentin's imagination; perhaps it did not need to be excited; at any rate, one Sunday morning he decided to put into execution his great *projét de voyage*.

His mother was accustomed to hide the key to the cabinet where she kept her money under her pillow. While she was at mass, Quentin seized the key, opened the cabinet, stuffed the seventy dollars that he found there into his pocket, and a few minutes later was calmly increasing the distance between himself and his home.

Fifteen days after his escape he was apprehended in Cadiz just as he was about to set sail for America, and was brought back to Cordova in the custody of the *guardia civil*.

Then his mother took him to a monastery, but Quentin had made up his mind to run away from everything, so he attempted to escape several times. At the end of a month, the friars intimated that they did not wish to keep him any longer.

To the boys of his age, Quentin was now the prototype of wildness, impudence, and disobedience. People predicted an evil future for him.

At this point his mother said to him one day:

"We are going to a certain house. Kindly answer politely anything they may ask you there."

Quentin said nothing, but accompanied his mother to a palace on the Calle del Sol. They climbed some marble stairs, and entered a hall where a white-haired old man was sitting in a large, deep armchair, with a blond little girl who looked like an angel to Quentin, by his side.

"So this is the little scamp?" inquired the little old man with a smile.

"Sí, Señor Marqués," replied Quentin's mother.

"And what do you wish to do, my boy?" the Marquis asked him.

"I!—Get out of here as soon as I possibly can," replied Quentin in a dull voice.

"But, why?"

"Because I hate this town."

The little girl must have looked at him in horror; at least he supposed she did.

His mother and the old man chatted a while, and at last the latter exclaimed:

"Very well, my boy. You shall go to England. Get his baggage ready," he added, turning to the mother, "and let him go as soon as possible."

Quentin departed, making the journey sometimes in the company of others, sometimes alone, and entered Eton School, near Windsor. In a short time he had forgotten his entire former life.

In the English school the professor was not the enemy of the scholar, but rather one of his schoolmates. Quentin met boys as daring as he, and stronger than he, and he had to look alive. That school was something like a primitive forest where the strong devoured the weak, and conquered and abused them.

The brutality of the English education acted like a tonic upon Quentin, and made him athletic and good-humoured. The thing of paramount importance that he learned there, was that one must be strong and alert and calm in life, and ready to conquer always.

In the same way that he accepted this concept on account of the way it flattered him, he rejected the moral and sentimental concepts of his fellow-pupils and masters. Those young men of bulldog determination, valiant, strengthened by football and rowing, and nourished by underdone meat, were full of ridiculous conventions and respect for social class, for the hierarchy, and for authority.

In spite of the fact that he passed for an aristocrat and a son of a marquis in order to enjoy a certain prestige in the school, Quentin manifested a profound contempt for the principles his schoolmates held in such respect. He considered that authority, wigs, and ceremonies were grotesque, and consequently was looked upon as the worst kind of a poser.

He used to maintain, much to the stupefaction of his comrades, that he felt no enthusiasm for religion, nor for his native land; that not only would he not sacrifice himself for them, but he would not even give a farthing to save them. Moreover, he asserted that if he should ever become rich, he would prefer to owe his money to chance, rather than to constant effort on his part; and that to work, as the English did, that their wives might amuse themselves and live well, was absurd—for all their blond hair, their great beauty, and their flute-like voices.

A man with his ideas, and one, moreover, who followed women—even servant girls—in the street, and made complimentary remarks to them, could not be a *gentleman*, and for this reason, Quentin had no intimate friends. He was respected for his good fists, but enjoyed absolutely no esteem....

During his last years at school, his only real friend was an Italian teacher of music named Caravaglia. This man communicated to Quentin his enthusiasm for Bellini, Donizetti, Rossini, and Verdi. Caravaglia used to sit at the piano and sing. Quentin listened to him and was much softened by the music. The *Alma innamoratta* from *Lucia,* and *La cavattina* from *Hernani,* made him weep; but his greatest favourites, the songs that went straight to his heart, were the manly arias from the Italian operas like that in *Rigoletto,* that goes:

*La constanza teranna del core.*

This song, overflowing with arrogance, merry fanfaronade, indifference, and egoism, enchanted him.

On the other hand, to his psalm-singing comrades, this merry and swaggering music seemed worthy of the greatest contempt.

In the farewell banquet which Quentin gave to his four or five companions, and to the Italian professor, there were several toasts.

"I am not a Protestant," said Quentin at the last, somewhat befuddled with whiskey, "nor am I a Catholic. I am a Horatian. I believe in the wine of Falernus, and in Cécube and his wines of Calais. I also believe that we mortals must leave the task of calming the winds to the gods."

After this important declaration, nothing more is known, except the fact that the diners all fell asleep.

# CHAPTER IV

## BLUE EYES, BLACK EYES

"SEE here, Quentin," said his mother, "you ought to go and call on the Marquis."

"Very well," Quentin answered, "must I go today?"

"You'd better."

"Then I shall."

"Do you remember where he lives?"

"Yes, I think I can find the house."

"It's in the Calle del Sol; any one will point out the palace to you."

Quentin left the house, turned into the Plaza de la Corredera, and from the Calle del Poyo, by encircling a church, he came out upon the Calle de Santiago. It was a moderately warm day in January, with an overcast sky. A few drops of rain were falling.

Quentin was very much preoccupied by the visit he was about to make.

So far, he had not asked what relation he was to that man. Surely some relationship did exist; a bastard kinship; something defamatory to Quentin.

Sunk deep in these thoughts, Quentin wandered from his way, and was obliged to ask where the street was.

The palace of the Marquis of Tavera stood in a street in the lower part of town, which with different names for its different parts, stretched from the Plaza de San Pedro to the Campo de la Madre de Dios.

The Marquis' palace was extremely large. Five bay-windows, framed in thick moulding, with ornate iron-work and brass flower-pots, opened from a façade of a yellow, porous stone. On either side of the larger centre balcony, there rose two pilasters surmounted by a timpanum, in the middle of which was the half-obliterated carving of a shield. The decayed iron-work of the balustrade was twisted into complicated designs.

On the ground floor, four large gratings clawed the walls of the palace, and in the centre was a large opening closed by a massive door studded with nails, and topped by a fan-shaped window.

Before the palace, the street widened into a small-sized plaza. Quentin entered the wide entrance, and his footsteps resounded with a hollow sound.

Some distance ahead of him, through the iron bars of the grating at the end of a dark gallery, he could see a sunny garden; and that shady zone, terminating in such a brilliant spot of light, recalled the play of light and shade in the canvases of the old masters.

Quentin pulled a chain, and a bell rang in the distance with a solemn sound.

Several minutes elapsed without any one coming to the entry, and Quentin rang again.

A moment later the vivid sunlight of the distant garden, which shone like a square patch of light at the end of the shadowy corridor, was dimmed by the silhouette of a man who came forward until he reached and opened the grating. He was small in stature, and old, and wore overalls, an undershirt, and a broad-brimmed hat.

"What did you wish?" asked the old man.

"Is the Señor Marqués at home?"

"Sí, Señor."

"May I see him?"

"I don't know; ask upstairs." The old man opened the grating, and Quentin passed through.

Through a door on the right he could see a deserted patio. In the centre of it was a fountain formed by a bowl which spilled the water into a basin in six sparkling jets. On the left of the wide vestibule rose a monumental stairway made of black and white marble. The very high ceiling was covered with huge panels which were broken and decayed.

"Is this the way?" Quentin asked the old man, pointing to the stairway.

"Sí, Señor."

He climbed the stairs to the landing, and paused before a large, panelled, double door. In the centre of each half, he discerned two large and handsomely carved escutcheons. To the left of this door there was a window through which Quentin peeped.

"Oh, how beautiful!" he murmured in astonishment.

He saw a splendid garden, full of orange trees laden with fruit. In the open, the trees were tall and erect; against the walls they took the form of vines, climbing the high walls, and covering them with their dark green foliage.

A light rain was falling, and it was a wonderful sight to see the oranges glistening like balls of red and yellow gold among the dark, rain-soaked leaves. The glistening brilliancy of the foliage, and of the golden fruit, the grey sky, and the damp air created an extraordinary effect of exuberance and life.

Silence reigned in the shady garden. From time to time, from his hiding-place in a tree, some bird poured forth his sweet song. A pale yellow sunbeam struggled to illuminate the spot, and as it was reflected upon the wet leaves, it made them flash with a metallic brilliancy....

Above the opposite wall, rose the silhouette of a blackened and moss-covered belfry, surmounted by the figure of an angel. In the distance, over the house-tops, rose the dark sierra, partially hidden by bluish mists. These mists were moved about by the wind, and as they drifted along, or dissipated into the air, they disclosed several white orchards which heretofore had been concealed by the haze.

On the mountain-top, as the white penants of mist floated among the trees, they left tenuous filaments like those silver threads woven among the thorn bushes by lemures.

Quentin was gazing tirelessly upon the scene, when he heard footsteps behind him. He turned and saw a little girl of ten or twelve years, with her hair down her back.

"Good-afternoon," said the child with a marked Andalusian accent, as she came up to him.

Quentin removed his hat respectfully, and the child smiled.

"Have you rung?" she asked.

"No."

She rang the bell, and a large, over-grown servant girl opened the door and asked Quentin what he wanted.

"Give the Señor Marqués my card," he said, "and tell him that I have come to pay him my respects."

"Come in, Señor."

Quentin entered. He rather wished that the Marquis would not care to receive him, hoping in this way to avoid making a tiresome call, but his wish was not granted, for in a short time, the over-grown servant girl asked him to kindly follow her.

They traversed a gallery whose windows looked out

upon the patio of the fountain; then, after crossing two large, dark rooms, they came to a high-ceilinged hall panelled in leather, and with a red rug, tarnished by the years, upon the floor.

"Sit down, Señor; the master will be here directly," said the maid.

Quentin seated himself and began to examine the hall. It was large and rectangular, with three broad and widely-separated balcony windows looking out upon the garden. The room possessed an air of complete desolation. The painted walls from which the plaster had peeled off in places, were hung with life-size portraits of men in the uniforms and habiliments of nobility: in some of the pictures the canvas was torn; in others, the frames were eaten by moths: the great, rickety, leather-covered armchairs staggered under the touch of a hand upon their backs: two ancient pieces of tapestry with figures in relief, which concealed the doors, were full of large rents: on the panels in the ceiling, spiders wove their white webs: a very complicated seventeenth century clock, with pendulum and dial of copper, had ceased to run: the only things in that antique salon that were out of harmony, were the French fire-place in which some wood was burning, and a little gilt clock upon the marble mantel, which, like a good parvenu, impertinently called attention to itself.

When he had waited a moment, a curtain was pulled aside, and an old man, bent with age, entered the salon. He was followed by a little bow-legged hunchback, crosseyed, grey-haired, and dressed in black.

"Where is the boy?" asked the old man in a cracked voice.

"Right in front of you," replied the hunchback.

"Come closer!" exclaimed the Marquis, addressing Quentin. "I do not see very well."

Quentin approached him, and the old man seized his hand and looked at him very closely.

"Come, sit by me. Have you enjoyed good health at school?"

"Yes, Señor Marqués."

"Don't call me that," murmured the old man, patting Quentin's hand. "Have you learned to speak English?"

"Yes, sir."

"But, well?"

"I speak it as well as I do Spanish."

"English is very hard," said the hunchback, who had seated himself upon the floor. "Yes means yesca (tinder); *verigüel* means muy bien (very well), and as for the rest—when you can say, 'I catch, I go, I say'—you know English."

"Hush, Colmenares," said the Marquis, "don't be a fool."

"You're more of a fool than I am," replied the dwarf.

The old man, paying no attention to him, said to Quentin:

"I already know, I already know that you have not been up to any more foolishness."

The hunchback burst into noisy laughter.

"Then he doesn't belong to your family," he exclaimed, "because every one of your family, beginning with you, is a fool."

"Hush, buffoon, be quiet; I'll warm your ribs for you if you don't."

This threat from the lips of the sickly octogenarian, was absolutely absurd; but the hunchback appeared to take it in earnest, for he began to make faces and grin in silence.

"Oh, Colmenares," said the old man, "kindly call Rafaela, will you?"

"Very well."

The hunchback went out, leaving the Marquis and Quentin alone.

"Well, my boy, I have asked your mother about you very often. She told me that you were well, and that you were working hard. I am very glad to see you"—and again he pressed Quentin's hand between his own weak and trembling ones.

Quentin regarded the old man tenderly, without knowing what to say. At this moment, the hunchback returned, followed by a young lady and a little girl. The little girl was the one Quentin had greeted upon the stairs; the young lady was the same girl he had seen several years before—probably in that very same room.

Quentin rose to greet them.

"Rafaela," said the old man, addressing the older girl, "this boy is a relative of ours. I am not going to recall incidents that sadden me: the only thing I want is that you should know that you are related. Quentin will come here often, will you not?"

"Yes, sir," answered he, more and more astounded at the direction the interview was taking.

"Good. That is all."

At this point, the hunchback, clutching the Marquis by the sleeve, asked:

"Would you like me to play for you?"

"Yes, do."

The hunchback brought a small, lute-shaped guitar, drew up a tabouret, and sat at the feet of the Marquis. Then he began to pluck the strings with fingers as long and delicate as spiders' legs. He played a guitar march, and then, much to Quentin's astonishment, the old Marquis began to sing. He sang a patriotic song in a cracked voice. It was a very old one, and ended with the following stanza:

*Ay mi patria, patria mía,*
*y tambien de mi querida;*
*luchar valiente por patria y amor,*
*es el deber del guerrero español.*

(Ah, my country, country of mine, and also of my sweetheart; to fight for country and love, is the duty of the Spanish warrior.)

When the old man had finished the song, his grand-daughters embraced him, and he smiled most contentedly.

Quentin felt as though he had been transported to another century. The shabby house, the old Marquis, the buffoon, the beautiful girls—everything seemed unusual.

The two sisters were pretty; Rafaela, the older sister, was extremely attractive. Some twenty-three or twenty-four years of age, she had clear, blue eyes—eyes the colour of pale blue satin—blond hair, a straight nose, and an enchanting smile. Lacking the freshness of her first youth, there was a suspicion of marcidity in her face, which, perhaps, enhanced her attractiveness.

The face of Remedios, the child, was less symmetrical, but more positive: she had large, black eyes, and an expression of mixed audacity, childishness, and arrogance. Now and then she smiled silently and mischievously.

When Quentin felt that he had stayed long enough, he rose, gave his hand to the two girls, and hesitantly approached the old man, who threw his arms about his neck and tearfully embraced him.

He saluted the hunchback with a nod of his head which was scarcely answered; descended the stairs, and upon reaching the vestibule, the man who had let him in, asked:

"Excuse me, Señor, but are you the man who got back from England a little while ago?"

"Yes."

"That's what I thought. Are you going to stay in Cordova?"

"I believe so."

"Then we shall see you?"

"Yes, I shall call from time to time."

The two men shook hands, and Quentin stepped into the street.

"The old man is my grandfather," said Quentin, "that's *just* what he is. His emotion, his harrowed look—that's *just* what he is."

Perhaps the best thing to do would be to ask his mother exactly what the circumstances of his birth were; but he feared to offend her.

He soon forgot about that, and began to think about the blond-haired girl Rafaela. She was pretty. Indeed she was! Her clear, soft eyes; her pleasant smile; and above all, her opaque voice had gone straight to Quentin's heart: but as Quentin was not a dreamer, but a Bœotian, a Horatian, as he himself had remarked, he associated with Rafaela's soft, blue eyes, the ancestral home, the beautiful garden, and the wealth which her family must still possess.

Quentin devoted the days following this visit to cogitating upon this point.

Rafaela was an admirable prize—pretty, pleasant, and

aristocratic. He must attempt the conquest. True, he was an illegitimate child. He had a desire to laugh at that thought, it seemed so operatic to him: now he could sing the aria from *Il Trovatore:*

*Deserto sulla terra.*

Bastard or no bastard, he considered that the thing was possible. He was tall, handsome, and above all, strong. In Eton, he had noticed that after all, the greatest attraction in a man for women is strength.

They said that the Marquis' house was going to ruin: he would save it from ruin and restore it splendidly. Then—into the street with those who got in his way! It was a great plan.

Truly, Rafaela was an admirable prize. To marry her, and live in that sumptuous house with the two sisters until the place was completely repaired, would be a life indeed! He would write his school friends and tell them about his marriage to an Andalusian descendant of the Cid, and describe the patios filled with orange trees.... Then he could say with his poet: "Let them serve us quickly this bottle of Falernus in the neighbouring gorge." After that... then came new chapters, as yet scarcely outlined in his imagination....

He would represent himself from the very first as a romanticist, an idealist, a scorner of the impurities of reality. He would manifest a respectful enthusiasm for her, like that of a man who dares not even dream of so much felicity.

"You'll win, Quentin, you'll win," he said to himself joyously. "What do you desire? To live well, to have a beautiful home, not to work. Is that a crime, forsooth? And if it were a crime, then what? They do not carry one off to jail for that. No. You are a good Bœotian, a good swine in the herd of Epicurus. You were not born for

the base bodily wants of a merchant. Dissemble a little,
my son, dissemble a little. Why not? Fortunately for you,
you are a great faker."

# CHAPTER V

## NOBLE AND ANCIENT ANCESTRAL HOMES!

A WEEK later, on a rainy day which recalled that of his first visit, Quentin approached the palace. In spite of his Epicureanism and his Bœotianism, he dared not enter; he passed by without stopping until he reached the Campo de la Madre de Dios.

He leaned over the railing on the river bank. The Guadalquivir was muddy, clay-coloured: some fishermen in black boats were casting their nets near the Martos dam and mill: others, with poles, perched upon the rocks of the Murallón, were patiently waiting for the shad to bite.

Quentin returned to the Calle del Sol disgusted with his weakness, but as soon as he reached the house, his energy again disappeared. Fortunately for him, the man who had opened the gate for him a few days before was seated on a stone bench in the vestibule.

"Good-afternoon," said Quentin.

"Good-afternoon, Señor. Did you come to see the Marquis?"

"No; I was just out for a walk."

"Won't you come in?"

"Very well, I'll come in for a while."

The old man opened the gate, shut it again, and they went down the long gallery. At the end of it, after climbing two steps, they came into the garden. It was large and beautiful: the walls were hidden by the fan-shaped foliage of the orange and lemon trees. Close-trimmed myrtles lined the walks, and underfoot, yellow and green moss carpeted the stones.

"I have taken care of this garden for fifty years," said the man.

"*Caramba!*"

"Yes; I began to work here when I was eight or ten years old. It is rather neglected now, for I can't do much any more."

"Why are those orange trees in the centre so tall?"

"Orange trees grow taller when they are shut in like that than they do in the country," answered the gardener.

"And what do you do with so many oranges?"

"The master gives them away."

At one end of the garden was a rectangular pool. On one of its long sides rose a granite pedestal adorned with large, unpolished urns which were reflected in the greenish and motionless water.

Quentin was contemplating the tranquil water of the pool, when he heard the halting notes of a Czerny étude on the piano.

"Who is playing?" he asked.

"Señorita Rafaela, who is giving her sister a lesson. Why don't you go up?"

"Why, I think I shall."

And with throbbing heart, Quentin left the garden and climbed the stairs. He rang, and a tall, dried-up maid led him through several rooms until he reached one in which Remedios was playing the piano while Rafaela, just behind her, was beating time upon an open book of music.

An old woman servant was sewing by the balcony window.

Quentin greeted the two sisters, and Rafaela said to him:

"You haven't been here for several days! Grandfather has asked for you again and again."

"Really?" asked Quentin idiotically.

"Yes, many times."

"I couldn't come; and besides, I was afraid I would be an annoyance, that I would bother you."

"For goodness' sake!"

"Well, you see you have already stopped the lesson on my account."

"No; we were just about to finish anyway," said Remedios. "Go on," she added, turning to Rafaela, "why don't you play for us?"

"Oh! Some other day."

"No. Do play," urged Quentin.

"What would you like me to play?"

"Anything you like."

Rafaela took a book, placed it on the rack, and opened it.

Quentin could read the word *Mozart* upon the cover. He listened to the sonata in silence: he did not know very much about classical music, and while the girl played, he was thinking about the most appropriate exclamation to make when she had finished.

"Oh! Fine! Fine!" he exclaimed. "Whose is that delicious music?"

"It is Mozart's," replied Rafaela.

"It's admirable! Admirable!"

"Don't you play the piano, Quentin?"

"Oh, very little. Just enough to accompany myself when I sing."

"Ah! Then you sing?"

"I used to sing a little in school; but I have a poor voice, and I use it badly."

"Very well, sing for us; if you do it badly, we'll tell you," said Rafaela.

"Yes, sing—do sing!" exclaimed Remedios.

Quentin sat down at the piano and played the introductory chords of Count di Luna's aria in *Il Trovatore:*

*Il balen del suo sorriso*
*d'una stella vince al raggio.*

Then he began to sing in a rich, baritone voice, and as he reached the end of the *romanza*, he imparted an expression of profound melancholy to it:

*Ah l'amor, l'amore ond' ardo*
*le favelli in mio favor*
*sperda il sole d'un suo sguardo*
*la tempesta, ah!… la tempesta del mio cor.*

And he repeated the phrase with an accent that was more and more expressive. Any one listening to him would have said that truly, *la tempesta* was playing havoc with his heart.

"Very good! Very good!" cried Rafaela. Remedios applauded gleefully.

"It's going to rain," announced the old woman servant as she glanced at the sky.

"That's because I did so badly," said Quentin with a smile.

They went to the window. The sky was darkening; it was beginning to rain. The heavy drops fell in oblique lines and glistened on the green leaves of the orange trees, and on the moss-covered tiles; the continuous splashing of the drops in the pool, made it look as if it were boiling….

The rain soon ceased, the sun came out, and the whole garden glowed like a red-hot coal; the oranges shone among the damp foliage; the green hedge-mustard spotted the glittering grey roof tiles with its gay note; water poured from the dark, ancient belfry of a near-by tower; and several white gardens smiled upon the mountain side.

"That is a regular gipsy sun," lisped Remedios, who at times had an exaggerated Andalusian pronunciation.

Quentin laughed; the little girl's manner of speech amused him immensely.

"Don't laugh," said Rafaela to Quentin with mock gravity; "my little girl is very sensitive."

"What did you say to him?" demanded Remedios of her sister.

"Oh, you rascal! He's heard it, now," Rafaela exclaimed humorously; and seizing the child about the waist, she kissed the back of her neck.

It was beginning to clear up; the dark clouds were moving off, leaving the sky clear; a ray of sunshine struck a tower formed by three arches set one above the other. In the three spaces, they could see the motionless bells; a figure of San Rafael spread its wings from the peak of the roof.

"What is that figure?" asked Quentin.

"It belongs to the church of San Pedro," replied the servant.

"Is it hollow like a weather-vane?"

"No; I think it is solid."

"It's stopped raining now," said Remedios. "Have you seen the house yet," she added, turning to Quentin, and using the familiar second person.

"No," he replied.

"She uses 'thou' to everybody," explained Rafaela.

They left the music-room, and in the next room, they showed Quentin various mirrors with bevelled edges, a glass cabinet full of miniatures with carved frames and antique necklaces, two escritoires inlaid with mother-of-pearl, bright-coloured majolica ware, and pier-glasses with thick plates.

"It is my mother's room," said Rafaela; "we've kept it exactly as it was when she was alive."

"Did she die very long ago?"

"Six years ago."

"Come on," said Remedios, seizing him by the hand, and looking into her sister's face with her great, restless eyes.

The three descended the stairs and traversed the gallery that connected the vestibule with the garden. On either side of them were an infinite number of rooms; some large and dark, with wardrobes and furniture pushed against the walls; others were small, with steps leading up to them. At the end of the gallery were the stables, extremely large, with barred windows. They entered.

"Now you'll see what kind of a horse we have here," said Rafaela. "Pajarito! Pajarito!" she called, and a little donkey which was eating hay in a corner came running up.

In the same stable was an enormous coach, painted yellow, very ornate, with several very small windows, and the family coat-of-arms on the doors.

"Grandfather used to ride in this coach," said Rafaela.

"It must have taken more than two horses to draw it."

"Yes; they used eight."

"These girls are admirably stoical," thought Quentin.

After the stables, they saw the corrals, and the cellar, which was huge, with enormous rain-water jars that looked like giants buried in the ground.

"We can't go in there," said Rafaela ironically.

"Why not?"

"Because this little idiot," and she seized her sister, "is afraid of the jars."

Remedios made no reply; they went on; through crooked passages that were full of hiding-places, and labyrinthic corridors, until they came to a large, abandoned garden.

"Would you like to go in?" Rafaela asked Remedios.

"Yes."

"Aren't you afraid of the genet any more?"

"No."

"What is it?" inquired Quentin.

"The gardener keeps a caged animal in here, and it frightens us because it looks like such a monster."

"You're a naughty girl," said Remedios to her sister. "What will you bet that I won't go to the genet, take it out of the cage, and hold it in my hand?"

"No, no; he might bite you."

"Where is this monster?" asked Quentin.

"You'll soon see."

It was a specie of weasel with a long tail and a fierce eye.

"The animal certainly has an evil look," said Quentin.

They walked about the abandoned garden: a thick carpet of burdock and henbane and foxglove and nettles covered the soil. In the middle of the garden, surrounded by a circle of myrtles, was a summer-house with a decayed door; inside of it they could see remnants of paint and gilt. On the old wall, was a tangled growth of ivy. Enveloped in its foliage, and close to the wall, they could make out a fountain with a Medusa head, through a dirty pipe in whose mouth flowed a crystalline thread which fell sonorously into a square basin brimful of water. There were two broad, moss-covered steps leading up to the fountain, and the weeds and wild figs, growing in the cracks, were lifting up the stones. From among the weeds there rose a marble pedestal; and a wild-orange tree near by, with its little red fruit, seemed spotted with blood.

"There are all sorts of animals here in the summer," said Rafaela. "Lizards come to drink at the fountain. Some of them are very beautiful with their iridescent heads."

"They are woman's enemies," warned Remedios.

Quentin laughed.

"Some of the foolishness the servant girls tell her," explained Rafaela. "I've forbidden them to tell her anything now."

The three returned to the corridor.

"What about the roof? We haven't showed him the roof," said the little girl.

"Juan must have the key; I'll go and ask him for it."

Remedios ran out in search of the gardener, and returned immediately.

They climbed the main stairs until they reached a door near the roof.

"What panels!" exclaimed Quentin.

"They are full of bats," said Rafaela.

"And thalamanderth,' lisped Remedios.

53

Quentin suppressed a smile.

"How funny! How very funny!" murmured the child somewhat piqued.

"I am not laughing at what you said," replied Quentin, "I was just remembering that that is the way we boys used to talk."

"She talks like the rowdies in the streets," said Rafaela.

"Well, I don't want anything more from you," cried Remedios. "You're always saying things to me."

"Come, girlie, come; the genet isn't coming here to eat you."

"He couldn't."

From the door, and through a corridor, they came out upon a broad, tiled terrace with an iron railing.

"Let's go up higher," said Remedios.

They climbed a winding staircase inside a tower until they came out upon a small azotea, whence they could command a view of nearly the entire city.

The wind was blowing strongly. From that height, they could see Cordova, a great pile of grey roofs and white walls, between which they could make out the alleys, which looked like crooked lines inundated with light. Sierra Morena appeared in the background like a dark wave, and its round peaks were outlined in a gentle undulation against the sky, which was cloudless. The gardens stood out very white against the skirts of the mountain, and upon a sharp-pointed hill at the foot of the dark mountain wall, stood a rocky castle.

Toward Cordova la Vieja, pastures glistened, a luminous green; in the country, the sown ground stretched out until it was lost in the distance, interrupted here and there by some brown little hill covered with olive trees.

"I'm going to fetch the telescope," announced Remedios suddenly.

"Don't fall," warned her sister.

"*Ca!*"

Rafaela and Quentin were left alone.

"How charming your sister is," said he.

"Yes; she's as clever as a squirrel, but more sensitive than any one I know. The slightest thing offends her."

"Perhaps you have petted her too much?"

"Of course. I am years older than she. She is like a daughter to me."

"You must be very fond of her."

"Yes; I put her to bed and to sleep even yet. Sometimes she has fits of temper over nothing at all! But she has a heart of gold."

At this point the little girl returned, carrying a telescope bigger than she was.

"What a tiny girl!" exclaimed Rafaela, taking the telescope from Remedios.

They rested the instrument on the wall of the azotea and took turns looking through it.


The afternoon was steadily advancing; yellow towers and pink belfries rose above the wet roofs, their glass windows brilliant in the last rays of the setting sun; a broad, slate-covered cupola outlined its bulk against the horizon; here and there a cypress rose like a black pyramid between great, white walls, and the thousands of grey tiled roofs; and the iron weather-vanes, some in the shape of a peaceable San Rafael, others in the form of a rampant dragon with fierce claws and pointed tongue, surmounted the gables and sheds, and decorated the ancient belfries, covered with a greenish rust by the sun of centuries....

Toward the west, the sky was touched with rose; flaming clouds sailed over the mountain. The sun had set; the fire of the clouds changed to scarlet, to mother-of-pearl, to cold ashes. Black night already lurked in the city and in the fields. The wind commenced to murmur in the trees, shaking the window blinds and curtains, and rapidly drying the roofs. A bell clanged, and its solemn sound filled the silent atmosphere.

Slowly the sky was invaded by a deep blue, dark purple in some places; Jupiter shone from his great height with a silver light, and night took possession of the land; a clear, starry night, that seemed the pale continuation of the twilight.

From the house garden arose a fresh perfume of myrtles and oranges; of the exhalations of plants and damp earth.

"We must go now," said Rafaela. "It's getting cold."

They descended the stairs. Quentin took leave of the two girls and stepped into the street.

## CHAPTER VI

### CONCERNING AN ADVENTURE OF QUENTIN'S IN
### THE NEIGHBOURHOOD OF EL POTRO

FOR a whole week Quentin walked through the Calle del Sol day and night, hoping to see Rafaela without going to her house. It did not seem expedient to him to call again so soon; he was afraid of being considered inopportune; and he would have liked it had chance—more apparent than real—granted him a meeting with Rafaela while he was strolling about the neighbourhood of the palace.

One warm night in January, Quentin left his house with the intention of walking by the palace in the Calle del Sol.

It was a beautiful, serene night, without a breath of air stirring. The great, round face of the moon was shining high overhead, its light dividing the streets into two zones—one white, and the other bluish black.

Some of the plazas seemed covered with snow, so white were the walls of the houses and the stones of the pavements.

Absently strolling along, Quentin approached the Mosque; its walls rose as solemn and black as those of a fortress; above their serrated battlements, the moon floated giddily in the deep, veiled blue of the sky.

"All this contains something of the stuff that dreams are made of," he thought.

No one was passing there, and his footsteps echoed loudly on the pavement.

Quentin started toward El Potro in order to reach the Calle del Sol, which was nearly at the other end of the town, and he was thinking of the thousand and one possibilities, both for and against his plans, when a little hunchback boy came running up to him, and said:

"A little alms, Señorito, my mother and I have nothing to eat."

"You come out at this time of night to ask alms!" murmured Quentin. "You'll have a fine time finding any people here."

"But my mother has fainted."

"Where is she?"

"Here, in this street."

Quentin entered a dark alley, and had no sooner done so, than he felt himself seized by his arms and legs, and tied by his elbows, and then blind-folded with a hand-kerchief.

"What's this? What do you want of me?" he exclaimed, trying vainly to disengage himself. "I'll give you all the money I have."

"Shut up," said a gruff voice with a gipsy accent, "and come with us—Somebody wants to settle a little account with you."

"With me! Nobody has any accounts to settle with me."

"Be quiet, my friend, and let's be going."

"Very well; but take off the handkerchief; I'll go wherever you tell me to."

"It can't be done."

When Quentin found that he was overpowered, he felt the blood rush to his head with anger. He began to stumble along. When he had gone about twenty paces, he stopped.

"I said that I would go wherever he is."

"No, Señor."

Quentin settled himself firmly on his left leg, and with his right, kicked in the direction whence he had heard the voice. There was a dull thud as a body struck the ground.

"Ay! Ay!" groaned a voice. "He hit me on the hip. Ay!"

"You'll either go on, or I'll knock your brains out," said the gipsy's voice.

"But why don't you take off this handkerchief?" vociferated Quentin.

"In a minute."

Quentin went on stumblingly, and they made several turns. He was not sufficiently acquainted with the streets near El Potro to get his bearings as he went along. After a quarter of an hour had elapsed, the gipsies stopped and made Quentin enter the door of a house.

"Here's your man," said the voice of the gipsy.

"Good," said a vigorous and haughty voice. "Turn him loose."

"He wounded Mochuelo bad," added the gipsy.

"Was he armed?"

"No, but he gave him a kick that smashed him."

"Good. Take off the handkerchief so we can see each other face to face."

Quentin felt them remove his bandage, and found himself in a patio before a pale, blond, little man, with a decisive manner, and a calañés hat on his head. The moonlight illuminated the patio; jardinières and flower-pots hung upon the walls; and overhead, in the space between the roofs, gleamed the milky veil of the blue night sky.

"Whom have you brought me?" exclaimed the little man. "This isn't the sergeant."

"Well! So it isn't! We must have made a mistake."

"You are lucky to have escaped, my friend," exclaimed the little man, turning to Quentin. "If you had been the sergeant, they would have had to pick you up in pieces."

"Bah! It wouldn't be that bad," said Quentin as he gazed in disgust at the boastful little man.

"Wouldn't it?"

"Of course not."

"Do you know to whom you are speaking?"

"No; and the most curious thing about it is that I don't care. Still, if you want us two to fight it out alone, come with me, and we'll see if it is your turn to win or to lose."

"I never lose, young man."

"Neither do I," replied Quentin.

"We'll have to give this lad a lesson," said the gipsy, "to teach him how to talk to quality folk."

"Be quiet, Cantarote," said the little man in the calañés. "This gentleman is a man, and talks like a man, and we are going to drink a few glasses this very minute to celebrate our meeting."

"That's the way to talk," said Quentin.

"Well, come on. This way, please."

Quentin followed the little fellow through a small door and down three or four steps to a corridor, through which they reached a dark cellar. It was dimly lighted by several lamps which hung on wires from the ceiling. Seated upon benches about a long, greasy table, were gathered a dozen or so persons, of whom the majority were playing cards, and the rest drinking and chatting. Upon entering the cellar, Quentin and the little man in the calañés made their way to a small table, and sat down facing each other. The blackened lamp, hanging by a wire from a beam in the ceiling, distilled a greenish oil drop by drop, which fell upon the greasy table.

The little man ordered the innkeeper to bring two glasses of white wine, and while they waited, Quentin observed him closely. He was a blond individual, pale, with blue eyes, and slender, well-kept hands. To Quentin's scrutinizing glance, he responded with another, cool and clear, without flinching.

At this point, a queer, ugly-looking man who was talking impetuously, and showing huge, yellow, horselike teeth, came toward the table and said to Quentin's companion:

"Who is this bird, Señor José?"

"This 'bird,'" replied the other, "is a hard-headed bull—understand?—The best there is."

"Well, that's better."

Quentin smiled as he gazed at the man who had called him a bird. He was an individual of indefinite age, clean-shaven, a mixture of a barber and a sacristan, with a forehead so low that his hair served him as eyebrows, and with a jaw like a monkey's.

"And this chap, who is he?" asked Quentin in turn.

"He? He is one of the most shameless fellows in the world. He wanders about these parts to see if they won't give him a few pennies. Though he is old and musty, you will always find him with sporting women and happy-go-lucky folk. Ask any one in Cordova about Currito Martín, and no matter where you are, they can tell you who he is."

"Not everywhere, Señor José," replied Currito, who

had listened impassively to the panegyric, gesticulating with a hand whose fingers resembled vine-creepers. "If you should ask the Bishop, he would not know me."

"Well, I would have taken him for a sacristan," said Quentin.

"I'm a sacristan of blackbirds and martens, if you must know," said Currito somewhat piqued. "The only places where I am known are the taverns, the huts in the Calle de la Feria, and the Higuerilla."

"And that's enough," said one of the card-players.

"That's right."

Two of the onlookers got up from the bench and began to chaff Currito. The sly rascal was at home among jests, and he answered the repartee that they directed at him with great impudence.

"That's a fine amber cigarette-holder, Currito," said one of them.

"The Marquis," he replied.

"A fine little cape, old boy," said the other, turning over the muffler of the scoundrel's cloak.

"The Marquis," he repeated.

"This Currito," said Señor José, "hasn't an ounce of shame in him; for a long time he has lived on his wife, who is kept by a marquis, and he has the nerve to brag about it. Come here, Currito."

Currito came to their table.

"Why do you keep boasting about your shame?" asked Señor José. "Don't you do it again in front of me. Do you understand? If you do, I'll skin you alive."

"Very well, Señor José."

"Come, have a glass, and then see if La Generosa is in any of the rooms here."

Currito emptied the wine-glass, wiped his mouth on the back of his hand, and left the cellar.

"Are you a foreigner?" Señor José asked Quentin.

"I was educated outside of Spain."

"Will you be in Cordova for some time?"

"I think so."

"Well, I'm glad, because I like you."

"Many thanks."

"I'll tell you who I am, and if after that, it doesn't seem a bad idea to you, we'll be friends."

"Before, too."

"No, not before. I am Pacheco, the horseman, or rather Pacheco, the bandit. Now, if you care to be Pacheco's friend, here's my hand."

"Here is mine."

"Well, you're a brave chap," exclaimed Pacheco. "That's the way I like to have a fellow act. Listen: any time you need me, you will find me here, in El Cuervo's tavern. Now let's see what these lads are talking about."

Pacheco got up, and followed by Quentin, went over to the card-players' table.

"Hello, Pajarote!" said Pacheco to the banker.

"Hello, Señor José! Were you here? I didn't see you."

"What's doing in Seville and the low country?"

"Nothing.... It's pretty slow. Everything is closed by hunger and poverty, and here I am with these thieves who would even steal a man's breath.... Why, I'm beginning to lose faith ever in San Rafael himself."

"Now you've spoiled my luck, comrade," said one of the players, throwing down his cards angrily. "What business did you have ringing in that angel? Look here, I'm not going to play any more."

Pajarote smiled. He was a scoundrel and a card sharp, and he always took delight in pretending to be unlucky while he was cleaning his friends of their money. He dealt the cards.

"I'll bet," said a man with one eye higher than the other whom they called Charpaneja, in the thin voice of a hunchback.

"I'll bet six," gruffly replied a charcoal-burner nicknamed El Torrezno.

More cards were tossed upon the table, and, as before, Pajarote won.

"I don't want to play," squeaked Charpaneja.

"Why not?" asked the banker.

"Because your hands are always lucky."

"The fact is, you haven't any spirit," replied Pajarote coldly. "You start out like a Cordovese colt, and quit like a donkey of La Mancha."

At this point Currito returned, and coming up to Señor José, said:

"La Generosa hasn't come yet, but Señora Rosario with her two girls, and Don Gil Sabadía are in the next room."

"Well, let's go in," said Pacheco.

He and Quentin again came out into the patio, and entered a room illuminated by a brass lamp set upon a round table. By the light of the lamp he could see a frightful-looking old woman with a hooked nose and moles on her chin, two young girls with flowers in their hair, and a bushy-haired old man with a long beard.

"The peace of God be with you," said Pacheco as he entered. "How is Don Gil? Good evening, Señora Rosario; what's the news?"

"Nothing: we just came here so these girls could have a drink of something."

"You mean these rosebuds," interrupted Currito.

"Thanks, Currito," said one of the girls with a smile.

"Child!" exclaimed Pacheco, "be very careful of Currito, for he's dangerous."

"He!" replied the old woman, "he is already among the down-and-outs."

"I'm like the old guide in the Mosque," replied Currito. "Every time he saw me, he used to say, 'Let me have an old suit of clothes—I'm more dead than alive.'"

"Heavens! What little wit you have!" said one of the girls with a gesture of contempt.

"Well, I live by my wits, my girl," answered Currito, piqued.

"Then, confound them, my man," she replied with the same gesture of contempt.

Currito peevishly fell silent, and Pacheco presented Quentin to the bushy-haired man.

"This gentleman," and he indicated Quentin, "is a brave chap whom I have had the pleasure of meeting this evening by mistake. This man," and he nodded to the old man with the long beard, "is Don Gil Sabadía, the only person in Cordova who knows the history of every street, alley, and by-way in the city."

"Not as much as that, man, not as much as that," said Don Gil with a smile.

"If there is anything you don't know," Pacheco went on, "nobody in Cordova knows it. Well, if you and the girls would like to drink a bottle of the best Montilla, I'll treat."

"Accepted."

"Cuervo!" shouted Pacheco, stepping outside the door.

The innkeeper appeared; a man of some fifty years, stoop-shouldered, ill-shaven, with hatchet-shaped side whiskers, and a red sash about his waist.

"What does Señor José wish?" he inquired.

"Bring a few bottles of your best."

While they were waiting for the wine, the ill-tempered girl and Currito resumed their quarrel.

"Look out for that girl," said Currito, "she hasn't much sense."

"Did anybody speak?" she asked in disgust.

"I believe the girl is suffering from jaundice."

"My goodness! What a bad-tempered old uncle he is!" said she.

"Listen, my child," continued Currito, "I'm going to make you a present of a sugar-plum to see if we can't sweeten your mouth."

"Currito, we don't need any sugar around here," answered the other girl easily.

"Girls! There's no need of getting scared," said the old woman in a gruff voice.

"I've left her hanging like a fresco painting, haven't I?" Currito remarked to Quentin.

"I've never noticed that fresco paintings were hung."

"He's a fool," explained the contemptuous girl.

The innkeeper arrived with the bottle and the glasses, and Currito seized the former and served every one.

"You know so much, Don Gil, what will you bet that you don't know what that Italian bishop said when he saw the Mosque?" said Currito.

"What did he say? Let's hear it," inquired Don Gil with an ironic smile.

"Well, the canon Espejito went up to him, and pointing out the Christ of the Column, explained to him how it was made: 'A prisoner made that Christ with his finger-nails,' and the Bishop said to him, 'The man who did it must have had good nails.'"

"He must be a heretic," said Señora Rosario.

"And who told you that fake?" asked Don Gil.

"El Moji told me."

"Well, he fooled you like a Chinaman."

"No, sir, he did not fool me," replied Currito. "El Moji was a man's man, El Moji never lied, and El Moji...."

"But you are trying to tell me what the Bishop said, when I was there at the time," exclaimed Don Gil.

"You there! Why, it was the time you went to Seville!"

"Very well, I was not there. Blas told me, and there's an end to it."

"But of what importance is all this?" asked Quentin.

"Let them be," interrupted the ill-tempered girl; "they're two disagreeable old uncles!"

"Don Gil," said Pacheco, smiling and winking his eye, "permits no one to be informed of anything he does not know about himself."

"Well, what will you bet," Currito presently broke out, "that you don't know what El Golotino said when he had the lawsuit with El Manano?"

"Let's hear, let's hear. This is most important," remarked Pacheco.

"Well, there isn't much to it. El Golotino, as you know, had a herd of a couple of dozen goats, and El Manano, who was a charcoal-burner, had rented a hill; and to find out whether the goats had wandered on the hill or not, they had a lawsuit, which El Golotino lost. Don Nicanor, the clerk, was making an inventory of the property of the owner of the goats, and was adding: 'two and four are six, and four are ten—carry one; fourteen and six are twenty, and three are twenty-three—carry two; twenty-seven and eight are thirty-five, and six are forty-one—carry four.' El Golotino thought that when the clerk said, 'carry one,' he meant that he was going to carry off one goat, so he shouted tearfully: 'Well, for that, you can carry off the whole bunch of them!'"

"That is not the way it was," Señor Sabadía started to remark, but every one burst out laughing.

"Come, girls, we must go home," announced Señora Rosario.

"I'm going out," said Don Gil, annoyed by the laughter.

"I am too," added Quentin.

They took leave of Pacheco, and the innkeeper accompanied the three women and the two men to the door with the lamp. They went through several alleys and came out in the lower part of the Calle de la Feria. They stopped, before a miserable white hut, the old woman knocked on the door with her knuckles, it was opened from within, and Señora Rosario and the three girls entered. Through a small window next the door could be seen a very small, whitewashed room, with a glazed tile pedestal, a varnished bureau, and flower-pots full of paper flowers.

"What a cage! What a tiny house!" said Quentin.

"All the houses on this side of the street are like this," answered Señor Sabadía.

"Why?"

"On account of the wall."

"Ah! Was there a wall here?"

"Of course! The wall that separated the upper city from the lower. The upper city was called Almadina, and the lower, Ajerquía."

"That's curious."

They walked up the Calle de la Feria. The sloping street, with its tall, white houses bathed in the moonlight, presented a fantastic appearance; the two lines of roofs were outlined against the blue of the sky, broken here and there by the azoteas on some of the houses.

"Oh, yes," continued the archæologist, "this wall used to extend from the Cruz del Rastro, to the Cuesta de Luján; then it stretched on through the Calle de la Zapatería and the Cuesta del Bailío, until it reached the tower on the Puerta del Rincón, where it ended."

"So it cut the town in two, and one could not go from one side to the other? That was nice!"

"No. What nonsense! There were gates to go through. Up there near the Arquillo de Calceteros, was the Puerta de la Almadina, which in the time of the Romans, was called Piscatoria, or Fish Gate. The Portillo did not exist, and when they built against the wall, in the place it now occupies, there stood a house which the city bought in 1496 from its owner, Francisco Sánchez Torquemada, in order to open up an arch in the wall. This data," added Don Gil confidentially, "comes from an original manuscript which is preserved in the City Hall. It's curious, isn't it?"

"Most curious."

They climbed the Cuesta de Luján. The neighbouring streets were deserted; within some of the houses they could hear the vague sound of guitars; lovers whispered to each other at the grated windows.

"See?" said Don Gil, looking toward the lower end of

the Calle de la Feria, "the fosses of the wall followed the line the moon makes in the street."

"Very interesting," murmured Quentin.

"Have you noticed how high the houses are in this street?"

"Yes, indeed; why is that?"

"For two reasons," answered Don Gil, turned domi-nie. "First, to gain the height the wall deprived them of; and second, because in times gone by, the majority of the spectacles were celebrated here. Here is where executions were held; where they baited bulls; and broke lances; and where, during the week preceding the Day of the Virgin of Linares, the hosiers held a grand fair. That is why there are so many windows and galleries in these houses, and why the street is called the Calle de la Feria."

The archæologist seized Quentin's arm and proceeded to relate several stories and legends to him. The two men traversed narrow alleys, and plazoletas lined with white houses with blue doors.

"You know no one here?" inquired the archæologist.

"Not a soul."

"Absolutely no one?"

"No. That is... I know a Cordova boy who was educated with me in England. His name is... Quentin García Roelas. Do you know him?"

"Not him; but I know his family."

"He is a silent, taciturn chap. It seems to me that there is something unusual connected with his life. I've heard something...."

"Yes, there is an interesting story."

"Do you know it?"

"Of course," replied Don Gil.

"But you are so discreet that you will not tell it?"

"Naturally."

"Very well, Don Gil I'm going; I'm sorry to leave your agreeable company, but...."

"Must you go?"

"Yes, I must."

"My dear man; don't go. I must show you a most interesting spot, with a history...."

"No, I cannot."

"I'll take you to a place that you will have to like."

"No, you must excuse me."

"Moreover, I'll tell you the story of your friend and schoolmate."

"You see...."

"It's early yet. It's not more than one o'clock."

"Very well, we'll go wherever you say."

They passed through very nearly the whole city until they came to the Paseo del Gran Capitán.

"What a city this is!" exclaimed Don Gil. "They can't talk to *me* about Granada or Seville; for look you, Granada has three aspects: the Alhambra, the Puerta Real, and the Albaicín—three distinct things. Seville is larger than Cordova, but it is already more cosmopolitan—it's like Madrid. But not so Cordova. Cordova is one and indivisible. Cordova is her own sauce. She is a city."

From the Paseo del Gran Capitán, they followed Los Tejares, and on the right hand side, Señor Sabadía paused before some little houses that were huddled close to a serrated wall. There were four of them, very small, very white, each with only one story, and all closed up except one, which merely had its door shut.

"Read this placard," said Don Gil, pointing to a sign in a frame hanging on one side of the door.

Quentin read by the light of the moon:

> Patrocinio de la Mata dresses
> corpses at all hours of the day
> or of the night in which she is
> notified, at very regular prices.

"The devil! What a lugubrious sign!" exclaimed Quentin after reading it.

"Do you see this hut?" asked Don Gil. "Well, every intrigue that God ever turned loose, goes on here. But let us go in."

They entered, and a cracked voice shouted:

"Who is it?"

"I, Señora Patrocinio, Don Gil Sabadía, who comes with a friend. Bring a light, for we're going to stay a while."

"One moment."

The old woman descended with a lamp in her hand, and led the two men into a small parlour where there was a strong odour of lavender. She placed the lamp on the table and said:

"What do you want?"

"Some small olives, and a little wine."

The old woman opened a cupboard, took out a dish of olives, another of biscuits, and two bottles of wine.

"Is there anything else you want?"

"Nothing more, Señora Patrocinio."

The old woman withdrew and shut the door.

"How do you like the place, eh?" asked Don Gil.

"Magnificent! Now for the history of my friend Quentin."

"Before the history, let's drink. Your health, comrade."

"Yours."

"May all our troubles vanish into thin air."

"True," exclaimed Quentin. "Let us leave to the gods the care of placating the winds, and let us enjoy life as long as fortune, age, and the black spindle of the Three Sisters will permit us."

"Are you a reader of Horace?" asked Don Gil.

"Yes."

"One more reason for my liking you. Another glass, eh?"

"Let us proceed. Go on with the story, comrade."

"Here goes."

Don Gil cleared his throat, and commenced his story as follows....

# CHAPTER VII

## IN WHICH IS TOLD THE HISTORY OF A TAVERN ON SIERRA MORENA

TOWARD the first part of last century, upon one of the folds of Sierra Morena, stood a tavern called El Ventorro de la Sangre (Bloody Tavern). It was half way between Pozo Blanco and Cordova, in a fertile little pasture near an olive orchard.

Its name arose from a bloody encounter between the dragoons and guerillas in that spot at the time of the French intervention.

The tavern was situated on a small clearing that was always kept green. It was surrounded by tall prickly-pears, a ravine, and an olive orchard in which one could see ruins—vestiges of a fortress and a watch-tower. This land belonged to a village perched upon the most rugged and broken part of the mountain.... Its name does not at present concern the story.

The tavern was neither very large, nor very spacious; it had neither the characteristics of a hostelry, nor even of a store. Its front, which was six metres long, white-washed, and pierced by a door and three windows, faced a bad horse-shoe road strewn with loose stones; its humble roof leaned toward the ground, and joined that of a shed which contained the stables, the manger, and the straw-loft.

One passed through the entrance of the little tavern from whose lintel hung a bunch of sarment—which indicated, for your enlightenment, that in the house thus decorated wine was sold—and entered a miserable vestibule, which also served as a kitchen, a larder, and, at times, a dormitory.

During the years 1838 and '39, the proprietor of El Ventorro de la Sangre was a man named El Cartagenero, who, so evil tongues asserted, had been a licentiate—though not of philosophy—in a university with mayors for professors, and sticks for beadles. No one knew the truth—a clear indication that the tavern was not run badly; the man paid well, behaved himself as a man should, and was capable, if the occasion arose, of lending a hand to any of the neighbouring farmers.

El Cartagenero demonstrated in his delightful and entertaining conversation, that he had travelled extensively, both by land and by sea; he knew the business of innkeeping—which has its secrets as well as anything else in the world; robbed very little; was hard-working, sensible, upright, and if need be, firm, generous, and brave.

El Cartagenero was to all appearances a fugitive; and that very condition of his made him most reserved and taciturn, in no way a prier, and very little given to mixing himself in other people's affairs.

When he had run the little tavern for six years, El Cartagenero rented an oil-press; he then installed a tile-kiln, and by his activity and perseverance, was getting along splendidly, when one day, unfortunately for him, while he was loading a cart with bricks, he fell in such a way that he struck his head on the iron-shod wheel, and was instantly killed.

From that very day, the tavern began to run down; La Cartagenera did not care to continue the renting of the press, because, as she said, she could not attend to it; she abandoned the kiln for the same reason, and neglected the tavern for no pretext at all, though, if there was no pretext or motive, there was an explanation; and this was La Cartagenera's vice of drinking brandy, and the laziness and idleness of her daughters—two very sly and very slothful un-belled cows.

The elder of El Cartagenero's daughters made her arrangements with a swaggering rascal from Cordova; and the other, not to be outdone by her sister, took for her good man, one of those country loafers—and what with the sweetheart of the former, and the friend of the other, and the brandy of the mother, the house began to run down hill.

The muleteers soon guessed what was up; they no longer found good wine there as before; nor a diligent person to prepare their meals and feed their animals; so now because the hosier had left the place swearing mad, again because the pedlar had quarrelled with them, all of their customers began to leave; and for a whole year no one dismounted at the tavern; and the mother and her daughters, with the two corresponding swains, passed the time insulting and growling at each other, stretched out in the sun in the summer, toasting sarment at the fire-place in the winter, and in all the seasons hurling bitter complaints against an adverse destiny.

After a year of this régime, there was nothing left in the house to eat, nor to drink, nor to sell—for they had sold everything including the doors—the family determined to get rid of the tavern. The girls' two friends came to Cordova and opened up negotiations with all their acquaintances, and were about despairing of making a sale, when a farmer from these parts by the name of El Mojoso, presented himself at the tavern. He was a clever, sensible chap, and the owner of a drove of five very astute little donkeys.

El Mojoso entered into negotiations with the widow, and for less than nothing, became possessed of the establishment. El Mojoso was very sagacious, and immediately comprehended the situation at the tavern; so he began to think about conducive methods of restoring the credit of the house. The first thing that occurred to him after he had been installed a few days, was to change its name, and he had a painter friend of his paint in huge letters upon the whitewashed wall above the door, this sign:

THE CROSS-ROADS STORE

El Mojoso had a wife and three children: one, employed as a miner in Pueblo Nuevo del Terrible; and two girls, with whom and his wife he established himself in the store.

His wife, whom they called La Temeraria, was a tall, strong, industrious, and determined matron. The daughters were splendid girls, but too refined to live in that deserted spot.

El Mojoso himself was a tough sort of a chap, crazy about bulls, slangy, and somewhat of a boaster. As a man who had spent his childhood in the Matadero district, which is the finest school of bull-fighting in the world, he knew how to differentiate the several tricks of the bull-ring.

At first, El Mojoso did not abandon his drove; the returns from the inn were very small, and it did not seem expedient to him to quit his carrying business. But instead of walking the streets of Cordova, he devoted himself to going to and from the mountain villages carrying wheat to the mill, farming utensils to the farms, and doing a lot of errands and favours that were gaining him many friends in the neighbourhood.

When he had no errands or favours to do, he carried stones to his house on his donkeys and piled them under the shed. After a year of this work, when he had gathered together the wherewithal, he got a mason from Cordova, and under his direction, La Temeraria and he and his daughters, and a youth whom they had hired as a servant, lengthened the house, raised it a story, tiled the roof, and whitewashed it.

El Mojoso had to sell his donkeys to pay the costs— only keeping one. The muleteers were already resuming their old custom of stopping at the store.

During the first months, the wine was pure, and there was a *pardillo* and a claret such as had not been known in those parts for many years. Little by little the store commenced to grow in fame; lively and genial folk met there; the wine grew worse, according to the opinion of the intelligent, but good wine was not lacking if the customer who asked for it had the means of paying without protest or objection three or four times its worth. During the slaughter season there was pork chine when they wanted it, and at other times of the year, pork sausage, blood pudding and other such delicacies.

El Mojoso learned his new business very quickly. Without doubt, he was a thief *a nativitate*. He watered the wine and perjured himself by swearing that it was the only pure wine that was sold in the entire mountain district; he put pepper in the brandy; he cheated in grain and hay; tangled up the accounts, and—always came out ahead.

Nearly every day he went to the city with his donkey under the pretext of shopping; but the truth is that his trips were to carry instructions and orders from a few timid men who went about the mountain, blunderbuss in hand, to some poor chaps in prison.

La Temeraria knew how to help her husband. She was a quiet, hard-working woman as long as no one interfered with her; but if any one dared to fail her, she was a she-wolf, more vengeful than God. She had enough spirit to look upon robbing as a pardonable and permissible thing, and even to the extent of not considering it extraordinary for a man to bring down a militia-man and leave him on the ground chewing mud.

In fine, the husband and wife were the most artful... innkeepers in these parts. At the Cross-roads Store, the traveller could spend the night in peace, whether he was an orderly person or had some little account to settle with the police; or whether he was a merchant or a horseman, he could be sure of being undisturbed. One day....

............

"But tell me, my friend," Don Gil asked Quentin; "how does the beginning of the story strike you?"

"Very well."

"Did you like the exposition?"

"I should say so! You are a master."

"Thanks!" exclaimed Don Gil, satisfied. "To your health, comrade."

"To yours."

"Now you'll hear the good part."

............

One rainy day in the month of February, just at dusk, there was gathered in the kitchen of the Cross-roads Store, a group of muleteers from the near-by village. Some of them, imbued with a love of heat, were seated upon two long benches on either side of the hearth; others were seated upon chairs and stools of wicker and lambskin, further away from the fire.

By the light of the blackened lamp and the flame of the candle, the whole circumference of the kitchen, which was a large one, could be seen: its enormous mantel, its rafters twisted and blackened with smoke, the big stones in the floor, and the walls adorned with a collection of pot-covers, saucepans, wooden spoons, and coloured jars hung upon nails.

The muleteers were engaged in an animated conversation while they waited for the supper which La Temeraria was at that moment preparing in two frying-pans full of pork chine and potatoes; El Mojoso was filling the measure with barley which he took from a bin; then, pouring the grain into a leather sieve, he handed it to a youth who was going to and from the kitchen and the stable.

Night had already fallen, and it was raining torrents, when repeated knocks sounded upon the door.

"Who is it?" shouted El Mojoso in a loud voice. "Come in, whoever it is."

This said, the host took a lantern, lit it with a brand from the fire, crossed the kitchen, and stood in the vestibule with the light held high to see who was coming in. The vestibule was as narrow as a corridor; it had board walls, and upon them, hanging from wooden pot-hooks, could be seen several kinds of pack-saddles, panniers, headstalls, and other harness of leather, cloth, and esparto-grass. Upon the slanting stone floor, several muleteers who had made their beds there were sleeping peacefully.

The knock on the door was repeated.

"Come in!" said El Mojoso.

The wooden half-door opened with a screech, and a man appeared on the threshold, wrapped in a Jerez shawl which was drenched with water.

"Is there lodging here?" the man asked.

"There's good will," answered the innkeeper. "Did you come on horseback?"

"Yes."

"Come in. I'll take your horse to the stable. Walk right in there."

The man went to the kitchen.

"The peace of God be with you, gentlemen!" he said.

"May He keep you," they all answered.

The recent arrival went in, took off his long, tasseled shawl, and sat down upon a grass-bottomed chair near the fire.

The innkeeper's daughter, more out of curiosity than anything else, threw an armful of dry rose-wood upon the fire, which began to burn brilliantly, producing a large flame, and filling the kitchen with the odour of its incense.

By the light of the flames they could see that the recent arrival was a tall and strong young man of about twenty years, upon whose upper lip the down had not yet begun to appear. He looked like a gentleman of noble blood; he wore a short coat, knee breeches fastened with silver buttons, buckled leggings, a blue sash, a coloured silk handkerchief about his neck, and a small, creased calañés. The hostess noticed that his shirt studs were made of diamonds.

"You have bad weather for travelling," she said.

"Bad it is," replied the youth dryly, without removing his eyes from the fire.

The muleteers examined the young man in silence. El Mojoso came back from the stable where he had taken the horse, brought in a half-filled sack on his back, and emptied it into the bin, weighed the barley in the measure, and asked the horseman:

"What shall I give the animal?"

"Give him a good feed."

"Shall I give him two quarts?"

"Yes."

El Mojoso went out with the measure in one hand and the lantern in the other.

"This chap," he murmured into his cloak, "is a rich youngster who has been in some escapade in Cordova.

His horse is out there with an embossed saddle. The boy will pay well."

El Mojoso was a man who knew his profession. Convinced of the character of the young man, he returned to the kitchen with a broader smile than usual, and said:

"What would your worship like for supper?"

"Anything."

"And would you like a bed?"

"Have you one?"

"Sí, Señor."

"Good: Then I shall sleep in a bed."

"Very well; they'll get it ready for you directly."

The hostess took one of the large frying-pans from the fire and emptied its contents into a dish which she placed upon a low table.

The muleteers prepared themselves for the meal. La Temeraria took one of the blackened lamps from the grime of the mantel-piece, lit it, and seeing that it did not give a very good light, took a hairpin from her hair, stuck it into the wick to trim and ventilate it, and this done, fastened it with a wooden peg to a beam that stuck out of the wall.

"Bring wine, Mojoso," she then said to her husband.

The innkeeper passed behind a counter which he had at the right of the kitchen door, and filled two bottles from a wine-skin; then, from another skin, using great care lest he spill the wine, he filled a small Andújar jar. One of the large bottles he placed upon the table about which the muleteers had seated themselves as they chatted and waited for their supper to be prepared.

La Temeraria placed a tripod over the fire, and presently the older daughter of the house entered with a large lamp.

"The room is ready, father," she murmured.

Turning to the youth, the innkeeper said:

"You may go up now, if you wish."

The young man arose and followed the landlord, who lighted his way. They went into the vestibule, and, one behind the other, climbed up a steep stairway to a granary. The wind blew strongly through the cracks in the roof; by the flickering lamp-light they could see piles of walnuts and acorns upon the floor, and large gourds hanging in rows. El Mojoso pushed open a white door of freshly-painted wood, entered a room with an alcove attached, placed the lamp upon the table, and after trimming it by all the rules of the art, said:

"Supper will be served to you directly. If you need anything, call;" and he shut the door as he went out.

The youth listened to the innkeeper's footsteps in the attic, and when he found himself alone, drew two pistols from his sash, entered the alcove, and hid them on the bed under the pillow; he inspected the door, and found that it was solid with a strong lock; next he opened the window, and a gust of cold air made the flame of the lamp flicker violently. He looked out.

"This doubtless looks out upon the other side of the road," he said to himself.

He closed the outside shutter and paced back and forth, waiting for his supper. The room was narrow and low and whitewashed, with blue rafters in the ceiling, and an alcove at one end occupied by a bed covered with a red quilt. Pushed against the wall was a mahogany bureau with a Carmen Virgin in a glass case; opposite the bureau was a straw couch with a mahogany frame. There was a round table in the middle of the room upon whose coarse top were two plates, a glass, and the lamp. Upon the walls were several rough engravings and a gun.

The young man showed signs of impatience, listening attentively to the slightest distant noises. Tired of pacing to and fro, he sat upon the couch and thoughtfully contemplated the rafters in the ceiling.

A half hour had elapsed since El Mojoso's departure, when there came a shy knock at the door. The youth was so preoccupied that he heard nothing until the third or fourth knock, and a voice saying:

"May I come in?"

"Come!"

The door opened and a girl entered—the landlord's second daughter—with a dish in one hand, and an Andújar jar in the other.

The youth was astounded at seeing such a pretty maid, and completely upset by the sight.

"What is it?" he asked.

"Your supper."

"Ah! You are the landlord's daughter?"

"Sí, Señor," she replied with a smile.

The girl set the dish upon the table, and he sat down without taking his eyes off her. She made a tremendous impression upon him. The child was truly charming; she had black, almond-shaped eyes, a pale complexion, and in her hair, which was cleverly done up and as black and lustrous as the elytra of some insects, was a red flower.

"What is your name, my dear, if I may ask?" said he.

"Fuensanta," she replied....

...........

"Ah! Her name was Fuensanta!" exclaimed Quentin involuntarily.

"Yes. It's a very common name in these parts. Why does it surprise you?"

"Nothing, nothing: proceed...."

"Well, I shall."

...........

The youth sighed, and as his admiration had doubtless not taken away his appetite, he attacked the slices prepared by La Temeraria with his fork, and after several drinks from the jar, he succeeded in emptying it, and doing away with the portions of the savoury country food.

The little girl returned directly to his room to bring the traveller his dessert, and they talked.

He asked her if she had a sweetheart, and she said she hadn't; he asked her if she would like to have him, and she answered that gentlemen could not very well love poor girls who lived in taverns, and then they talked for a long time.

The next day, the young horseman left the tavern to proceed on his journey, and El Mojoso went down to Cordova to his business...

...........

"And who was that young man?" asked Quentin.

"Wait, comrade. Everything in its time. How do you like the way I tell it, eh?"

"You certainly are a past master."

"Well, now comes the best part of it. You'll see...."

# CHAPTER VIII

## A FIGHT IN AN OLIVE ORCHARD

SEVERAL days afterward, just at dawn, El Mojoso was returning from Cordova to his tavern, when, at a turn in the road, he came upon a small cavalcade made up of six men—five of whom were soldiers, and the other, an elegantly dressed young man.

El Mojoso, who had little liking for evil encounters, pricked up his beast in order to get into the paths ahead of the group, but the chief, who wore the insignia of a sergeant, when he noticed the innkeeper's intention, shouted to him:

"Hey, my good man, wait a moment!"

El Mojoso stopped his donkey.

"What do you want?" he asked ill-humouredly.

"We've got something to say to you."

"Well, I can't lose anything by listening to it."

"You are the owner of the Cross-roads Store, aren't you?"

"Yes, sir: what else do you want?"

"Why, just don't go so fast, friend, we feel like going along with you."

"Are you going to Pozo Blanco?"

"No, sir."

"To Obejo, perhaps?"

"No. We're going to the Store."

"To the Store!" exclaimed El Mojoso, overcome with astonishment. "Whom are you looking for in my house?"

"We're looking for the Marquesito."

"The Marquesito? What Marquesito?"

"Don't you know him?"

"Upon my word I do not! I hope to die if I'm not telling you the truth."

"Well, it seems that your daughter knows him very well," replied the soldier meaningly.

El Mojoso's face darkened, not that it had ever been exactly light, and looking back at the sergeant, he murmured in a dull voice:

"You've either said too much or too little."

"I've said all that was necessary," answered the soldier gruffly.

El Mojoso fell silent and urged on his donkey, while the soldiers and the unknown young gentleman followed him.

The sun came out from behind the mountain; in the distance they could see a series of low-lying hills and the Cross-roads Store in its little green clearing near the ravine.

When they reached the Store, El Mojoso dismounted from his donkey and began to pound furiously upon the door. He beat frantically with hands and feet.

"Open! Open!" he shouted impatiently.

"Who is it?" came from within.

"Me," and El Mojoso ripped out a string of angry oaths.

A lock screeched, the door opened, and La Temeraria appeared half-dressed on the threshold.

"Why didn't you open sooner?" El Mojoso vociferated.

"What's the matter?" she asked as she drew a short skirt over head and fastened it rapidly about her waist.

"A whole lot's the matter. Are there any travellers in the house?"

"The young man who was here a few days ago passed the night here."

The unknown gentleman and the chief of the soldiers exchanged a look of understanding. El Mojoso entered his house, and La Temeraria followed behind him.

"Go and see if there is a horse in the stable," said the sergeant to one of his men, "and if there is, bring it here."

The soldier dismounted, went into the stable, and returned after a little, leading a horse by the bridle.

La Temeraria, who had heard the noise, intercepted the soldier.

"Where are you taking that horse?" she asked.

"The sergeant ordered me to bring him out."

"What for?"

"So the man who is here can't escape."

"What has the young man done?" asked La Temeraria, looking contemptuously at the soldier.

"He killed a man in Cordova about a month ago."

At this moment, the innkeeper, who had been inside the house, returned shouting to the vestibule.

"Where is Fuensanta?" he asked his wife.

"She must be in her room."

"She isn't there."

"Not there?"

"No. I just looked."

El Mojoso and La Temeraria looked at each other furiously and understandingly.

Meanwhile the sergeant, followed by one of his soldiers, went up the stairs to the garret. When the fugitive heard the noise their boots and spurs made, he must have realized his danger, for they heard the thud of a body as he threw himself against the door, then the turning of a key in the lock, and then a murmur of voices.

The sergeant drew his sword, went up to the door behind which he had heard the voices, and knocked with the hilt of his weapon.

"Open in the name of the law!" he shouted in a thundrous voice.

"Wait a moment, I'm dressing," came the answer from within.

After a minute had elapsed, the sergeant exclaimed impatiently:

"Come, come! Open the door!"

"Wait just a second."

"I won't wait a minute longer. Open: I promise not to hurt you."

"Words are air, and the wind carries them all away," replied the fugitive ironically.

"Will you open, or will you not?"

"I will not; and he who contradicts me is in danger of his life. You'll have to kill me here."

At the risk of breaking his neck, the sergeant ran down the stairs three steps at a time, and addressing his soldiers, said:

"Boys, come upstairs with your guns. We've got to

break down the door. One of you stay here on guard, and if any one tries to escape, fire on him."

Two of the men dismounted rapidly, crossed the vestibule, and, preceded by the sergeant, rushed headlong upstairs, reached the garret, and began to beat upon the door with the butts of their heavy guns.

"Surrender!" shouted the sergeant again and again.

No one answered.

"Quick now! Throw down the door."

The door was new and did not yield to the first blows, but little by little the panels gave way, and at last, a formidable blow with the butt broke the lock....

The soldiers entered:—stretched upon the floor lay a half-dressed woman. The window was open.

"The scoundrel escaped through that," said one of the men.

"My God! We can't let him escape," shouted the sergeant, and sticking his head through the window, he saw a man running across a field half hidden among the olive trees. Without making sure whether it was the man they were after or not, he drew a pistol from his belt and fired.

"No—he's gone. We've got to catch him."

They all left the room; there came a devilish noise of boots and spurs on the stairs, and they crossed the vestibule.

"To your horses," said the sergeant.

The order was obeyed instantly.

"You, Aragonés, and you, Segura, get behind that haystack," and the chief indicated a great pile of black straw. "You two, ride around that field, and this gentleman and I will go and look for the Marquesito face to face."

The two pairs of troopers took their appointed places, and the sergeant and the unknown gentleman advanced through the middle of the olive orchard.

Aragonés and Segura were the first to see the fugitive, who was running along hiding behind the olive trees, with a gun in his hand. The two soldiers cocked their guns and advanced cautiously; but the youth saw them, stopped and waited for them, kneeling upon one knee. The soldiers attempted to make a detour in order to get near their game, but as they described an arc, the youth kept the trunk of an olive tree between him and them. Seeing that he was making sport of them, the soldiers advanced resolutely. The Marquesito aimed his gun and fired, and one of the horses, that of Aragonés, fell wounded in the shoulder, throwing his rider. Segura, the other soldier, made his horse rear, in order to guard against a shot, but the Marquesito fired a pistol with such good aim, that the man fell to the ground with blood pouring from his mouth.

Then the youth, realizing that the other pursuers would immediately come to the spot where they had heard the shots, ran until he came to a century-old olive tree with a great, deformed trunk whose gnarled roots resembled a tangled mass of snakes. He took advantage of the respite to load his gun and pistol. Then he waited. Presently a shot was fired behind him, and he felt a bullet enter his leg. He turned rapidly and saw the sergeant and the gentleman approaching on horseback.

"My death will cost you dear," murmured the Marquesito angrily.

"Surrender!" shouted the sergeant, and approached the fugitive at a trot.

The Marquesito waited, and when the sergeant was twenty paces from him, he fired his gun and pierced him with a bullet.

"Hey, boys!" shouted the sergeant. "Here he is. Kill him!" Then he put his hand to his breast, began to bleed at the mouth, and fell from his horse murmuring, "Jesus! He's killed me!"

One of the sergeant's feet caught in the stirrup, and the horse, becoming frightened, dragged his rider's body for some distance over the ground.

"Now it's your turn, coward!" shouted the Marquesito, addressing the gentleman.

But that person had turned on his croup and couldn't get away fast enough.

The youth began to think that he was safe: the blood was flowing copiously from his wound, so he took the handkerchief from about his neck and bound his leg firmly with it. Next, he reloaded his weapons, and limping slowly, sheltering himself behind the olive trees and glancing from side to side, he advanced.

When he had reached a little plaza formed by a space that was bare of trees, he saw one of the soldiers in ambush. Perhaps it was the last one.

When they saw each other, pursuer and pursued immediately took refuge behind the trees. The soldier fired; a ball whistled by the Marquesito's head; then he rested his gun against a tree trunk, fired, and the soldier's helmet fell to the ground.

They both concealed themselves while they reloaded their weapons, and for more than a quarter of an hour, they kept shooting at each other, neither of them making up his mind to come out into the open.

The Marquesito was beginning to feel faint from the loss of blood; so he decided to risk all for all.

"Let's see if we can't finish this business," he murmured between his clenched teeth; and he advanced, limping resolutely toward the soldier. After a few steps he discharged his gun point blank, and immediately after, his pistol.

When he saw that his enemy had not fallen, that he was still standing, he tried to escape, but his strength failed him. Then the soldier took aim and fired. The Marquesito fell headlong... he was dead. The ball had struck him in the back of the neck and had come out through one of his eyes, shattering his skull.

"He was a brave chap," murmured the soldier as he gazed at the corpse; then he kneeled by his side and searched his clothes. He wrapped his watch and chain, his shirt studs, and his money, in a handkerchief, tied it in a knot, and made his way back to the tavern.

As he drew near, he heard a voice wailing in despair:

"Oh, mother! Oh, mother! Oh, my dearest mother!"

In the clearing before the house was Fuensanta, half-undressed, livid, with her face black and blue from the beating her father had given her. The girl was moaning upon the ground, terror-stricken. La Temeraria, with her arms lifted tragically, was shouting:

"She has dishonoured us! She has dishonoured us!"

The innkeeper's other daughter stood in the doorway, watching her sister as she dragged herself along the ground, exhausted by her beating.

"Don't beat the girl like that," said the soldier.

"Don't beat her!" shouted El Mojoso. "No, I won't beat her any more," and seizing his daughter by the arm he pushed her brutally from him, shouting:

"Go... and never come back!"

The bewildered girl hid her face in her hands, and then the poor little thing began to walk away, weeping, and not knowing what she was doing, nor where she was going.

Months later, a woman from an Obejo mill came to El Mojoso and announced that Fuensanta had given birth to a son, and that she desired to be forgiven and to return home; but the innkeeper said that he would kill her if she ever came near him.

. . . . . . . . . . . . .

"The scoundrel! The bandit!" exclaimed Quentin, striking the table a blow with his fist.

"Who is a scoundrel?" asked Señor Sabadía in surprise.

"That Mojoso fellow, the dirty thief... his daughter dishonoured him because she loved a man, yet he did not dishonour himself, though he robbed every one that came along."

"That's different."

"Yes, it's different," cried Quentin furiously. "To the hidalgos of Spain it is a different matter; to all those commonplace and thoughtless men, a woman's honour is beneath contempt. Imbeciles!"

"I see that you are enraged," said Don Gil with a smile. "Does the story interest you?"

"Very much."

"Shall I proceed?"

"Please do."

"Then kindly call Señora Patrocinio and ask her to bring more bottles of wine, for my throat is very dry."

"But you are a regular cask, my dear Don Gil."

"Yes I'm the Cask of the Danaides. Call her, please."

"Señora Patrocinio! Señora Patrocinio!" called Quentin.

"Isn't she coming?"

"No. She is probably busy with her witchcraft. Perhaps

this very minute she is burning in her magic fire the sycamore torn from the sepulchre."

"Or the funereal cypress, and the feathers and eggs of a red owl soaked in toad's blood," added Don Gil.

"Or the poisonous herbs which grew in such abundance in Iolchos, and in far-off Iberia," continued Quentin.

"Or the bones torn from the mouth of a hungry bitch," added the archæologist.

"Señora Patrocinio! Señora Canidia!" shouted Quentin.

"Señora Patrocinio! Señora Canidia!" echoed Señor Sabadía.

"What do you want?" asked the old woman as she suddenly entered the room.

"Ah! She *was* here!" exclaimed Quentin.

"She *was* here!" echoed Señor Sabadía. "We want some more bottles."

"What kind do you want?"

"I believe, venerable dame," Quentin ejaculated, "that it is all the same to my friend here, whether it be wine from the vines of Falernus, Phormio, or Cécube, as long as it is wine. Is that not true, Don Gil?"

"Of course. I see that you are a sagacious young man. Bring them, old woman," said the archæologist, turning to Señora Patrocinio, "bring fearlessly forth that excellent wine that you have guarded so jealously these four years in the Sabine pitchers."

The old woman brought the bottles, Quentin filled Don Gil's glass and then his own, they emptied them both, and Señor Sabadía went on with his story in these words:

# CHAPTER IX

## IN WHICH SEÑOR SABADÍA ABUSES WORDS AND WINE

YEARS ago in the Calle de Librerías, in a little corner near the Cuesta de Luján, there stood a silversmith's shop, with an awning stretched over the doorway, a very narrow show-case in which a number of rosaries, rings, medals, and crosses were displayed, and a miserable half-obliterated sign with these words: "Salvador's Shop." From one end of this sign, symbolically, hung a pair of pasteboard scales.

Salvador, the proprietor of this silversmith's shop, was a wealthy bachelor who had lived with a sister for many years before her death.

At the time of my story, Don Andrés, as the silversmith was called, was a man of some sixty years, small, clean-shaven, with white hair, rosy cheeks, clear eyes, and smiling lips. He resembled a silver medal.

With all his sweet, beatific countenance, Don Andrés was at heart, an egoist. Possessing little intelligence and less courage, life made a coward of him. He had an idea that things advanced too rapidly, and was, therefore, an enemy to all innovations. Any change whatever, even if it were beneficial, disturbed him profoundly.

"We have lived like this so far," he would say, "and I can see no necessity for any change."

Don Andrés Salvador was equally conservative in his business: all he had was an ability for work that required patience. Rosaries, crosses, rings, and medals left his house by the gross, but everything manufactured in his shop was always the same; unchanged, and unimproved—wrought with the same old-fashioned and decadent taste.

Besides being a conservative, Don Andrés was distrust personified; he did not want any one to see him at work. At that time, repoussé work was still something mysterious and secret, and the silversmith, to prevent any one from surprising his secrets, shut himself up in his own room when he was about to make something of importance, and there worked unseen.

One morning when Don Andrés was standing in the doorway of his shop, he saw a girl running toward him along the Calle de la Feria, pursued by an old woman.

His instinct as a law-abiding citizen made him go out and stop the girl.

"Let me go, Señor," she cried.

"No. Is that your mother following you?"

"No, she isn't my mother," and the child began to cry disconsolately. In a broken voice she told him how she had been ill for some time in a hut on the Calle de la Feria, and how, when she had become well, the mistress of the house had tried to force her to remain as her ward, and how she had escaped.

By this time the old woman had come up behind the girl, and as a group of children began to form around the shop door, the silversmith led the two women inside.

He asked the old woman if what the girl had said was true, and the Celestina in her confusion said that it was, but defended herself by declaring that she had kept the girl because she had not paid for what she had spent on medicines during her illness, and for dresses, stockings, and underclothes with which to clothe her.

The silversmith realized that it was a matter of an infamous exploitation, and whether he was indignant at this, or whether he was touched by the girl's appearance, the fact is, he said with more vehemence than he was accustomed to use:

"I see, Señora Consolación, that you are trying to exploit this child in an evil way. Leave her alone, for she will return your clothes, and go back to your house; for if you don't, I shall warn the authorities, and you will rest your old bones in jail."

The old woman, who knew the influence and prestige the silversmith enjoyed in the district, began once more to complain of the great prejudice they had against her, but Don Andrés cut her argument short by saying:

"Either you get out, or I will call the alguacil."

The Celestina said not another word, but tied her handkerchief about her neck as if she wished to strangle herself with it, and moved off down the street, spouting curses as she went.

The girl and the silversmith were left alone in the shop. He followed the old woman with his eyes as she went screaming along the Calle de la Feria among the noisy people who came running to their doorways as she passed. When she was out of sight, he said to the girl:

"You can go now. She's gone."

When she heard this, the girl began to sob again.

"For God's sake, don't send me away, Señor! For God's sake!"

"I'm not going to send you away. You may stay a while if you wish."

"No. Let me stay here always. You are good. I'll be your servant, and you won't have to give me a thing for it."

"No, no—I cannot," replied the silversmith.

Then the child knelt on the floor, and with her arms thrown wide apart, said:

"Señor! Señor! Let me stay!"

"No, no. Get up! Don't be silly."

"Then if I kill myself," she cried as she regained her feet, "it will be your fault."

"Not mine."

"Yes, yours," and the girl, changing her tone, added, "But you don't want me to go. You won't throw me out; you'll let me live here; I'll serve you, and take care of you; I'll be your servant, and you needn't give me a thing for it; and I will thank you and pray for you."

"But, what will people say?" murmured Don Andrés, who foresaw a complication in his life.

"I swear to you by the Carmen Virgin," she exclaimed, "that I won't give them a chance to talk, for nobody shall see me. You'll let me live here, won't you?"

"How can I help it! You stick a dagger into one's heart. We'll give it a try. But let me warn you about one thing: the first time I notice a failing—even if it is only a man hanging around the house—I'll throw you out immediately."

"No one will hang around."

"Then I shall give you some old clothes this very minute, and you may send those to Señora Consolación's house. Then go to work in the kitchen immediately."

And so it was done; and Fuensanta, for the girl was Fuensanta, the daughter of El Mojoso, entered the house of the silversmith as a servant, and became, as she had promised, circumspect, submissive, silent and industrious.

Little by little the silversmith grew fond of her; Don

Andrés' sister had been a basilisk, a violent and ill-tempered old maid for whose fits of bad temper he had always suffered. Fuensanta paid the old man delicate attentions to which he was unaccustomed, and he looked forward to an old age in an atmosphere of affection and respect.

"See here," Don Andrés once said to her, "you must not be separated from your son. Bring the boy here."

Fuensanta went to Obejo, and returned the following day with the boy. He was three years old, and a regular savage. Fuensanta, who realized that such a wild creature would not please such an orderly and meticulous person as the silversmith, always kept him segregated on the roof, where the little lad passed the long hours in play.

After she had been in Don Andrés Salvador's house for three years, Fuensanta got married.

Among the agents and pedlars who were supplied in the shop, there was a young man, Rafael by name, whom they nicknamed El Pende.

This Rafael was at that time a gracious, pleasant chap of some twenty-odd years; he had the reputation of being lazy—firstly because he came from the Santa Marina district, and secondly because he was the son of Matapalos, one of the biggest loafers in Cordova.

Matapalos, a distinguished member of the Pende dynasty, was a carpenter, and such a poor one, so they said, that the only things he could make were wedges, and even these never came out straight.

El Pende junior, in spite of his reputation as a loafer, used to work. He took up the business of peddling from town to town; selling necklaces and rosaries throughout the entire highlands, and buying old gold and lace wherever he went.

He was a gaudy and elegant lad, who spent nearly everything he earned on jewels and good clothes.

"I'd rather wear jewels than eat," he said.

Rafael, or El Pende, as you will, began promptly to pay court to the girl. She duly checked his advances, but he grew stronger under punishment, and she, seeing that the man persisted, told him the story of her misfortune.

El Pende made light of it all. He was very much enamoured, or perhaps he saw something in the woman that others had missed for, though she had no money, nor any possibility of inheriting any, he did not give up trying until he succeeded in persuading her to marry him.

"Now I've got to persuade the master," said Fuensanta, after coming to an understanding with her sweetheart. "Because, if he opposes us—I won't marry you."

Slowly, insinuatingly, Fuensanta prepared the ground day by day. Allowing herself to stumble, she suggested the idea of marriage to the silversmith, until Don Andrés himself advised his servant to marry, and pointed out to her the advantages she would have should she join herself to Rafael.

They were married, and lived in an attic next the roof. The silversmith gladly granted them the attic, for they scared away thieves, and he liked to have a young man around to look after the house.

Fuensanta continued to serve him as before. El Pende made his trips; he had made advantageous terms with the silversmith in his commissions, and he and the old man understood each other admirably.

Fuensanta began to behold a useful collaborator in her husband. He was intelligent and sagacious; he had a latent ambition which was awakened with real violence at his marriage.

The child was an obstacle to the peace of the household. Quentin was stupid, brutal, proud, and meddle-some.

After two years of matrimony, Fuensanta gave birth to a son whom they called Rafael, after his father. Quentin had no use for the boy, a fact that caused El Pende to hate his stepson.

Quentin did not go to school, so he knew nothing. He played about the streets in rags with rowdies and toughs. One day, when El Pende saw him with some gipsies, he seized him, carried him home, and said to his mother:

"We've got to do something about this child."

"Yes, we must do something," she agreed.

"Why don't you ask the master if he knows of a cheap school?"

Fuensanta spoke to the silversmith, who listened to her attentively.

"Do you know what we'll do?" said Don Andrés.

"What?"

"We'll find out who his father's family are. How long ago was he killed?"

"Seven years."

"Good. Then I'll find out."

On that same street, on the corner of the Calle de la Espartería, in a house upon whose chamfer was an iron cross, there lived a retired captain of militia, Don Matías Echavarría. The silversmith called on him, related what had happened in the Cross-roads Store, and asked the captain if he remembered the affair, and if he knew the name of the protagonist.

"Yes," said Don Matías, "the boy who ran away and was killed on the Pozo Blanco road, was the son of the Marquis of Tavera. When the thing happened, they hushed it up, saying that he had met his death by a fall from his horse, and no one ever knew anything about it."

When the silversmith returned to his house, he said nothing to Fuensanta, but, shut up in his room, he wrote a letter to the old Marquis, giving him a detailed account of the facts, and telling him that a grandson of his was living in his modest home.

He had to wait for the answer. At the end of two weeks, Don Andrés received a message from the Marquis telling him to send Fuensanta to his house to talk with him, and to bring the boy with her.

Fuensanta made Quentin as presentable as possible, and went with him to the Marquis' palace. The old man received her very pleasantly, bade her tell him her story, caressed the child, and murmured from time to time:

"He's just like him, just like him...." Then he added, turning to the mother, "Are you in needy circumstances?"

"Sí, Señor Marqués."

"Very well; take one hundred dollars for the present. We shall see what we can do for the boy."

Fuensanta told her husband what had happened in the Marquis' house, and El Pende immediately took possession of the hundred dollars.

The economical chap already had a like amount, and he believed that the moment had arrived to realize his plans of establishing himself. Consequently, a little later, he rented a store in the Calle de la Zapatería.

. . . . . . . . . . . . .

"What's the matter with you, Don Gil?" asked Quentin, as he saw the narrator looking about for something.

"Why, you're not pouring wine for me."

"There's none left."

"Then call Señora Patrocinio."

"What will you have, Don Gil? Falernus? Or shall we devote ourselves this time to the vines of Calais?"

"No, no; Montilla."

"Can't we make a change?"

"Mix one wine with another? Never! It's very dangerous. But are you, or are you not going to call that old woman? If you do not, I will not go on with my story."

"Do go on with it, Don Gil," said Señora Patrocinio, opening the door and placing two bottles upon the table. "I was almost asleep out here, and was amusing myself by listening to what you were saying."

"Eh!" exclaimed Don Gil, "I must be a great historian if even Sister Patrocinio listens to my tale. Allow me to wet my throat. Now for it, ladies and gentlemen, now for it!"

# CHAPTER X

## DON GIL FINISHES HIS STORY

SEÑORA PATROCINIO seated herself at the table. She was a thin, lean old woman, with a yellow complexion, a hooked nose which was on friendly terms with her chin, grey hair, and a wrinkled skin.

Don Gil took a drink, and continued as follows:

The store was located in a large, antique house, painted blue. On the ground floor were four grated windows, a door, and two little shops. One of these was a mat store, and the other was the one El Pende had rented.

It was a tiny apartment, scarcely three metres square, with a few living-rooms beyond a dark back room.

El Pende put neither signs nor decorations on his shop; he placed a counter painted with red ochre in the middle of the floor, set up a few pine shelves, and commenced business.

All kinds of things to eat and to drink and to burn were sold at the store; a heterogeneous assortment was heaped upon the shelves; there were soaps, silks, taffy of all kinds, and dyes from the most distinguished factory in the whole world, which is that of the Calle de Mucho Trigo; there were hemp-seeds roasted in honey, candied pine-nuts, almond paste, and those thin little wafers that you must have seen, that look like priests' hats.

. . . . . . . . . . . . .

"Come, don't get tiresome," said Señora Patrocinio.

"If you interrupt me, Sister Patrocinio, I shall refuse to go on," answered the narrator.

"You are losing the thread of your story. Come to the point, Don Gil, come to the point."

"Very well, then—I refuse to continue."

"Go on, man, go on; you're crankier than a wheat-sifter," said the old woman.

"Where was I?" murmured Don Gil. "I believe I've forgotten."

"You were telling us what the store contained," suggested Quentin.

. . . . . . . . . . . . .

Of drinkables (the archæologist continued), there were all sorts of brandies and refreshing beverages; *rossolis,* which they call ressolis here; Cazalla, and wild cherry brandy in green jars which some call *parrots*, and others *greenfinches.*

The little store in the Calle de la Zapatería soon had customers. Country folk used to go there to take a little nip in the morning; a few servant girls and a great many children used to stop there to buy sweets.

El Pende stayed behind the counter where he received his friends, who sometimes spent a little money. The most assiduous in his attendance at these gatherings, was a ruined hidalgo by the name of Palomares, whom El Pende had known since childhood, and who, having nothing to do, used to take refuge in the shop. In order not to be in the way, and at the same time to make himself useful, he used to wait on customers himself.

This hidalgo, Diego Palomares, was an adventurer, a son of Lucena. He had departed from his home town for the first time when he was eighteen years old, to attend the Seville Fair. He lost all his money and his desire to return to his native city, by gambling, and acquired, in exchange, a desire to see the world; so he went to Cadiz and embarked for America. There he had his ups and downs successively: he was a merchant, a super-cargo on a ship, and after many years of hard and fatiguing work, he returned to Cordova, thirty-six years old, penniless, and prematurely aged.

When Diego Palomares saw that his friend was getting on well with the store, he joined him.

While El Pende sat at the counter tending the store, Fuensanta continued to help the silversmith.

Six months after the first gift, the old Marquis sent for Fuensanta and gave her another hundred dollars.

From the wife's hands they passed into those of her husband, who used them all in the store.

El Pende asked the landlord to give him another room, and to remove one of the grated windows, that he might enlarge his store. His request was granted, and in place of the grating, they installed a show-window.

Then El Pende had a sign painted, and hanging from the board, a gilt, many-pointed star.

How many arguments he and Palomares had as to whether the star was right or not!

I remember that one day, when I was on my way to the Casino, they called me in to elucidate the question for them; and you ought to have heard me give them a talk about office-signs of all kinds! It is a matter to which few people pay any attention.

"Come, there you go again, wandering away from your subject," said the old woman.

"Be quiet," Don Gil ejaculated. "This matter of signs is very interesting; don't you think so?" he asked Quentin.

"I don't know anything about it."

"Oh, don't you? Well, for example, some night you may see a closed store with a sign which reads 'Perez,' with two red hands hanging from the board. What kind of business do those red hands indicate?"

"A glove store, perhaps?" asked Quentin.

"That's right. How clever the lad is! What does a basin indicate?"

"That's well known—a barber shop."

"And a rooster on top of a ball?"

"That I don't know."

"Why, a poultry shop. And a red or blue ball in a show-case?"

"A drug store."

"Very good. And a little tiny mattress?"

"A mattress-maker's store."

"And one or two black hands holding a bunch of keys?"

"I think I have seen that in front of locksmiths' shops."

"That's right. And a large book?"

"A bindery."

"But what a clever chap he is! And large eyeglasses—very large?"

"An optician's."

"And the bust of a woman leaning from a balcony as though taking the air?"

"I don't know."

"A ladies' hair-dressing salon: but they don't have as many here as they do in Madrid. And a horse-shoe?"

"You're the one that ought to be horse-shoed," ejaculated Señora Patrocinio. "Are you going on with the story or not, Don Gil?"

"But you two are confusing me! You make me lose the thread. Where was I?"

"You were telling us," said Señora Patrocinio, "about how they fixed up the store with the Marquis' money."

"Ah! That's so."

. . . . . . . . . . . . .

They widened the store; left off several articles that were not very productive, and devoted themselves exclusively to selling comestibles. They bought casks of Montillo wine, Montero oil, sugar, coffee, and hired some chocolate makers to make chocolate.

Palomares, whom El Pende had engaged as a clerk when he saw the prosperity of the establishment, spent the day wrapping up cakes of chocolate, toasting coffee, and mixing peanuts and chicory.

Palomares had a great talent for labelling his mixtures. When he had faked up something, he called it "Extra-Superior"; if the fake was so complete that one could not tell what kind of a product it was, then he called it "Superior" or "Fine."

Besides these hyperbolical names, there were other more modest ones, such as "First Class," "Second Class," and "Third Class." These divisions were hard to define; yet Palomares asserted, not that they were good, but that one could easily distinguish a difference between them.

According to him, it was clear that the "Second Class" was worse than the "First Class," and that the "Third Class" was worse than the "Second Class"; but this was not saying that the "First Class" and the "Second Class" were good, or even passably so.

In spite of the chemistry that El Pende and his assistant

employed, the store grew in reputation. The show-window was full of sausages wrapped in tinfoil, prunes, and tins of preserves. On the shelves were loaves of sugar, bottles of sherry, and jugs of gin. Upon the floor in sacks, were rice, kidney-beans, and casks of sardines.

Money began to flow into the store in such a quiet and unobtrusive manner that no one was aware of it. The old silversmith grumbled at the thought that some fine day they would leave him; but Fuensanta deceived him by telling him that the store was not getting along very well, and that they would get rid of it if they had a chance.

El Pende, who lacked the patience of his wife, wished to emancipate himself completely from the old man, so he rented the first floor of the house in which the store was located, giving the back room to Palomares.

Then Fuensanta hired a servant girl, and every minute she had free, she went to keep the old silversmith company. This procedure was very much praised by the old wives of the community, and Fuensanta enjoyed much popularity. At the same time, El Pende succeeded in making people forget his family nickname, and everybody called him Rafael, or Señor Rafael, and some even called him Don Rafael.

The family was progressing economically, and acquiring more respectability, when the lad Quentin began to make trouble. He ran away from home; he stole; once he came near poisoning the whole family; he did terrible things.

Then the old Marquis, to whose knowledge his grandson's escapades had come, had him brought before him and sent him away to school in England.

Quentin left, and the family continued their progress. Fuensanta had her fourth child, a daughter; and during the confinement, Don Andrés Salvador, the silversmith, died from heart failure.

When they opened the old man's will, they found that his fortune, almost in its entirety, with the exception of a few bequests to two distant relatives, was left to Fuensanta. The fortune, including the money and the house, amounted to somewhere near thirty thousand dollars.

Then Fuensanta and El Pende tried to rent the whole lower floor of the house on the Calle de la Zapatería, with the idea of converting it into a large warehouse. The landlord was willing, but the man who rented the mat store said that he would not move, that he had a ten-year contract with the landlord, and that he did not intend to leave. They offered to pay him an indemnity, but he persisted in his recalcitrant attitude.

And maybe the fool wasn't stubborn! El Capita was a man of evil intent with a magnificent history. Some time ago he lived with a widow who had two daughters in school. When the elder daughter graduated, the man fell in love with her, and married her; though he continued his relations with her mother. El Capita was an artful chap. His wife found out about the affair, and was indignant. She ran away with her husband's clerk out of revenge; but El Capita did not worry about the matter. Along came the second daughter, and El Capita, who was very astute, began to make advances to her, which she, more accommodating than her elder sister, willingly accepted.

El Capita was very content with his store; doubtless he had an affection for all those panniers and headstalls— mute witnesses of his drunken parties and tempestuous love affairs, and he got it into his head that he was not going to move. But the man reckoned without his hostess; and in this case, his hostess was Fuensanta, who when she said that she was going to do a thing, did it regardless of all obstacles.

Fuensanta very quietly transferred the inherited silver-smith's shop; then she sold the house in the Calle de

Librerías, and with the money from the transfer and the sale, bought the house in the Calle de la Zapatería; and El Capita had to get out in a hurry, willy nilly, with all his pack-saddles and panniers.

Fuensanta and El Pende converted the whole lower floor into a warehouse. They furnished the barracks and the prison with goods at wholesale; but as they did not wish to kill their retail trade, they rented a store in the Calle de la Espartería near the Arco Alto and the Calle de Gitanos. This place, which was known in ancient times by the name of El Gollizno on account of its extreme narrowness, is one of the busiest corners in Cordova. Certainly there....

. . . . . . . . . . . . .

"Good lord! Another digression?" exclaimed Quentin. "Haven't you finished yet?"

"Yes."

"Tell us the rest," said the old woman. "What happened to that El Pende fellow?"

"Nothing: they elected him to the council, then they made him lieutenant-mayor, and now he is a wealthy merchant, a banker; and we who were rich once, haven't a penny now. Eh? Well, that is the story. Come—pass me some more wine."

Don Gil seized the bottle with one hand, brought it to his mouth, and began to drink.

"Enough, man, enough," said Señora Patrocinio.

The archæologist paid no attention to her, and never stopped until he had emptied the bottle. Then he gazed about the room, shut his eyes, leaned his head upon the table, and an instant later, commenced to snore noisily.

"The compadre is rather intoxicated," said Quentin as he looked at Don Gil.

"Come, you're feeling pretty good yourself," replied the old woman.

"I? I was never so calm in my life. It takes a lot to get us people from England drunk."

"Ah! Are you English?"

"No; I come from here."

"And are you a friend of the Quentin of whom there has been so much talk tonight?"

"Ha... ha... ha!"

"What are you laughing at?"

"Why, that Quentin... is me!"

"You?" and she used the familiar *tu*.

"Ha... ha! Now the old dame is beginning to 'thee and thou' me!"

"Is it you, Quentin?"

"Yes."

"I am a relative of yours."

"Really? I'm very glad to hear it."

"I can't explain anything to you now, because you are drunk. Come some other day and we'll talk it over. I'll help you."

"Very good; I shall take advantage of your protection.... Ha, ha!"

"You shall see. You won't have to work."

"Work! Ha... ha... ha! That is an idea that never occurred to me, good dame. Far from me is that vulgar thought.... Ah!... Ha... ha... ha!"

Señora Patrocinio seized Quentin by the arm and led him to the street.

"Now, go home," she said to him; "some other day I shall tell you something that may interest you. Should you need money, come here before you go anywhere else."

This said, she pushed Quentin into the middle of the street. The coolness of the night air cleared his head. Day had not yet dawned; the sky was clean and cloudless; the moon was low in the heavens—just touching the horizon.

# CHAPTER XI

## MORE INCOMPREHENSIBLE THAN THE HEART OF
A GROWN WOMAN, IS THAT OF A GIRL-CHILD

QUENTIN did not abandon the idea of becoming intimate with Rafaela.

He now knew the close relationship that united them.
They were of the same family. Things would have to
turn out badly indeed not to be advantageous to him.

One morning Quentin again went to his cousin's
house. He found the gate open, and went as far as the
interior of the garden without ringing. He found Juan,
the gardener, busily occupied in trying to turn the key
which let the water out of the pool; an undertaking in
which he was not successful.

"What are you trying to do?" Quentin asked him.

"To turn this key; but it's so dirty...."

"Let me have it," said Quentin; and taking a large
crowbar, he turned the key with scarcely an effort. A jet
of water ran into a small trough, from which it flowed
through the various ditches that irrigated the different
parts of the garden.

"Where are the young ladies?" asked Quentin.

"At mass: they'll be back in a little while."

"What's doing here? How is everything getting on?"

"Badly. Worse every day," answered the gardener.
"How different this house used to look! Money used to
flow here like wheat. They said that every time the clock
struck, the Marquis made an ounce of gold. And such

luxury! If you had walked through these patios thirty years ago, you'd have thought you were in heaven!"

"What was here?"

"You would have met the armed house-guards, all gaudily attired—with short coats, stiff-brimmed hats, and guns."

"What did they do?"

"They accompanied the Marquis on his trips. Have you seen the coach? What a beauty it is! It will hold twenty-four persons. It's dirty and broken now, and isn't a bit showy; but you should have seen it in those days. It used to take eight horses and postillions *a la Federica* to haul it. And what a to-do when they gave the order to start! The guards, mounted on horseback, waited for the coach in that little *plazoleta* in front. Then the cavalcade started off. And what horses! He always had two or three of those animals that cost thousands of dollars."

"It must have cost him a lot to maintain a stable like that."

"Just think of it!"

"When did these grandeurs come to an end?"

"Not very long ago, believe me. When the Queen came to Cordova, she rode from the Cueva del Cojo to the city in our coach."

"How is it that the family could fall so far?"

"It has been everybody's fault. God never granted much sense to the members of this household; but the administrator and the Count, who is the young ladies' father, were the ones who brought on most of the ruin. The latter, besides being a libertine and a spendthrift, is a fool. People are always deceiving him; and what he doesn't lose through foolishness, he does through distrust. Once he bought twenty thousand gallons of oil in

Malaga at seventy *reales,* brought them here, and sold them in a few days, at forty."

"That certainly was an idiotic thing to do."

"Well, he's done lots more like it."

"What has become of him now? Where does he live?"

"He goes about the city with toreadors and horse-dealers. He has separated from his wife."

"Did he marry again?"

"Yes; the second time, he married the daughter of an olive merchant: a beautiful, but ordinary woman who is giving the town a lot to talk about. Since he is a fool, and she a sinner, after two or three years of married life, they separated—throwing things at each other's heads. Now he is living with a gipsy girl named La Mora, who relieves him of what pennies he has left. The girl's brothers and cousins go into retirement with him in taverns, and make him sign papers by threatening him with violence: why, they haven't left him a penny! And now that he has no money, they no longer love him. La Mora throws him out of his house, and I believe he crawls back to her on his knees."

"Meanwhile, what about his wife?"

"She gets worse and worse. She has been going about here with a lieutenant... she's a wild hussy."

The gardener took his spade and made a pile of earth in a ditch to keep the water away from a certain spot. While Juan worked, Quentin turned his ambitious projects over and over in his mind.

"What a superb stroke!" he was thinking "To marry the girl, and save the property! That surely would be killing two birds with one stone. To have money, and at the same time, pass for a romantic chap! That would be admirable."

"Here come the young ladies," said Juan suddenly, looking down the corridor.

Sure enough; Rafaela and Remedios, accompanied by the tall, dried-up servant, appeared in the garden. The two girls were prettier than ever in their mantillas and black dresses.

"See how pretty they are!" exclaimed Juan to Quentin, arms akimbo. "Those children are two slices out of heaven."

Rafaela laughed the laugh of a young woman utterly lacking in coquetry; Remedios looked at Quentin with her great, black eyes, waiting, perhaps, for a confirmation of the gardener's compliment.

Rafaela removed her mantilla, folded it, stuck two large pins in it, and gave it to the maid; then she smoothed her hair with her long, delicate-fingered white hand.

"I have a favour to ask of you," she said to Quentin.

"Of me?"

"Yes, sir."

"Command me: I shall consider myself most happy to be your slave."

Rafaela laughed musically and said:

"Goodness me! How quickly you take your ground!"

"I am not exaggerating; I am saying what I feel."

"Then be careful, for you seem to me to be a trifle restless for a slave, and I may have to put you in irons."

"It won't be necessary for you to do that. Tell me what you want me to do."

"Well, a very simple thing. My father, who is not all a gentleman should be, took a little silver jewelcase out of my room the other day. It is a souvenir of mother. I think he must have sold it, and I wish you would take the trouble of looking for it. You'll find it in some pawn-shop on the plaza. There is a coronet upon the cover of the case, and in the silk lining are the initials, R. S. If you find the little box, please buy it, and I shall pay you whatever it amounts to."

"No, not that."

"Oh, I don't want it under any other condition."

Apropós of the little box, Rafaela spoke sadly of her mother.

Remedios, who had taken off her mantilla, took a hoop from a corner and began to play with it.

"Remedios!" said Rafaela. "You have your new dress on. Change it, and study your lessons immediately."

"No, not today," replied the child.

"Why not? And she says it so calmly! Big girls don't play with hoops. If I don't watch this child, she plays all sorts of games, just like a little street urchin. Do you think that is right, girlie?"

Remedios looked at her sister impudently, and only whistled as an answer.

"Don't whistle, please."

"I will," answered Remedios.

"I'll shut you up in the dark room. We've had two days this week without our lessons. If you don't learn any more than that, you'll be a little donkey…. Just about as clever as Pajarito."

"No!" exclaimed the little girl, stamping her foot.

"Yes, yes," said Rafaela, smiling.

"No."—And throwing her arms about her sister's neck, Remedios climbed into her lap.

"I believe you have lost your moral strength," Quentin said to her.

"Yes; I think so too," added Rafaela.

Safe in her sister's lap, Remedios began to chatter, while Rafaela patted her like a baby. She told several stories in which Pajarito, Juan and the genet appeared.

"What a little story-teller you are!" said Rafaela, laughing.

When she grew tired of this, Remedios jumped from her sister's lap, and began to run about the garden. Presently she appeared riding astride of the donkey.

"The child is wild today," said Rafaela, gazing severely at Remedios.

The little girl noticed that her sister was annoyed, and jumping from the donkey at the risk of falling, she went up to her.

"Juan said that we can pick oranges now."

"Girlie, will you kindly be less of a busybody, and a little more quiet?"

"Well, that's what he said!" exclaimed Remedios, making an expressive gesture, and rolling her great, black eyes.

Quentin began to laugh. Rafaela joined him.

"What are you laughing at?" demanded Remedios of her sister.

"I'm not laughing, child."

"Yes, you are. Let's get out of here."

"But, why?"

"Yes; come on."

"It's just a little notion the girl has taken," murmured Quentin.

"What business is it of yours?"

"My dear child, if you grow up like this, no one will be able to resist you."

Remedios remained frowning by Rafaela's side; then she saw Juan's little dog, took it in her arms, and running to the pool, threw it into the water.

"What a creature!" said Rafaela, vexed.

They went to the pool; the dog swam to the edge and began to flounder about without being able to get out. Quentin knelt upon the ground, and stretching out his arm, lifted the little animal from the water.

"He's shivering," said Rafaela. "Do you see what you have done?" she added, turning to her sister—"He may die."

Remedios, who had watched the rescue impassively, went to a corner and sat upon the ground with her face to the wall.

"Remedios!" called Rafaela.

The child made no reply.

"Come, Remedios," said Quentin, going over to her.

"Go away!"

"Come, you're exhausting my patience."

"I won't."

Rafaela tried to seize the girl, but she began to run, shouting:

"If you follow me, I'll throw myself into the pool."

And she was making for it when Quentin seized her firmly about the waist, and heedless of her shrieks and kicks, handed her over to Rafaela.

"No, no; you must go into the dark room. What a child!"

"No, I won't do any more, I won't do any more," sobbed Remedios, hiding her head on her sister's shoulder, overcome with shame, and weeping like a Magdalene.

"When the tears are over, she'll be a little lamb. Will you undertake my mission?" Rafaela asked Quentin.

"If the little box is in Cordova, you may be sure that I shall find it."

"Good! Adiós. We are going in to get over this," said Rafaela, smiling ironically.

Rafaela and Remedios went up to their rooms, and Quentin went out into the street.

# CHAPTER XII

## IN SEARCH OF A JEWEL-CASE

"IN those days," asserted Don Gil Sabadía in a notable article in *El Diario de Cordova*, "La Corredera was a large, rectangular plaza surrounded by houses with heavy balconies and porticos supported by thick columns. At that time the plaza had no dirty and ugly brick market-place; nor were the houses as neglected as they are today; nor did so much hedge-mustard grow on the balconies. With a daily open-air market, a plaza used on great occasions for bull-fights and jousts, La Corredera constituted a commercial, industrial, and artistic centre for Cordova. In that spot were celebrated regal fiestas of great renown in our locality; there *autos da fé* were consummated; there Señor Pedro Romero and Pepe Hillo fought bulls when Charles IV visited the city; there the Tablet of the Constitution was set up in 1823 with great enthusiasm, only to be torn down and dragged about that same year; there the bodies of a few splendid youths were exposed, killed in the hills with their guns in their hands; there also the last executioners of Cordova, the two Juans—Juan García and Juan Montano—both masters of the art of hanging their fellow men. had splendid opportunities to perform the extremely important duties that had been conferred upon them. Lastly, from there, from La Corredera, sprang the rogues of Cordova, relatives of the rascals of Zocodover and Azoguejo, fathers of the scoundrels of Perchel, and of the lancers of Murcía, and remote ancestors of the Madrid *golfos*."

And Don Gil, after enumerating the beauties of La Corredera, terminated his article with the following lament: "One more reason we have for thanking our much-boasted-of progress!"

Quentin had been told that nearly all of the pawn shops in Cordova were situated in La Corredera, and the morning after his conversation with Rafaela, he appeared there, resolved to leave no stone unturned until he had discovered the little box which he had been entrusted to find.

He entered La Corredera through the Arco Alto. From this spot, the plaza presented a pleasing and picturesque spectacle. It was like a harbour filled with yellow and white sails shaking in the breeze, shining with light, and filling the whole extent of the plaza. Under the dark and sombre porticos, in the tiny shops and booths, there were little piles of black objects.

Quentin walked through the centre of the plaza. He saw permanent booths, like large huts, where they sold grains and vegetables; and some that were portable, like great umbrellas with long sticks, which belonged to green-grocers and fruit-sellers. Other booths were a bit more simple, being merely wide, awningless tables upon which walnuts and hazelnuts were heaped. Others, simpler still, were upon the ground, "upon the stone counters," as the itinerant pedlars called them.

Quentin left the centre of the plaza and entered the arcade, resolved to leave no second-hand store or pawn-broker's establishment unvisited. Each space beneath the arcade was occupied by a booth, and each column had a little stand at its base. On the inside of the covered walk were the gateways of inns with their classic patios, and their splendid old names; such as the Posada de la Puya, or the Posada del Toro.... The sandal stores displayed coils of plaited grass as signs; the drink establishments, shelves full of coloured bottles; the saddleries, headstalls, cinchas, and cruppers; the tripe shops, bladders, and sieves made of the skins of Lucena donkeys. Here a cane weaver was making baskets; there, a pawnbroker was piling up several greasy books; and near him, an old fright of a woman was taking a piece of hakefish from a frying-pan and placing it upon a tin plate.

Even the sidewalks were occupied; a vendor of Andújar ware was pacing up and down before his dishes: large water-jars, and small, green jugs which were arranged in squares upon the stones. An old country-woman was selling rolls of tinder for smokers; a man with a cap was exhibiting cigar cases and shell combs upon a folding table.

At each column there was a grinder with his machine, or a hatter with his caps in a large basket, or a fritter-maker with his caldron, or a cobbler with his bench and cut leather and a basin to dampen it in. There were notes of gaiety which were struck by stockings and handkerchiefs of vivid colours; and sinister notes: rows of different sized knives tied to a wall, on whose blades were engraved mottoes as suggestive as the following:

*Si esta víbora te pica,*
*No hay remedio en la botica.*

(If this viper should sting thee, there is no cure for it in the drugstore.)

Or as that other legend, laconic in its fidelity, written below a heart graven in the steel:

*Soy de mi dueño y señor.*

(I am of my lord and master.)

Although he visited every pawn shop and second-hand dealer in the plaza, Quentin failed to find the jewel-case. Somewhat dazed by the sun and the noise, he stopped and leaned against a column for a moment. It was a babel of shouts and voices and songs—of a thousand sounds. The hardware dealers struck horse-shoes with their hammers in a queer sort of rhythm; the knife-grinders whistled on their flutes; the vendor of medicinal herbs emitted a melancholy cry; the pine-nut seller shouted like a madman: "Boys and girls, weep for pine-nuts!"

There were cries that were languid and sad; others that were rapid and despairing. Some vendors devoted themselves to humour; like the seller of rolled wafers who began his advertisement by saying: "Here's where you get your wafers... they came from El Puerto—all the *way for* you!" and then mixed up a lot of sayings and refrains. Other merchants added a scientific touch; like the seller of tortoises, who dragged the little animals along the ground tied to a string, and shouted in a voice made husky by brandy: "Come and buy my little sea-roosters!"

All this rabble of vendors, of farmers, of women, of naked children, and of beggars; talked, shouted, laughed, gesticulated; it flowed from the Arco Alto to the Calle de la Espartería, where the orchardists from El Ruedo waited to bargain with the farmers; it entered the Plaza de las Cañas, and while the multitude moved about, the winter sun, yellow, brilliant as gold, fell upon and reverberated from the white awnings.

Quentin went through the Arco Bajo to a plazoleta where a group of old men were sunning themselves, with their cloaks tied to their bodies and their stiff, broad-brimmed hats pulled down over their eyes. The majority of them were so preoccupied in their noble task of doing nothing, that Quentin dared not bother them with questions, so he made his way toward a lupine-seller who was seated beneath a small awning which sheltered him from the sun.

The man had fastened a frame to the wall which served him as an awning. As the red disk of the sun descended in the heavens, the man changed the angle of the frame, always keeping himself in the shade.

This wise fellow, who was reading a paper at the moment through a pair of glasses, wore a high-crowned, sugar-loaf hat; he had the small, gentle eyes of a drunkard, a long, twisted, red nose, and a white, pointed beard. When Quentin accosted him, he lifted his eyes with indifference, looked over his glasses, and said:

"Sweetmeats? Lupine?"

"No; I would like you to tell me if there is a pawn shop around here besides those in La Corredera."

"Sí, Señor; there is one in the Plaza de la Almagra."

"Where is that?"

"Near here. Would you like me to go with you?"

"No, thanks. They might steal your wares."

"Pish! What would they want them for?" And the ingenious chap with the sugar-loaf hat came out from behind his awning, tipped his hat toward one ear, caressed his goatee, and flourishing a white stick, abandoned his basket of lupine to fate, and accompanied Quentin until he left him in front of a second-hand store.

"Thank you very much, *caballero,*" said Quentin.

The wise man smiled, shifted his high-crowned hat from his left ear to his right, swung his stick, and, after bowing ceremoniously, departed.

Quentin entered the shop and explained to the clerk what he was looking for. The man, after listening to him, said:

"I've got that jewel-case."

"Will you show it to me?"

"I don't know why I shouldn't."

The man opened a writing-desk, and from the bottom of one of the drawers took out a small, blackened box. It had a coronet upon the cover, but the lining had been torn out, so they could not see the initials that Rafaela had mentioned to Quentin. Nevertheless, it was probably the right box. Quentin wished to make sure.

"Do you mind telling me," he asked, "where this box came from?"

"Are you so interested in it?" questioned the pawnbroker rather sarcastically.

"Yes; but it is because I wish to make sure that it is the one I am looking for."

"Well, I don't mind saying where it came from, for I am sure that the man who sold it to me owned it."

"Is it from the house of a marquis?"

"Sí, Señor."

"Of one who lives on the Calle del Sol?"

"Sí, Señor."

"How much do you want for it?"

"Seventy dollars."

"The devil! That's a good deal."

"It's worth it. A man who knew about such things would give me a hundred dollars for it; perhaps more...."

"Very well. If I cannot come and get it today, I shall be here tomorrow."

"Very well."

Quentin went home deep in thought. Where was he going to get those seventy dollars? He entered the store and went to see Palomares.

"Could you let me have seventy dollars today?" he inquired.

"Seventy dollars! Where am I going to get it?"

"Don't you know any one who lends money?"

"You've got to have a guarantee if you want any one to lend you money; and what guarantee are you going to give?"

128

"The fact is, I've got to have the money today."

"Look here; come to the store on the Calle de la Espartería this evening, and we'll see what we can do."

At six o'clock, Quentin went to the store. He had never been there before. It was small, but overstocked with goods, and, at that hour, crowded with purchasers.

"Is Don Rafael in?" Quentin asked a clerk.

"There, in the back room."

Quentin went in, and found himself in a small room with various shelves full from top to bottom of tins of all kinds and colours, bottles, flasks, and jars. One breathed there a mixed odour of cinnamon, petroleum, coffee, and cod-fish. In that little shop of nutritious produce, three persons were engaged in conversation with Don Rafael. Quentin greeted them and sat down.

One of the three persons was a prebendary by the name of Espego, whom they called Espejito on account of his small stature. Espejito had a sly look, and was pacing about the back room with his hands behind his back.

The second member of the coterie was a lean man with very thin legs, which were wide apart like those of a compass; he had a face like a tunny-fish, with a fixed, penetrating, and suspicious glance. He was called Camacha, and was a solicitor. He wore a short moustache, side-whiskers that reached to the bottom of his ears, a broad-brimmed hat tipped to one side, and very tight trousers.

The third member was leaning back in a chair; he was a sexagenarian with a roman profile; his face was full of fleshy wrinkles; his nose, crooked and aquiline hung over his upper lip like a vulture over its prey; his eyes were staring and sunken; his mouth contemptuous and bitter, and his skin, lemon-coloured. He wore

Pío Baroja

a black handkerchief tied about his head; over it, a broad-brimmed hat, also black; and over his shoulders, a roomy, dark-brown cloak with large folds.

This gentleman, the owner of a number of farms about Cordova, was called Don Matías Armenta.

The four men talked slowly and disjointedly.

"I believe there are guarantees," murmured one of them from time to time.

"That's what I think."

"The condition of the house...."

"Is not satisfactory, that's certain; but to respond...."

"That's what I think."

"We'll speak of that some other day."

"I'm in the way here," thought Quentin, and he went into the store and sat down upon a bench, waiting for Palomares to appear.

Palomares went into the back room, and at the end of a short time, came out and said to Quentin:

"Well, my lad, it can't be done."

Quentin went into the street cursing his stepfather and the old cronies who were with him for a trio of usurers of the worst kind. He was walking along the streets wondering how he was to get the money, when he remembered the offer Señora Patrocinio had made to him the night he and Don Gil Sabadía were in her house.

"Let's go there," he said to himself. "We'll see if she makes good her offer."

He made his way to Los Tejares where Señora Patrocinio lived. The door of the house was open. Quentin knocked, and, as no one answered, he walked in.

"Señora Patrocinio!" he cried.

"Who is it?" came from above.

"A man who comes to ask for something."

"Well, we give nothing here."

"I am Quentin."

"Ah! It's you? Come in and wait for me."

"What beautiful confidence!" said Quentin, seating himself in the vestibule, which was nearly in darkness.

Just then he heard footsteps upon the stairs, and a woman veiled in a black mantilla descended with Señora Patrocinio.

The veiled lady looked at Quentin as she passed; he returned the look with curiosity, and would have gone to the door to see her better, had not Señora Patrocinio seized him by the arm.

"Come," said the old woman, "what's the matter?"

"Señora Patrocinio," Quentin stammered, "send me away and take me for an idiot if my request seems stupid to you. I have come to ask for money."

"Have you been gambling?"

"No."

"How much do you need?"

"Seventy dollars."

"Come, that's not much. Follow me."

Quentin and the old woman climbed to the second floor and entered a room which contained a large bed. Señora Patrocinio took a key from her pocket, and opened a cabinet. She clawed inside of it with her deformed hands until she brought forth a bulging purse. She opened it, removed from it a roll of coins wrapped in paper, broke it over the bed, and scattered several gold-pieces upon the coverlet. The old woman counted out twenty twenty-peseta pieces and offered them to Quentin.

"Take them," she said.

"But you're giving me too much, Señora Patrocinio."

"Bah! They won't weigh you down."

"Thanks very much!"

"You must not thank me. I only want one thing, and that is that you come to see me now and then. Some day I'll explain our relationship and what I expect of you."

"Very well."

Quentin took the money and left the house joyfully. It was night, and he thought that the pawn shop on the Plaza de la Almagra might be closed, but he went by to make sure, and found it still open. He took the jewelcase and went home.

"The truth is, I'm a lucky man," he murmured gleefully.

Quentin slept peacefully, rocked by sweet expectations. The next afternoon he went to the Calle del Sol.

He found the gate open, and passed on into the garden. The gardener was not there. He went upstairs and rang the bell. The tall, dried-up servant who came to the door, said:

"The young ladies are in the kitchen."

"Well, let's go there."

They went through a series of corridors and entered the kitchen. It was an enormous place, with a high skylight through which at that moment there filtered a ray of sunlight that fell upon the blond, somewhat mussed-up hair of Rafaela.

Rafaela and Remedios turned at the sound of footsteps.

"Oh, is it you? You have found us in a pretty mess," said Rafaela, showing him her hands covered with flour.

"What are you making?" asked Quentin.

"Some fried-cakes."

"It smells deliciously in here."

"Have you a sweet tooth?" asked Rafaela.

"Somewhat."

"This is the one with a sweet tooth," said Rafaela, indicating Remedios. "Let's get out of here, she'll have indigestion if we don't."

Rafaela washed her hands and arms, dried them carefully, and led the way from the kitchen into the drawing-room.

"I've got the little box here," announced Quentin.

"Oh, really? Give it to me. Thank you! Thank you very much indeed! How much did it cost you?"

"Nothing.... A mere trifle."

"No, no, that's not possible. Please tell me how much you paid for it."

"Won't you accept this small favour from me?"

"No; for I realize that it must have cost you a lot."

"Bah!"

"I'll find out, and then we'll talk about it further."

Remedios, approaching Quentin mysteriously, said to him:

"Is it true that there is a store in your house?"

"Yes."

"Are there sweets in it?"

"Yes."

"Will you bring me some?"

"What do you want me to bring you?"

"Bring me some white taffy, some hard candy, a lady-finger, and a sugar-plum."

"But, child, you want a whole candy shop!" said Rafaela.

"Then just some taffy and cake, eh?"

"Very well."

"But lots of it."

"Yes."

"Fine: now sing for us!"

"Gracious, what a bold little girl!" exclaimed Rafaela.

They opened the drawing-room windows, and Quentin sat at the piano and played the opening chords of the baritone aria from *Rigoletto*. Then, in a hearty voice, he began:

*Deh non parlare al misero*
*del suo perduto bene....*

He suddenly recalled his school, his friends; then he felt sentimental, and put a real sadness in his tones. When he sang, *Solo, difforme, povero,* he felt almost like weeping.

After *Rigoletto* came the song from *Un ballo*:

*Eri tu che machiavi....*

Quentin exhausted his repertoire; he sang all the songs from the Italian operas that he knew; and then, exaggerating his English accent, he sang *Rule Britannia!* and *God Save the Queen!*

134

The two sisters and the old servant sewed as they listened to Quentin, who kept up a steady stream of conversation like a stage comedian. They laughed at his stories and clownish tricks.

He had an inexhaustible supply, and related many anecdotes and adventures that were mostly invented by himself....

The afternoon passed very quickly. From the balcony they could see the dark mountain outlined strongly against the blue of the sky. The sun, very low in the horizon, was leaving long shadows of chimneys and towers on the grey roofs, and reddening the belfries with an ideal light that grew paler with each passing moment.

They could scarcely see within the room; the old servant brought in a lamp and placed it upon the table. Quentin took leave of the two sisters.

On his way out, he paused before the window overlooking the garden. The atmosphere was unusually clear; the sky was deepening to an intense blue. Distant objects; the white gardens upon the hillside, the hermitages among the cypress trees, the great round-topped pine trees upon the summit,... all could be seen in detail.

It grew darker; in the black, rectangular patch of the pool, a star commenced to twinkle, then another, until a multitude of luminous points trembled in its deep, quiet waters.

# CHAPTER XIII

## A PICNIC AND A RIDE

"AREN'T you going to Los Pedroches?" Remedios asked Quentin one day. The two sisters and the old woman were sewing in the drawing-room.

"What's doing there?" he asked.

"The Candelaria Picnic," answered Rafaela.

"Are you going?"

"Yes, I believe so. We are going with our cousins."

Quentin fell silent for a moment.

"Aren't you going?" Remedios asked again.

"I? No. I don't know any one."

"Don't you know us?" she asked.

"Yes; but I'd bother you...."

"Why?" asked Rafaela pleasantly.

"And if I did not bother you, I should be certain to annoy your cousins; perhaps they wouldn't like me to bow to you."

Rafaela became silent; implying, though perhaps unwittingly, that what Quentin had said might be true. So, somewhat embarrassed, he said:

"What do they do there?"

"Not much nowadays," answered the old woman. "There are a few dances and supper parties... but the best thing about it used to be the return home: it was the custom for every lad to bring a lass back to town on his horse's croup."

"Has that custom died out?" asked Quentin.

"Yes."

"Why don't they still follow it?"

"On account of the fights they had coming back," answered the old woman. "Boys, and men too, took to scaring the horses, and some of the riders fell off and began to fight furiously with both fists and guns."

"You seem to know all about it," said Rafaela to the old woman. "Have you ever been in Los Pedroches?"

"Yes; with a sweetheart of mine who carried me behind him on his horse."

"My! What a rascal!... What a rascal!" exclaimed Rafaela.

"When we reached Malmuerta," the old servant continued, "they frightened our horse, so my sweetheart, who had a short fowling-piece on his saddle, made as if to shoot it, and the people couldn't get away fast enough...."

Quentin decided to go to the picnic.

"I'm going to Los Pedroches, mother," he said to Fuensanta.

"That's good, my son," she replied, "go out and have a good time."

"To tell you the truth, I haven't any money."

"I'll give you what you need; and I'll find you some riding clothes, too."

Quentin hired a big horse with a cowboy saddle; then, following his mother's instructions, he put on a short jacket covered with ribbons and braid, fringed leggings, a tasseled shawl across the saddle bow, and a broad-brimmed hat.

He mounted at the door of his house. He was a good horseman, and as he jumped into the saddle, he made his horse rear. He brought him down at once, waved to his mother who was on the balcony, and rode off at a smart pace.

He went out through the Puerta de Osario to the Campo de la Merced, under the Arco de la Malmuerta and turned his horse's head toward the Carrera de la Fuensantilla. There he noticed the unusual exodus of people making their way in groups toward Los Pedroches.

It was a splendid February afternoon. The sun poured down like a golden rain upon the green countryside, and smiled in the fields of new wheat which were dotted with red flowers and yellow buds. Here and there a dark hut or a stack of straw surmounted by a cross arose in the broad expanse of cultivated lands.

Quentin rode swiftly along the highway, which was bordered at intervals by large, grey century-plants, from among whose pulpous branches rose flocks of chirping birds.

He reached the picnic-grounds: a meadow near the Los Pedroches ravine. The people were scattered over the meadow in groups. The bright and showy dresses of the girls shone in the sun afar off against the green background of the field. As Quentin drew near the fiesta-grounds, some groups were eating supper, and others were playing the guitar and dancing.

In some places, where the dancers were doubtless experts, curious onlookers crowded about them. An old man with side-whiskers was playing the guitar with great skill, and a dancer in a narrow-waisted suit was pursuing his graceful partner with his arms held high in the air; and one could hear the clacking of castanets, and the encouraging applause of the onlookers.

It was a peaceful happiness, dignified and serene. Girls in showy dresses, Manilla shawls, and with flowers in their hair, were strolling about, accompanied by sour-visaged dueñas and proud youths.

A little apart from the centre of the picnic, the more wealthy families were lunching peacefully; while little boys and girls were screeching as they swung in the swings hung from the trees.

There were vendors of oranges and apples and walnuts and chestnuts; and taffy women with their little booths of sweets and brandy.

Quentin went around the grounds looking all about him, searching for his cousins; and at last, in a little unpopulated grove, he caught sight of them among a group of several boys and girls.

Remedios recognized Quentin when he was still some distance away, and waving her hand at him, she rose to meet him. Quentin rode up to her.

"Where are you going?" the girl inquired.

"For a little ride."

"Do you want a cake?"

"If you will give…."

"Come on."

Quentin dismounted, walked up to the group, gave his hand to Rafaela, and greeted the others with a bow. Undoubtedly Rafaela had informed her friends who the horseman was, for Quentin noticed that several of the girls looked at him curiously.

He took the cake that Remedios gave him, and a glass of wine.

"Won't you sit down?" Rafaela asked him.

"Thank you, no. I'm going for a ride along the mountain."

As he drew near Rafaela, Quentin noticed the look of hatred that one of the young men present cast at him.

"He's a rival," he thought.

From that instant, the two boys were consumed with hatred for each other. The young man was tall, blond, with a certain rusticity about him in spite of his elegant clothes. Quentin heard them call him Juan de Dios. The youth spoke in a rather uncultured manner, converting his *s's* into *z's*, his *r's* into *l's*, and vice versa. He gazed fixedly at Rafaela, and from time to time said to her:

"Why don't you drink a little something?"

Rafaela thanked him with a smile. Among the girls were Rafaela's two cousins; the elder, María de los Angeles, had a nose like a parrot, green pop-eyes, and a salient under lip; Transito, the younger, was better looking, but her expression, which was half haughty and half indifferent, did not captivate one's sympathies. Like her sister, she had green eyes, and thin lips with a strange curve to them that gave her a cruel expression.

Transito questioned Quentin in a bantering and sarcastic tone; he replied to her pleasantly, with feigned modesty, and in purposely broken Spanish. Presently he announced his intention of going.

"What, are you going?" asked Rafaela.

"Yes."

"Are you afraid of us?" said Transito.

"Afraid of being enchanted," replied Quentin gallantly, as he bowed and went in search of his horse.

"Wait! Take me on the croup," Remedios shouted.

"No, no; you'll fall," said Rafaela.

"No, I won't," replied the child.

"The horse is gentle," Quentin put in.

"Very well then; you may take her for a while."

Quentin mounted rapidly, and Remedios climbed upon the step of the carriage that stood near. Quentin rode up to her and stuck out his left foot for her to use as a support. The little girl stepped upon it, and seizing Quentin about the waist, leaped to the horse's croup and threw her arms about the rider.

"See how well I do it," said she to her sister, who was fearfully watching these manœuvres.

"I see well enough."

"Where shall we go?" Quentin asked the girl.

"Right through the picnic-grounds."

They rode among the groups; the arrogance of the rider and the grace of Remedios with her red flower in her hair, attracted the attention of the crowd.

"There's a pair for you!" said some as they watched them ride by; and she smiled with her shining eyes.

Following Remedios' orders, Quentin rode back and forth among the places which she pointed out to him.

"Now let's go to the mountain."

Quentin rode up hill for half an hour.

The afternoon was drawing to a close; the shadows of the trees were lengthening on the grass; white clouds, solid as blocks of marble, with their under sides ablaze, floated slowly over the mountain; the air smelt of rosemary and thyme. Cordova appeared upon the plain enveloped in a cloud of golden dust; beyond her undulated low hills of vivid green, stretching in echelon one behind the other, until they were lost in the distance in a golden haze of vibrating light. Over the roofs of the city rose church towers, slate-covered cupolas, black, sharp-pointed cypresses. From between the walls of a garden, with a very tall and twisted trunk, a gigantic palm tree raised its head—like a spider stuck to the sky....

Quentin turned back with the idea of leaving Remedios with her sister.

"Well, well!" Rafaela exclaimed. "You certainly can't complain. We've been waiting for you to go home with us. Come, get down."

"No; he's going to take me home—aren't you, Quentin?"

"Whatever you wish."

"Well, let's be going."

"We're off!"

"Look out for jokers," warned Rafaela's cousin Transito.

They took the road cityward, riding among the groups who were returning from the fiesta.

They could see Cordova in the twilight with the last rays of the sun quivering upon its towers. In some houses the windows were commencing to light up; in the dark blue sky, the stars were beginning to appear.

Neither Quentin nor the girl spoke; they rode along in silence, swaying with the motion of the horse. They reached the Carrera de la Fuensantilla, and from there followed Las Ollerías. At the first gate they came to, El Colodro, Quentin thought he saw a group that might have stationed itself there with the intention of frightening the horses of the passers-by; so he went on through the Arco de la Malmuerta to the Campo de la Merced.

Here there was a group of little boys and young men, one of whom had a whip.

"Be careful, child; hold on to me tightly," said Quentin.

She squeezed the rider's waist with her arms.

"Are you ready?"

"Yes."

The group of young people came toward Quentin, one of them brandishing the whip. Before they had time to frighten his horse, Quentin drove in his spurs and slackened his reins. The animal gave a jump, knocked down several of the jokers, and broke into a gallop, spreading consternation among the youngsters. When they had passed the Campo de la Merced, Quentin reined in his horse and began to walk again.

"How did you like that, little girl?" asked Quentin.

"Fine! Fine!" exclaimed Remedios, brimming over with delight. "They wanted to shoot us."

"And they fell down."

The girl laughed delightedly. Quentin guided his horse to the Puerta del Osario, and once through it, threaded his way along lonely alleyways. The horse went at a walk, his iron shoes resounding loudly on the pavement.

"Would you like me to treat you?" asked Quentin.

"Yes."

They were passing a tavern called El Postiguillo; so Quentin stopped his horse, clapped his hands loudly twice, and the innkeeper appeared in the doorway.

"What does the little girl want?" said the man.

"Whatever you have," answered Remedios.

"A few cakes, and two small glasses of Montilla?"

"Would you like that?" asked Quentin.

"Very much."

They ate the cakes, drank the wine and went on their way. Just as they reached the Calle del Sol, a carriage stopped at the door, from which Rafaela, her cousins, and the blond young man descended. The latter, who helped the girls down, called to Remedios: "I'll be with you in a moment!" But the girl pretended not to hear him, and called Juan. Quentin took the child by the waist and lifted her into the arms of the gardener; then he bowed, and turned his horse up the street.

When he reached his house, he found that his family had not yet returned from the picnic. He saw Palomares in the street and joined him; gave his horse to a boy to take to the livery stable, and, in the company of the clerk, entered a café. He told him how he had passed the afternoon, and then began to speak casually of his grandfather's family.

"It looks as if they were about ruined, eh?"

"Yes; completely."

"Still they must have *some* cash haven't they?"

"Oof! The old man was very rich; more through his wife than himself. He is a fine man but very extravagant. When the rebel leader Gomez took possession of Cordova the old Marquis, who was then a Carlist, took him in and gave him thousands of dollars. He has always spent his money lavishly."

"What about the son?"

"The son is nothing like his father. He is a disagreeable profligate."

"And the son's wife?"

"La Aceitunera? She's a sinner of the first water."

"Pretty, eh?"

"Rather! A fine lass with unbounded wit. When she left her husband, she went to live with Periquito Gálvez; but now they say she is trotting about with a lieutenant. Just pull Juan the gardener's tongue a bit, and he'll tell you some curious things."

"Didn't the family ever have any relative clever enough to save it from ruin?"

"Yes; the Marquis has a brother called El Pollo Real; but he is a selfish sort who doesn't want to mix in anything for fear they will ask him for money. Have you never seen him?"

"No."

"Well, El Pollo Real has been a Tenorio. Now he is a half paralytic. They say that he is devoting himself to writing the history of his love affairs, and has hired a painter to paint pictures of all his mistresses. He's been at it for years. The first artist he had was a friend of mine from Seville, and he used to tell me that El Pollo Real would give him a miniature or a photograph for him to enlarge, and then he would explain what the subjects looked like: whether blondes or brunettes, tall or short, marchionesses or gipsies."

"Do you know Rafaela?"

"Do I know her! Rather! Poor little girl!"

"Why 'poor little girl'?" exclaimed Quentin, feeling cold from head to foot.

"The girl has had hard luck."

"Why, what happened to her?"

"Oh, affairs of a wealthy family, which are always miserable. After she was thirteen or fourteen years old, Rafaela was engaged to the son of a Cordovese count. It seemed as if the two children loved each other, and they made a fine couple. They were always seen together; going for walks, and in the theatre; when it began to be rumoured that the Marquis' family was on its way to ruin.

Then her sweetheart went away to Madrid. Month after month went by, and the lad did not return; finally some one brought the news that he had married a young millionairess in Madrid. Rafaela was ill for several months, and since that time she has never been as well or as gay as she used to be."

Quentin listened to this story profoundly mortified. He no longer cared to ask questions; he arose, left the café, and took leave of Palomares.

He was unable to sleep that night.

"Why this anger and mortification?" he asked himself. "What difference does it make whether Rafaela has had a sweetheart or not? Aren't you going to work out your problem, Quentin? Aren't you going to follow out your plan in life? Aren't you a good Bœotian? Aren't you a swine in the herd of Epicurus?"

In spite of Quentin's efforts to convince himself that he ought not to be irritated, it was impossible to do so. Merely to think that a man, probably a young whipper-snapper, had scorned Rafaela, offended him in the most mortifying manner.

# CHAPTER XIV

## SPRING

NO; he was no Bœotian; he was no Epicurean; he could not say that in his heart, he followed the admirable advice of the great poet: "Pluck today's flower, and give no thought to the morrow's."

He was passing through all of the most common and most vulgar phases of falling in love; he had moments of sadness, of anger, of wounded and maltreated self-esteem.

He tried to analyze his spiritual condition coldly, and he considered it best and most expedient to make an effort not to appear at Rafaela's house for a long time.

"I must be active," he said to himself. At other times his reason appealed to him: "Why not go to see her as I used to? What is it that I want? Do I want her to cease having a sweetheart she has already had? That would be stupid. We must accept things that have already been."

At this, his wounded pride responded with fits of anger, obscuring his intelligence; and the pride generally came out victorious.

Quentin did not appear at Rafaela's house for some time. Alone, with nothing to occupy him, friendless; he was desperately bored. How the Andalusian spring oppressed him! He wandered about from place to place, without plans, without an object, without a destination.

The sun inundated the silent, deserted streets; the sky, a pure, opaque blue, seemed something tangible—a huge turquoise, or sapphire in which roofs and towers and terraces were embedded.

Everything gave the impression of profound lethargy....
The houses: blue, yellow, pale rose, cream-coloured, all
hermetically sealed, seemed deserted; the irrigated vesti-
bules flowed with water; one smelt vaguely the odour of
flowers, and a penetrating perfume of orange blossoms
arose from the patios and gardens.

The plazas, like white whirlpools of sunlight, were
blinding with the reverberation of light against the walls.
In the alleys, tenebrous, narrow, shadowy, one felt a
damp, cave-like cold.... Everywhere silence and solitude
reigned; in some lonely spot, a donkey, tied to a grating,
remained motionless; a hungry dog scratched in a heap
of refuse; or a frightened cat ran with tail erect until it
disappeared in its hiding-place.

In the distance, the crowing of a cock rang out like
a bugle call in the silent air; one heard the melancholy
cry of the vendors of medicinal herbs; and through the
deserted plazoletas, through the narrow and tortuous
alleys, there rose the song of love and death that a
*grancero* was singing as he rode along on his donkey.

In La Ribera, some vagabonds and gipsies were sunning themselves, while others played quoits; little children with brown skins ran about bare-legged, covered
only by a scanty shirt; sunburned old women came to
the windows and gratings; and along the white, the very
white highway, which resembled a great chalk furrow,
there passed gallant horsemen, raising clouds of dust.

The river wound peacefully along—blue at times, at
times golden; wagons and herds passed slowly over the
bridges—so slowly that from a distance they seemed
motionless.

An oppressive calm, a tiresome somnolence weighed
down upon the city; and in the midst of this calm, of this
death-like silence, there sounded a bell here, another
there—all extremely languid and sad....

At nightfall, the magic of the twilight touched the city

and the distant landscape with gold——'d lights; splendid colours of extraordinary magnificence. The clouds
became rosy, scarlet.... The country was tinged with
gold, and the last rays of the sun set fire to the rocks
and peaks of the mountain-tops.

In the streets, which were bathed with light, a narrow
strip of shadow appeared upon the walks, which grew
and widened until it covered the whole pavement. Then
it slowly climbed the walls, reached the grated windows
and the balconies, scaled the twisted eaves.... The sunlight completely disappeared from the street, and there
only remained the last vestiges of its brilliancy upon the
towers, the high look-outs, and the flaming windows....

The air grew diaphanous, acquired more transpar-
ency; the horizon more depth; and the sides of the white
walls of garrets and corners, as they reflected the scarlet
or rosy sky, resembled blocks of snow animated by the
pale rays of a boreal sun....

Presently the lamps were lighted; their little red flames
flickering in the shadows; and squares of lighted windows punctured the façades of the houses.

At this hour on work days, women visited the stores;
wealthy families returned in their coaches from their
orchards; youths rode back and forth on horseback; and
the nocturnal life of Cordova poured through the central
streets, which were lighted by street lamps and shop
windows.

Quentin wandered from place to place, ruminating
on his sadness; walked indifferently along streets and
plazas; watched the young ladies coming and going
with their mammas, and followed by their beaux. When
his irritation disappeared, he felt discouraged. The melancholy calmness of the city, the dreamy atmosphere,
produced within him a feeling of great lassitude and
laziness.

At times he firmly believed that Rafaela would trouble him no more; that his feeling of love had been a superficial fantasy.

In the morning Quentin often went to the Patio de los Naranjos where El Pende's father used to spend his time with a coterie of old men, beggars, and tramps, which all Cordova ironically called *La Potrá*, or the herd of young mares.

El Pende senior, or Matapalos, passed his time there chatting with his friends. He was an original and knowing fellow who spoke in apothegms and maxims. He dominated the meetings as few others could. No one could, like him, so slyly introduce a number of subjects in a conversational hiatus, or in the act of rolling a cigarette. Of course, for him, this last was by no means a simple affair; but rather an operation that demanded time and science. First, Matapalos took out a little knife and began to scrape a plug of tobacco; after the scraping came the rubbing of it between his hands; then he tore a leaf of cigarette paper from its little book, held it for a moment sticking to his under lip, and then began to roll the cigarette first on one end, and then on the other, until the manœuvre was happily consummated. This operation over, Matapalos removed his calañés, placed it between his legs, and from somewhere within the hat drew forth a little leather purse, from which he extracted flint and steel and tinder.

After this, he slowly covered himself and from time to time, in the midst of the conversation, struck the steel with the flint until he happened to light the tinder, and with the tinder, his cigarette.

The old man lived in a hut in the Matadero district; he knew everything that had occurred in Cordova for many years, and boasted of it. For Matapalos, there were no toreadors like those of his own time.

"I'm not taking any merit away from Lagartijo or

Manuel Fuentes," he said, "but you don't see any more toreadors like El Panchón, or Rafael Bejarano, or Pepete, or El Camará. You ought to have seen Bejarano! He was such a great rival of no less a person than Costillares, that in my time they used to sing:

*"Arrogante Costillares,*
*anda, vete al Almadén*
*para ver bien matar toros*
*al famoso Cordobés."*

(Proud Costillares, come, and go to the Almadén to see the famous Cordovese kill bulls right.)

In this subject Matapalos had a formidable adversary; another old man whom they called Doctor Prosopopeya, who, as a native of Seville, never admitted that a Cordovese toreador could come up to one from Seville.

Quentin found Matapalos very funny and very amusing, and he often went to listen to him.

While the old man related ancient history in his quiet, peaceful voice, Quentin contemplated the Patio de los Naranjos, sometimes listening to what was said, sometimes not.

The orange trees were in full blossom, and their penetrating perfume produced a certain giddiness; from time to time one could hear distant bells which the cathedral bell seemed to answer, clanging loudly.... Then silence again reigned; the birds chirped in the trees; the water murmured in the fountain; the butterflies bathed in the pure air; and the lizards and salamanders glided along the walls.

Among the shadows of the orange trees shone vivid splashes of sunlight; doves tumbled from the cathedral roof and flew softly through the blue and luminous air, making a slight sound of ripping gauze; sometimes they made a metallic whirr as they rapidly beat their wings.

The majority of the *Potrá* was made up of beggars and tramps. These beggars were neither emaciated, squalid, nor ill; but strong, vigorous men, hirsute, with long, matted locks, sunburned, covered with rags.... Some wore threadbare calañés hats; others, broad-brimmed sombreros worn over grass handkerchiefs; some, a very few, wore loose, yellowish coats with long sleeves; a good many wrapped themselves up in grey cloaks of heavy cloth and many folds. Nearly all of them had private homes where they were given leavings and cigarette butts; those who did not, went to the barracks, or to a convent; no one lacked the hodge-podge necessary for wandering on, though poorly, through the bitter adversities of life.

From time to time the *Potrá* came into a little money; and then ten or twelve of them got up a pool to play the lottery.

In that troop there was a beggar with a black beard, younger than the rest, bent almost double at the waist, who went about leaning on a short crutch. They called this man El Engurruñao. He had one shrunken leg wrapped in rags, although really he had no illness at all. He howled in a doleful voice after every decently-dressed passer-by, and he took in plenty of money.

Through the conversations of these tramps and beggars, Quentin came to know Cordova life, and that of the principal families of the town. Through them he learned that the majority of the great families were on their way to poverty.

One example of an economic catastrophe was that of a gentleman who walked through the arcade of the Mosque every morning. This gentleman was dressed like a dandy of other days: well-fitting coat, flowing black cravat, tall silk hat with a flat brim, and, on some cold days, a blue cape. The poor man was emaciated, had long, grey, bushy hair, and wore yellow gloves.

He was a ruined aristocrat. It was pitiful to see that living ruin walking up and down under the porticos, with his hands behind his back, talking to himself with a gesture of resignation and sadness....

# CHAPTER XV

## WHERE HIS BEAUTIFUL EXPECTATIONS WENT!

ONE morning Quentin met Juan, the gardener.

"You don't come to the house any more, Señorito."

"I've had lots to do these days."

"Have you heard the important news?"

"What is it?"

"The Señorita is going to be married."

"Rafaela?"

"Yes."

"To whom?"

"To Juan de Dios."

Quentin felt as if all his nerves had let go at once.

"The Marquis is getting worse every day," the gardener continued, "so he thought the Señorita ought to get married as soon as possible."

"And she.... What does she say?"

"Nothing, at present."

"But will she oppose it?"

"How do I know?"

"Are the family affairs in such bad shape that the Marquis was forced to take this course?"

"They are very bad. The grandfather hasn't much longer to live; the Señorita's father is a profligate; and El

Pollo Real doesn't care to do anything at all. To whom will they leave the girls? Their stepmother, La Aceitunera, is no good. Have you ever heard of a Señora Patrocinio who has a house in Los Tejares? Well, she goes there every day. Why, it's a shame."

"And this Juan de Dios... is he rich?" asked Quentin.

"Very; but he is very coarse. When he was a little boy he used to say: 'I want to be a horse,' and he used to go out to the stable, pick up some filth in his hands, and say to the people, 'Look, look what I did.'"

"He *is* coarse, then—eh?"

"Yes; but he's got noble blood in him."

Quentin left Juan and went home perplexed. Indubitably, he was no Bœotian, but a vulgar sentimentalist, a poor cadet, an unhappy wretch, without strength enough to set aside, as useless and prejudicial, those gloomy ideas and sentiments: love, self-denial, and the rest.

And he had thought himself an Epicurean! One of the few men capable of following the advice of Horace: "Pluck today's flower, and give no thought to the morrow's!" He! In love with a young lady of the aristocracy; not for her money, nor even for her palace; but for her own sake! He was on a level with any romantic carpenter of a provincial capital. He was unworthy of having been in Eton, near Windsor, for eight years; or of having walked through Piccadilly; or of having read Horace.

In the miserable state in which Quentin found himself, only nonsensical ideas occurred to him. The first was to go to Rafaela and demand an explanation; the second was to write her a letter; and he was as pleased with this idiotic plan as if it had been really brilliant. He made several rough drafts in succession, and was satisfied with none of them. Sometimes his words were high-sounding and emphatic; again, he unwittingly gave a clumsy and vulgar tone to his letter: one could read between the lines a common and uncouth irony, as often as extraordinary pride, or abject humility.

At last, seeing that he could not find a form clear enough to express his thoughts, he decided to write a laconic letter, asking Rafaela to grant him an interview.

He gave Juan the letter to give to his young mistress. He was waiting at the door for some one to answer his ring, when Remedios appeared.

"See here," said the child.

"What's the matter?"

"Don't you know? Rafaela is going to marry Juan de Dios."

"Does she love him?"

"No; I don't think she does."

"Then why does she marry him?"

"Because Juan de Dios is very rich, and we have no money."

"But will she want to do it?"

"She hasn't said anything about it. Juan de Dios spoke to grandfather, and grandfather spoke to Rafaela. Are you going to see sister?"

"Yes, this very minute."

"She's in the sewing-room."

They went to the door.

"Tell her not to marry Juan de Dios."

"Don't you like him?"

"No. I hate him. He's vulgar."

Quentin went in, glided along the gallery, and knocked upon the door of the sewing-room.

"Come in!" said some one.

Rafaela and the old woman servant were sewing. As Quentin appeared a slight flush spread over the girl's cheeks.

"What a long time it is since you have been here!" said Rafaela. "Won't you sit down?"

Quentin gave her to understand with a gesture that he preferred to remain standing.

"Have you been so very busy?" asked the girl.

"No; I've had nothing to do," answered Quentin gruffly. "I've spent my time being furious these days."

"Furious! At what?" said she with a certain smiling coquetry.

"At you."

"At me?"

"Yes. Will you let me speak to you alone a minute?"

"You may speak here, before my nurse. She will defend me in case you accuse me of anything."

"Accuse you? No, not that."

"Well, then, why were you so furious?"

"I was furious, first because they told me that you once had a sweetheart whom you loved; and second, because they say that you are going to get married."

Rafaela, who perhaps did not expect such a brusque way of putting the matter, dropped her sewing and rose to her feet.

"You, too, are a child," she murmured at length. "What can one do with what is gone by? I had a sweetheart, it is true, for six years—and I was in love with him."

"Yes; I know it," said Quentin furiously.

"If he acted badly," Rafaela continued, as if talking to herself, "so much the worse for him. There is no recollection of my childhood that is not connected with him. In his company I went to the theatre for the first time, and to my first dance. What little happiness I have had in my life, came to me during the time I knew him. My mother was living then; my family was considered wealthy.... Yet, if that man were free, and wished to marry me now, I would not marry him; not from spite, no—but because to me he is a different man.... I say this to you because I feel I know you, and because you are like my sister Remedios: you demand an exclusive affection."

"And don't you?" demanded Quentin brusquely.

"I do too; perhaps not as much as you; but neither do I believe that I could share my affection with another. I must not deceive you in this. You would be capable of being jealous of the past."

"Probably," said Quentin.

"I know it. I don't believe that I have flirted with you; have I?"

Rafaela spoke at some length. She had that graciousness of those persons whose emotions are not easily stirred. Her heart needed time to feel affection; an impulse of the moment could not make her believe herself in love.

She was a woman destined for the hearth; to be seen going to and fro, arranging everything, directing everything; to be heard playing the piano in the afternoons. In a burst of frankness, Rafaela said:

"Had I listened to your hints, I should have made you unhappy without wishing to, and you would have made me miserable."

"Then how is it that you are going to marry Juan de Dios?" asked Quentin brutally.

Rafaela was confused.

"That's different," she stammered; "in the first place, I have not decided yet; and besides, I have made my conditions. Then again, there is this great difference: Juan de Dios is not jealous of my past love affair... he wants my title. [In this moment, Rafaela is sure that she is calumniating her betrothed in order to get out of her difficulty.] Moreover, my whole family is interested in my marrying him. If I do so, my grandfather, poor dear, will be easy in his mind; Remedios will be sure of being able to live according to her station,—and so shall I."

"You are very discreet; too discreet—and calculating," said Quentin bitterly.

"No; not too much so. What would happen to us girls otherwise?"

"What about me?"

"You?"

"Yes, me; I would work for you if you loved me."

"That could never be."

"Why?"

"For many reasons. First of all, because I am older than you...."

"Bah!"

"Let me speak. First, because I am older than you; second, because you would be jealous of me and would continually mortify me; and lastly, most important of all, because you and I are both poor."

"I shall make money," said Quentin.

"How? With what? Why aren't you making it now?"

"Now?" questioned Quentin after a pause. "Now I have no ideal; it's all the same to me whether I'm rich or poor

But if you believed in me, you'd find that I could snatch money from the very bowels of the earth."

"Possibly, yes," said Rafaela calmly; "because you are clever. But those are my reasons. Some day, when you recall our conversation, you will say: 'she was right.'"

"You are very discreet," said Quentin as he turned toward the door; "too discreet; and you have discreetly torn asunder all my illusions, and have left my soul in shreds."

"Do you hate me now?" she said sadly.

"Hate you, no!" exclaimed Quentin with emotion, effusively pressing the hand Rafaela held out to him. "You are an admirable woman in every respect!"

And trembling violently, he left the room.

As he went down the stairs Remedios rushed up to him.

"What did she say to you?" she asked.

"It's no use; she's going to marry him."

"Did she tell you that herself?"

"Yes."

"And you. What are you going to do?"

"What can I do?"

"I'd kill Juan de Dios," murmured the girl resolutely.

"If she wished it, I would, too," replied Quentin, and he stepped into the street.

He walked along in a daze; he repeated Rafaela's words to himself, and discovered better arguments that he might have put forward in the interview, but which did not occur to him at the moment. Sometimes he thought, more rationally: "At least I came out of it well;" but this consolation was too metaphysical to satisfy him.

He spent a sleepless night at his window watching the stars and thinking. He analyzed and studied his moral problem, proposing solutions, only to reject them.

At dawn he went to bed. He believed that he had hit upon a definite solution—the norm of his existence. Condensed into a single phrase, it was this:

"I must become a man of action."

# CHAPTER XVI

## THE MAN OF ACTION BEGINS TO MAKE HIMSELF KNOWN

QUENTIN got up late, ate his breakfast and wrote several letters to his friends in England. In the evening he looked through the amusement section of the paper and saw that there was to be an entertainment in the Café del Recreo.

He asked Palomares where this café was, and was told that it was on the Calle del Arco Real, a street that ran into Las Tendillas.

The constant irritation in Quentin's mind troubled him so, that he calmly decided to get drunk.

"Tell me," he said to the waiter after seating himself at a table in the café, "what refreshments have you?"

"We have currants, lemons, blackberries, and French ice-cream."

"Fine! Bring me a bottle of cognac."

The waiter brought his order, filled his glass, and was about to remove the bottle.

"No, no; leave it here."

"Aren't you going to see the show?" asked the waiter with obsequious familiarity. "They are giving *La Isla de San Balandrán*: it's very amusing."

"I'll see."

After Quentin had emptied several glasses, he began to feel heartened, and ready for any folly. At a near-by table several men were talking about an actress who took the principal part in a musical comedy that had just been put on. One with a very loud voice was dragging the actress' name through the mire.

This man was extremely fat; a kind of a sperm whale, with the bulging features of a dropsical patient, a shiny skin, and the voice of a eunuch. He had a microscopic nose that was lost between his two chubby cheeks, which were a pale yellow; his hatchet-shaped whiskers were so black that they seemed painted with ink; his stiff, bluish hair grew low on his forehead, with a peak above the eyebrows. He wore diamonds upon his bosom, rings upon his pudgy fingers, and, to cap his offensiveness, he was smoking a kilometric cigar with a huge band.

The bearing, the voice, the diamonds, the cigar, the waddling, and the laughter of that man set Quentin's blood afire to such an extent, that rising and striking the table where the whale was talking to his friends, he shouted:

"Everything you say is a lie!"

"Are you the woman's brother or husband?" inquired the obese gentleman, staring into space and stroking his black sideburns with his much bediamonded hand.

"I am nothing of hers," replied Quentin; "I don't know her, and I don't want to know her; but I do know that everything you say is a lie."

"Pay no attention to him," said one of the fat man's companions; "he's drunk."

"Well, he'd better look out, or I'll strike him with my stick."

"You'll strike me with your stick!" exclaimed Quentin. "Ha... ha... ha!... But have you ever looked into a mirror?... You really are most repulsive, my friend!"

The fat man, before such an insult to his appearance, rose and endeavoured to reach Quentin, but his friends restrained him. Quentin quickly removed his coat and rolled up his sleeves, ready to box.

"Evohé! Evohé!" he thundered. "Come who will! One by one, two by two, every one against me!"

A thin, blond man with blue eyes and a golden beard, stepped up to him; not as though to fight, but with a smile.

"What do *you* want?" Quentin asked him rudely.

"Oh! Don't you remember Paul Springer, the son of the Swiss watch-maker?"

"Is that you, Paul?"

"Yes."

"Well, I'm sorry."

"Why?"

"Because I should have liked it had it been the fat man or one of his friends, so I could have cut him open with my fist."

"I see that you are just as crazy as ever."

"I, crazy? I'm one of the few people on this planet in their right senses! Moreover, I have decided to become a man of action. Believe me!"

"I can't believe anything of you now, my lad. What you ought to do is to put on your coat and go to bed. Come, I'll go with you."

Quentin assented, and went home with his friend.

"We'll see each other again, won't we?" said the Swiss.

"Yes."

"Then, until another day."

They took leave of each other. Quentin remained in his doorway.

"I'm not going in," he said to himself. "Am I not a man of action? Well, *adelante!* Where can I go? I'll go and see Señora Patrocinio. I'll take a few turns about here until my head is a little clearer...."

He knocked at the house in Los Tejares, and the door was immediately opened to him.

"Ah! Is it you?" said the old woman, as she lifted the candle to see who it was.

"Yes, it is I."

"Come in."

The old woman lit the lamp in the same room on the lower floor that Don Gil Sabadía and Quentin had occupied.

"What's the matter?" asked Señora Patrocinio. "Do you need money?"

"No. Do you, too, wish to offend me?"

"No; I just wanted to give you some."

"Thanks very much! You are the only person who takes any interest in me—why, I don't know.... I have come to see you tonight because I am unhappy."

"I know.... Rafaela is going to get married."

"And how do you know that that is the reason for my unhappiness?"

"Nothing is secret from me. You liked her, but you will get over it soon. She was fond of you, too."

"Do you think...?"

"Yes; but the poor girl had a bad beginning in life, and does well not to get mixed up in adventures; for the majority of men aren't even worth the trouble of looking in the face. Still, what her sweetheart did was disgraceful. Rafaela was brought up weakly,—too carefully guarded;

then she began to grow quite happy, what with taking care of her mother and her betrothal. Then her mother died; her father remarried immediately; in a few months it began to be rumoured that her family was on the verge of ruin, and her sweetheart skipped out. Think of it! The poor abandoned girl began to turn yellow, and thought she was going to die. I believe that she owes her cure to the trouble her younger sister gave her."

"Yes; I understand that she has no faith in men. Probably I ought not to have paid any attention to the fact," Quentin added ingenuously. "But won't this Juan de Dios make her suffer?"

"No. He's coarse, but good at heart. What are you going to do?"

"I! I don't know. We live in such a contemptible epoch. If I had been born in Napoleon's time! God! I'd either be dead by now or else on the road to a generalship."

"Would you have enlisted with Napoleon?"

"Rather!"

"And would you have fought against your own country?"

"Against the whole world."

"But not against Spain."

"Especially against Spain. It would be pretty nice to enter these towns defended by their walls and their conventionalities against everything that is noble and human, and raze them to the ground. To shoot all these flat-nosed, pious fakers and poor quality hidalgos; to set fire to all of the churches, and to violate all the nuns...."

"You've been drinking, Quentin."

"I? I'm as calm as a bean plant, which is the calmest vegetable there is, according to the botanists."

"You must not talk like that of your native land in front of me."

"Are you a patriot?"

"With all my heart. Aren't you?"

"I am a citizen of the world."

"It seems to me that you've been drinking, Quentin."

"No; believe me."

"I say this to you," added the old woman after a long pause, "because for me, this is a solemn moment. I have told no one the story of my life until this moment."

"The devil! What is she going to tell me?" mumbled Quentin.

"Are you vengeful?" asked the old woman.

"I?"

Quentin was not sure whether he was vengeful or not, but the old woman took his exclamation for one of assent.

"Then you shall avenge me, Quentin, and your family. We are of the same blood. Your grandfather, the Marquis of Tavera, and I are brother and sister."

"Really?"

"Yes. He doesn't know that he has a sister living. He thinks I died a long time ago."

Quentin scrutinized the old woman closely and discovered certain resemblances to the old Marquis.

She pressed Quentin's hand, and then commenced her story as follows:

"In villages, there are certain families in which hatred is perpetuated through century after century. In cities, after one or two generations, hatred and rivalry are gradually wiped out until they disappear altogether. Not so in the villages: people unconcerned in the quarrel carry the story of it from father to son, present the chapter of insults to different individuals, and go on feeding the flame of rancour when it tends to extinguish itself.

"I was born in a large, highland village, of such an illustrious family as that of Tavera. My mother died young, my older brother went to England, the other to Madrid to take up a diplomatic career, while I remained in the village with my father and two maiden aunts.

"My mother, whom I scarcely knew, was very good, but rather simple; so much so that they say that when the fishes in our pool did not bite, she called in a professional fisherman and gave him a good day's wages to teach them to do so.

"My family came from an important village in the province of Toledo, near La Puebla, where long ago there used to stand a tower and a castle and various strongholds, which are now nothing but ruins.

"According to my father, a harsh man, proud of his titles and lineage, we came from the oldest nobility, from the conquerors of Cordova, and were related to the whole Andalusian aristocracy: the Baenas, Arjonas, Cordovas, Velascos, and Gúzmans.

"In spite of our ancestry, our family did not enjoy any especial respect from the townspeople on account of the display we made, because our property had diminished somewhat, and also because the new liberal ideas were beginning to make themselves felt.

"My father owned nearly the whole village; he received a contribution from every chimney; he had the only interment chapel in the large church; and a patronage in several smaller churches and hermitages. In spite of the prestige of his lineage and his wealth, every one hated him—justly, I believe, for he was despotic, violent and cruel.

"That was about fifty years ago. My nose did not try to meet my chin then, nor did I lack any teeth; I was a lass worth looking at; graceful as a golden pine, and blonder than a candle. Any one seeing me in those days would have liked to know me! I lived with my father, who used to aim a blow at me every once in a while, and with my aunts, who were busybodies, meddlers, and crazy.

"As I have already said, my father had enemies; some openly avowed, others secret, but who all did the greatest amount of harm they could. Among them, the most powerful was the Count of Doña Mencia, whose family, much more recently come to the village than ours, was slowly acquiring property and power.

"The rivalry between the two houses was increased by a lawsuit which the Doña Mencias won against us, and it grew into a savage hatred when my father committed the offensive act of violating one of the rival family's little girls.

"The Doña Mencias took the child to Cordova; my father once heard a bullet whistle by his head as he was on his way to a farm—and this was the state of affairs, my family hated by our rivals and by nearly all of the townspeople, when I reached my eighteenth year, with no one to advise me but my aunts.

"I was, as I have said before, very pretty, and attracted attention wherever I went. Even at that age I had already had two or three beaux with whom I used to talk through my window-grating, when the Count of Doña Mencia's eldest son began to call upon me, and finally to ask for my hand. The whole village was surprised at this; I was disposed to pay no attention to him; moreover, I received several anonymous letters telling me that if I listened to the Count's son, very disagreeable consequences might arise, because the hatred was still latent between the two families. I was just about decided to refuse him, when my aunts, crazy novel readers that they were, insisted

169

that I ought to listen to him, for the boy's intentions were honourable, and in this way I could once and for all put an end to the rivalry and hatred.

"My father prided himself upon the fact that he never interfered with what was happening in the family; his only occupations were hunting, drinking, and chasing after farm girls, and if I had consulted him about the affair, he would have sent me harshly about my business.

"So, following my aunts' advice, I accepted the enemy of our home as a sweetheart, and received him for a year. One time in the garden, which was where we used to see each other, he threw himself upon me and attempted to overpower me; but people came in answer to my cries. My betrothed said that I had foolishly taken fright, as he was only trying to kiss me; I wanted to break the engagement, but instead of breaking off our relations, the affair only hastened the wedding.

"Grand preparations were made, but so sure were the townspeople that my sweetheart would never marry me, that servants, friends, every one, gave me to understand that the wedding would never take place, and that my betrothed would be capable of changing his mind at the very foot of the altar. Thus warned, I attempted to lessen the expense of the wedding, but my aunts tried to convince me not to do such a crazy thing.

"In fine, the day which was as dreaded as it was hoped for, arrived; my betrothed appeared at the church, and the wedding was celebrated. God knows how many hopes I had of being happy. The marriage feast was eaten; the ball was held. The festivities lasted until midnight, when we retired.

"The next morning when I awoke, I looked for my husband at my side, but did not find him. He never appeared all day long; they looked for him, but in vain. Days and days passed, and more days, while I waited for him, fearing an accident rather than an insult. After a long time, I received a mocking letter from him in which he told me that he would never come back to me.

"From that one wedding night, I became pregnant, and on this account suffered much anxiety. My father, in whom the affair had rekindled the anger at the rival family, assured me that he would strangle the child if it were born alive: my aunts did nothing but weep at every turn.

"I was restless; I don't know whether from pain or what, and gave premature birth at eight months to a dead boy.

"A short time after, my father died of a fall from his horse, the administrator started a lawsuit against us, and took all our property from us; my older brother was travelling, the other was in Rome; I wrote to them, and they did not answer; my aunts took refuge in the house of some relatives, and I went where the will of God took me.

"At first I was in mortal terror, but I soon got used to it, and did everything. I've lived like a princess and like a beggar; I've intrigued in high circles, and have been an army vivandière. I have been in a battle in the Carlist wars, and have walked among the bullets with the same indifference with which I walk the streets of Cordova today.

"After a while, with the pain I suffered, I forgot everything,—everything except my husband's infamy, and that of his whole family.

"That family has gone on implacably bringing disgrace to ours. When they killed your father there was a man pursuing him with the soldiers. Do you know who he was? My husband's son. And his grandson was Rafaela's sweetheart, the one who left her when he thought she was penniless.

"My husband married again. He is a bigamist, and probably falsified my death certificate. Today he moves in high circles, but the blow he gets from his downfall will be all the greater."

"What are you thinking of doing?" asked Quentin.

"Of denouncing him. I have not done so before on account of my older brother. I don't want to bring shame to him in his last days. As for the other brother, I don't mind; he is an egoist. When the Marquis dies, you'll see what I shall do. If I die before he does, you will avenge me. Will you, Quentin?"

"Yes."

"That's all I want. Your word is enough. Ask me for whatever you want, and come to see me."

Señora Patrocinio kissed Quentin's cheek, and he left the house confounded.

"Now," he murmured, "this woman turns out to be the sister of a marquis, married to a count, and my aunt. And she wants us to avenge ourselves. Why then let's do so... or let's not. It's all the same to me. You know your plan, Quentin," he said to himself. "Who are you?" he asked himself, and immediately replied, "You are a man of action. Very good!"

# CHAPTER XVII

## "I AM A LITTLE CATILINE"

THE coterie was the most select in the Casino. Its members used to meet there in order to speak ill of everybody. There were young men who did nothing but ride horseback, try the strength of young bulls by prodding them with long pikes from horseback, and gamble their souls away; old men whose sole occupation was talking politics; and a great variety of persons who had made a business of amusing themselves—a fact which did not prevent one from reading a gloomy weariness in their expressions.

This meeting of aristocrats and plebeians, of rich men and poor men, of vagrants employed and unemployed, possessed a rare character, which was produced by a preponderance of aristocratic prejudices, mixed with a great simplicity.

In this coterie, so democratic in appearance, high and low had their say; even the waiters in the Casino mixed in the conversation. It possessed those characteristics, partly affable, partly coarse, that the Spanish aristocracy had had until foreign ideas and customs began to transform and polish it.

In that meeting one gleefully flayed one's neighbour. Amid jests and laughter, flagellated by jovial satire, every person of significance in the town marched in review, either on account of their merits or their vices, their stupidity or their wit. If one believed what was told there, the city was a hot-bed of imbroglios, obscenities. wild escapades.

Among the members of aristocratic families there was a multitude of alcoholics and diseased individuals; the rotten produce of vicious living and consanguineous marriages. In these families there were a great many men who seemed to be obsessed with the idea of going through their fortunes, of ruining themselves quickly; others travelled the road to ruin without meaning to, through the robbery of their administrators and usurers; the majority were simply idiots; the clever ones, the clear-sighted ones, went to Madrid to play politics, leaving the old ancestral homes completely dismantled.

The scandals of the masses were mixed with those of the aristocracy; and the ingenuous jests of the charcoal-burners, and the dissolute wit of the Celestinas, were repeated and applauded with relish.

They spoke, too, and constantly, of the bandits of the Sierra; they knew who their protectors were in and out of Cordova, where their hiding-places were: and this friendship with bandits was not looked upon as a disgrace, but rather as something that constituted, if not a glorious achievement, at least a spicy and piquant attraction for the town.

"The gangs are organized in the very jail itself, while the bandits walk about the city."

"But, is that true?" asked some horrified stranger.

"Everything you hear is," they told him with a laugh. "Even the abductions of Malaga and Seville are planned here."

"And why don't you put an end to the evil?"

When the Cordovese heard this he smiled at the stranger, and added that in Cordova they had never looked upon the horsemen as an evil.

While the aristocrats and plebeians gave food for gossip, the middle class worked: lawyers, priests, and merchants enriched themselves, conducted their business, while a cloud of citizens from Soria fell like locusts upon the town, and took possession of the money and lands of the old, wealthy families by means of their evil skill at money-lending and usury.

One evening in the early part of autumn, several gentlemen were chatting in one of the salons of the Casino. They were members of the early coterie. Some were reading newspapers, and others were talking, seated upon divans, or walking to and fro.

Springer, the Swiss watch-maker's son, had come in to read a newspaper, and as he read, he heard them talking about his friend Quentin, whom he had not seen for some time. He listened attentively.

"But is it true he has come into some money?" asked a stout, red-faced gentleman with a grey moustache.

"I don't know," answered a bald-headed man with a black beard. "He undoubtedly has money. They say that he has bought a house for María Lucena."

"I don't believe that."

"Quentin is a child of good luck," added another.

"I should say he is," responded he of the black beard. "Lucky at cards, and lucky at love."

"Couldn't the Marquis have given him some money?" asked the stout gentleman.

"The Marquis! He hasn't a penny."

"But where does the boy get his money?"

"I don't know—unless he steals it."

"But that would be found out."

The members of the coterie were all silent for a moment while the stout gentleman took a short nap; then he said:

"Do you know if that paper that has just been published is his?"

"What paper? *La Víbora?*" asked he of the bald head.

"Yes."

"I don't think so."

"Well, they say it is."

"It strikes me that that paper is owned by the Masons."

"Oh, but don't you know that Quentin is a Mason?" said a small, dark man with a black moustache.

"Really?" asked every one at once.

"Yes, indeed. I know it for a fact; he joined the Lodge this summer."

"Perhaps he makes his living from that," said the fat gentleman.

"No one makes a living from that," replied the short man with a laugh. "It occurred to me when I was a student in Madrid to become a Mason, and do you know what happened? They carried me about from one place to another with my eyes bandaged, and ended by taking five dollars away from me."

Every one laughed. At this point a young man entered and stretched out in an arm chair with an air of deep gloom.

"What's up, Manolillo?" asked the bald-headed man.

"Nothing. Quentin is upstairs plucking everybody. If he quits in time, he's going to come out ahead; if he stays in, he may lose everything."

As Springer, who heard this, was a man of good intentions and a loyal friend, he arose, threw his paper upon the table, left the salon, went through a gallery paved with marble, up a flight of stairs, and entered the gambling hall.

Quentin was dealing; he had a pile of bills and gold coins before him. Springer went up to him, and put his hand upon his shoulder. Quentin turned.

"What is it?"

"I come," said Springer in a low voice, "to give you the advice of a gambler who just left here completely plucked. He said that if you quit in time, you'll come out ahead; if you stay in, you may lose everything."

"Really?" exclaimed Quentin, rising, as if he had just received important news. "Well, then, the only thing I can do is to leave. Gentlemen," he added, addressing the players, "I shall return in a little while," and placing the bills in his folder, he rapidly picked up the gold coins.

A murmur of indignation arose among the players.

"Come!" said Quentin to Springer.

They left the hall rapidly, descended the stairs, and did not stop until they had reached the street.

"But, what has happened to you?" the Swiss asked, utterly surprised.

"Nothing; it was a stratagem," answered Quentin with a smile. "I could not find the right moment to leave decorously. They were all after me like dogs; and there I was boasting like a man to whom four or five thousand dollars more or less are of little importance. They would have gone up in smoke soon."

By the light of a lamp, Quentin pulled out a handful of bills, sorted them, and put them into a folder; and then, unbuttoning first his coat, and then his vest, he put them in his inside pocket.

"Aren't you afraid something may happen to you in the street?" asked the Swiss.

"*Ca!*"

"Do you know that you are the talk of the town, Quentin?"

"Am I?"

"Really. Besides, you have a tremendous reputation."

"As what?"

"As a Tenorio, a dare-devil, a gambler, and a Mason."

Quentin burst out laughing.

"I heard in the Casino here," Springer went on, "that you were not living at home any more, but with an actress."

"That's true."

"Have you quarrelled with your family?"

"Yes; I got angry and left my stepfather. Usurers disgust me."

"It also seems that you have received a legacy from some relation or other of yours. Is that true?"

"Boy, I don't know," said Quentin ingenuously. "I've invented so many things, that now I don't know which is the truth and which is a lie." Then, turning melancholy, he added, "The trouble with me is that I am out of my element. I'm a Northerner."

"You!" said Springer; and he began to laugh so heartily that Quentin joined him.

"What are you laughing at?"

"At how well I know you. So you are a Northerner. What a faker you are!... What shocks me is that you have become a Mason. That's absurd."

"Yes; it's absurd to you and me, but it isn't to many people."

"Where is your Lodge?"

"In the Calle del Cister, near the Calle del Silencio. Would you like to come?"

"What for?"

"Man, we'll baptize you anew; we'll call you Cato, Robespierre, Spartacus...."

"I don't believe it's worth while...."

"As you wish."

"Your Masonry disgusts me."

"It *is* ridiculous, but it serves for something: it is useful for propaganda."

"What propaganda are you putting forward?"

"Just now I am a Federal Republican."

Springer burst out laughing again.

"You're a Federal Republican! Like my countrymen, the Swiss."

"You think it's funny?"

"Very, my lad. You couldn't live if you went to Switzerland."

"Well, then, there I would be a Monarchist. I am nothing at heart. I am a man of action who needs money and complications in order to live. Do you know what name they have given me at the Lodge?"

"What?"

"Catiline. They have hit the nail on the head. I am a little Catiline. What an admirable chap was that Tribune of the people! Eh? I am very enthusiastic about him."

"Then, Cicero would seem despicable to you."

"Ah! absolutely despicable. Charlatan, pedant, coward... in other words—he was a lawyer."

"Listen," said the Swiss. "They told me another and more serious thing: that you are the one who edits that newspaper, *La Víbora*. Is that true?"

"Yes."

"Are you the author of those very violent satires?"

"Not the author; the inspirer. Catiline turned libeller?... It would be unworthy of him."

"But don't you realize that you are exposing yourself to a very serious danger?"

"*Ca!* Don't you believe it. Men are more cowardly than they seem. Moreover, I am defended by a lot of people; first by those who rejoice over and enjoy the satires—as long as they are not directed against themselves; second, by my friends, of whom the majority are very powerful people; third and last, and this is what I place most confidence in, I am defended by these fists, and because I don't give a fig for anybody."

"Well, you certainly are acting without scruple or conscience."

"Is it worth while to live otherwise? I believe not."

"Man alive! That depends upon the way one looks at it."

"That's the way I look at it. The spectacle is dangerous, but amusing. Well? Are you coming to the Lodge?"

"What for?"

"You will hear several orators declaim their speeches, and I shall present you to Don Paco Sánchez Olmillo, Master Surgeon and Master Mason. If you wish I'll make a speech in your honour on human liberty. It is a discourse which I have learned by heart, and which, with a few trifling changes, I turn loose on all occasions, making it seem different each time."

"The plan does not tempt me."

"Then if you don't wish to go to the Lodge, I shall take you to the tavern in the Calle del Bodegoncillo."

"What are you going to do there?"

"I'm going to pay my retinue. Then I shall present you to Pacheco."

"To which Pacheco? To the bandit?"

"The same. He is my lieutenant."

"The devil! Shall I be safe with you?"

"Yes; safer than if you were with the Alcalde."

"But you keep very bad company."

"Whom do you mean by that? Pacheco? Pacheco is an unfortunate chap. Ask any one, and they will tell you that he was forced to take to the mountain merely on account of a rooster."

"Was that all?"

"That was all. On account of a rooster called Tumba-navíos or Tumbalobos, I don't exactly remember which. Pacheco used to go to the cock-fighting ring in the Calle de las Doblas, and one day he got mixed up in an argument with a fellow as to the relative merits of two fighting-cocks... and, well, they had words. Pacheco stuck a knife into the fellow, with bad results, and left him cold.... A man's affair!" added Quentin resignedly.

"Then one of those sergeants of the *guardia civil* who like to stick their noses into everything, insisted upon hunting Pacheco. He gave chase to him and caught up to him; but Pacheco, seeing that the game was about up, and remembering the words of Quevedo: that it is better to be ahead by a blow in the face than by all Castile, discharged his fowling-piece at the guard. This also had bad results, for he blew his skull open and sent him to join the other fellow."

The Swiss applauded the story, laughing quietly.

"And is that chap from this city?" he asked.

"I think he is from Ecija or thereabouts."

"What kind of a man is he?"

"A good fellow."

"Does he hurt any one in the country?"

"No. He appears at a farmhouse and asks the operator for a loan of ten or twelve dollars, and the operator gives it to him. He's a good man."

"Is he in Cordova now?"

"Yes."

"Why don't they arrest him?"

"They don't dare. Don't you see that I am protecting him?"

The Swiss looked at his friend, whom he admired deep down in his heart, and murmured again and again:

"My, what a faker!"

"It has been my custom to invite him to dine with me in the Café Puzzini and in the Rizzi Tavern," added Quentin, "and no one has dared to interfere with him."

Conversing in this manner, they had come out upon Las Tendillas, and were going up the Calle de Gondomar toward the Paseo del Gran Capitán. They walked past San Nicolás de la Villa, and followed the Calle de la Concepción toward the Puerta de Gallegos.

A strong breeze was blowing which made the blinds and windows rattle noisily.

"Where is that tavern?" asked Springer.

"Right here," answered Quentin. "This is the Calle del Niño Perdido, a sort of *cul-de-sac;* it is not ours. This other is the Calle de los Ucedas; nor is that the one we are looking for, either."

They walked on a few paces.

"This is the Calle del Bodegoncillo," said Quentin, "and here is the tavern."

# CHAPTER XVIII

## THE TAVERN IN THE CALLE DEL BODEGONCILLO

THE tavern was a small one; it had a red counter covered with zinc, a door at one side through which one passed into a large cellar lit by two smoky oil lamps and several black lanterns. That night there was a great concourse and influx of people in the place. Quentin and Springer entered, traversed the outer room, then crossed the cellar, where there were several occupied tables, and sat down at a small one in the light of an oil lamp.

"This is our table," said Quentin.

He clapped his hands, and the landlord, a man by the name of El Pullí, appeared; he ordered some crabs, a ration of fried fish, and a bottle of Montilla. Then he said:

"Bring me the bill for everything I owe."

El Pullí returned presently with the crabs, the fried fish, and the wine, and, upon a dish; a paper upon which several letters and figures had been scrawled in blue ink.

Quentin took the paper, pulled out several bills from his vest pocket, and proceeded to toss them upon the plate.

"Is that right?" he asked of El Pullí.

"It must be right if you counted it," replied the man.

"Here's something for the boy," added Quentin, putting a dollar upon the table.

"I have two boys, Don Quentin," answered El Pullí slyly.

"Well, then, here's something for the other one."

That clinking of silver produced an extraordinary effect in the tavern. Every one looked at Quentin, who, pretending not to notice the fact, began to eat and to carry on an animated conversation with his friend.

At this point two men approached the table: one was tall, smiling, some thirty years old, toothless, with a black beard and reddish, blood-shot eyes; the other was short, blond, timid-and insignificant-looking.

Quentin greeted them with a slight nod, and indicated that they should be seated.

"Here," said Quentin to Springer, indicating the man with the beard, "you have a thoroughgoing poet; the only bad thing about him is his name: he is called Cornejo. He is Corneille translated into Cordovese. But sit down, gentlemen, and order what you like; then we shall talk."

The two men seated themselves.

The poet looked something like a carp, with his dull, protruding eyes. He wore very short trousers, checked yellow and black, and carried a cane so worn by use that he had to stretch out his arm to touch the ground with it. From what Quentin said, Cornejo was a fantastic individual. He had on a blue, threadbare coat which he called his "black suit," and a ragged overcoat which he called his "surtout." He always had patches in his trousers; sometimes these were made of cloth, and sometimes of rawhide; he lived in the perpetual combination of a zealous appetite and an empty stomach; he fed only upon alcohol and vanity; hence his poetical compositions were so ethereal that they were windy, rather than wingèd verse.

Once when he was walking with a comrade who was also a poet and a ragamuffin, he said, pointing to some grand ladies in a carriage:

"My lad, they are looking at us with a contempt that is... inexplicable."

The fellow went through life wandering from tavern to tavern, reciting verses of Espronceda and Zorilla; sometimes between the madrigals and romances, he composed some terrible poems of his own in which he appeared as a ferocious person who cared for no liquid but blood, for no perfume but the odour of graveyards, and for no skies but tempestuous ones.

Cornejo was very popular among the workingmen, and he knew all the toughs and ruffians who swarmed in the taverns. The short, blond chap who accompanied him was nervous.

"This gentleman," said the poet to Quentin, pointing to the little fellow, "is the printer. If you can give him something...."

"Very well. How much do I owe you?" asked Quentin.

"Here is the invoice," said the little man humbly.

"Don't bring any invoices to me! How much is it?"

"Forty dollars."

"Good. That's all right."

Quentin filled a glass of wine, and the printer looked at him rather anxiously.

"How much do you need to assure the publication of the paper for three months?"

The printer took out paper and pencil and rapidly made some figures.

"Two hundred dollars," said he.

"Good," replied Quentin, and he took some bills from his pocket-book and put them upon the table. "Here are the two hundred dollars. I'll pay you the forty that I owe you when I can."

"That's all right," said the printer, picking up the money without daring to count it. "Would you like me to give you a receipt?"

"I—What for?"

The printer rose, bowed ceremoniously, and went out.

"How about you, Cornejo?" murmured Quentin. "Do you need some?"

"Throw me ten or twelve dollars."

"Here are twenty; but you've got to get to work. If you don't, I'll kick you out."

"Don't you worry." The poet stuck the bill carelessly into his pocket, and began to listen to the conversation of the persons at the next table. One of these was a man with a huge beard whom they called El Sardino; the other was a charcoal-burner with a grimy face called El Manano.

"Listen to this conversation," said the poet. "It's worth it."

"But what does that man give you?" El Manano was saying to El Sardino, making strange grimaces with his sooty face, and waving his arms.

"He gives me nothing," replied the other very seriously, "but he reports me."

"He reports you! You must be easy!"

"It's true."

"But what good has it done you to know him?"

"It's done me a lot of good, and I am grateful."

"That's almost like scratching a place to lie down in, comrade," said El Manano meaningly.

"Well, I'm like that," replied El Sardino. "Of course nothing gets ahead of me, and I always take my hat off so they can see the way my hair is parted."

"You've told me that before."

"I don't understand a word of what they are saying," said the Swiss with a smile.

"Nor do they understand each other," remarked Quentin.

"That's their way of talking," said the poet.

"And who are those fellows?" asked Springer.

"El Sardino is an itinerant pedlar," replied Cornejo. "He makes sling-shots for the children out of branches of rose-bay, and whistles out of maiden-hair ferns; the kind that have little seeds in them to make them trill. El Manano is a charcoal-burner."

"Of whom were they speaking?"

"Probably of Pacheco."

"The bandit?" asked Springer.

Cornejo fell silent; glanced at Quentin, and then, swallowing, murmured:

"Don't say it so loud; he has many friends here."

"That's what *we* are," replied Quentin.

The poet could not have been pleased by this turn of the conversation, for without saying another word, he addressed the charcoal-burner:

"Hello, Manano!" he cried. "It looks as if we'd caught it now, eh? Well, look out they don't take you to La Higuerilla!"

"Me!—to La Higuerilla?" exclaimed the drunkard; "nobody can do that!"

"Don't you want to go there any more?"

"No."

"Why not? You used to be glad to go."

"Because they used to treat a fellow right; but now, as you've said in poetry, they don't give you anything but water, a blow or two with a stick now and then, and that stuff that smells so bad... *pneumonia*."

The poet smiled at this testimony of his popularity.

El Sardino and El Manano had resumed their same parabolic manner of speech, when there came humming into the tavern a small, straight man with a short, black moustache that looked as if it were painted on his lip, a broad-brimmed hat pulled over his eyes, a huge watch chain across his vest, and a knotted and twisted stick.

When Springer caught sight of this ludicrous individual, he smiled mockingly, and the poet said:

"Here's Carrahola."

"What a funny chap!"

"He's a bully," replied Cornejo.

"Bah!" exclaimed Quentin, "he's a poor fellow, who because he is so small, has the fad of carrying everything extra large: his stick, his sombrero, his cigar-case."

And indeed, as if to demonstrate this, Carrahola pulled a silver watch, as white and as large as a stew-pan, from his vest pocket, and after ascertaining the time, asked the landlord:

"Has Señor José come yet?"

"No, Señor."

"But is he coming?"

"I can't tell you; I think so."

Carrahola went up to the table at which Quentin, Springer, and Cornejo were sitting, drew up a chair, and sat down without greeting them.

"This is a great night for finding lone jackasses, Carrahola," said the poet, turning to the little man.

189

The fellow turned his head as if he had heard the voice from the other side of the room, and paid no attention. Carrahola doubtless considered himself a great bully; he noted the expectancy in the tavern, so he seized Quentin's glass, held it up to the light, and emptied it with one swallow. Quentin took the glass, and, without saying a word, took careful aim, and tossed it through an open window. Then, clapping his hands, he said to El Pullí who came toward him:

"A glass; and kindly notify this person," and he pointed to Carrahola, "that he is in the way here."

"Move on," said the innkeeper; "this table is occupied."

Carrahola pretended not to understand; he took a plug of tobacco and a knife from his coat, and began to scrape tobacco; then he suddenly put the instrument upon the table.

"What do you do with that?" inquired Quentin, pointing to the blade with his finger. "Flourish it?"

Carrahola rose tragically from the table, put his knife away slowly, seized his enormous knotted stick, insinuated himself into his broad hat, gave a little pull to the lapels of his coat, and said dryly and contemptuously:

"Some one is talking in here who would not dare to speak thus in the street."

This said, he spat upon the floor, wiped away the spittle by rubbing it with the sole of his boot, and stood looking over his shoulder.

"And what does that mean?" asked Quentin.

"That means, that if you are a man, we'll have two glasses now, and then go and cut each other's hearts out."

Without replying Quentin stood up, seized Carrahola by the neck of his coat, lifted him like a puppet, and let him fall upon the soles of his boots, which struck the floor with a ludicrous sound. Everybody burst out laughing. Carrahola charged furiously at Quentin with lowered head; but the latter with the easy movement of a boxer, threw him over his hip into the air; then he took him in his two strong hands, pushed him up to the window, and watch, knife, broad-brimmed hat and all, tossed him into the street.

"You'll have to learn how to treat people politely," said Quentin after the operation was over.

"What a lad!" exclaimed El Manano. "He dropped him in the box like a letter!"

Murmurs of admiration were heard all over the tavern. Then a boy, or a small man (one could not determine his age easily), with reddish hair and a very freckled face, a mutilated calañés, and a twill coat, came hopping toward Quentin.

"Good evening," he said. "El Garroso, that carter over there, has some friends who say that if he 'tried wrists' with you, he could beat you. We say he couldn't do it. Would you like to try wrists with him, Don Quentin?"

"No, not now, thanks."

"Excuse me if I was wrong to ask you; but some are betting on you and others on him."

"Whom did you bet on?"

"On you."

"Good, then let's go over."

"El Rano is always making bets," said Cornejo.

"Is his name El Rano?"

"Haven't you noticed his face?"

The little man turned around, and Springer was forced to suppress a smile. Sure enough, he looked exactly like a frog, with his protruding, bulgy, stupid-looking eyes, his broad face, bottle-shaped nose, and mouth that spread from ear to ear.

"Where is El Garroso?" asked Quentin.

"At that table over there."

A man arose, smiling; he was round shouldered, with bow legs and arms, a square head, a bull neck, and a swelling something like a coxcomb in the middle of his forehead.

El Rano, El Garibaldino, and El Animero placed a table and two chairs in the middle of the tavern. El Garroso sat down, followed directly by Quentin.

"Well, as this is not a fighting matter," said Quentin to El Garroso, "we'll have two rounds, eh?"

"Sí, Señor."

They placed their elbows upon the table, clasped hands, and the chairs, the table, and even the bones of the adversaries began to creak.

El Garroso turned red; a vein in his forehead, as large as a finger, looked as if it were about to burst. Quentin was impassive.

"Do you think you are going to lose, Rano?" he said to the little man.

"No, indeed."

"That's right. Now you'll see." And without making an apparent effort—crack! El Garroso's arm fell to the table, his knuckles striking the boards forcibly.

Every one was astonished.

"Good, now let's try it again," said Quentin.

"No, no. You're stronger than I am," murmured El Garroso.

Quentin said that it was all a matter of practice, and was chatting away, when Carrahola, who could not have been hurt by his fall, doubtless lifting himself by his hands, and hoisting himself until his head reached the height of the window through which he had made his exit so brusquely, shouted with a prolongation of the "o":

*"Gallego!"*

"I'm going out and beat him up," said El Pullí. "I'll show him something pretty fine;" and the man closed the window and barred it with a stick.

Presently Carrahola shouted through the keyhole of the street door:

*"Oscurantista!"*

At this moment some one knocked at the door, Pullí opened it, and Pacheco and a friend, both wrapped in cloaks, entered, followed by Carrahola.

"The peace of God be with you, gentlemen," said Pacheco. "Who is it that is entertaining himself by throwing my friends through the window?"

"It was I," replied Quentin.

"Ah! Is that you? I didn't see you."

"Yes, sir; and I'll throw him out again if he bothers me."

"If it was you, that's another matter," said Pacheco. "I know that you don't like to stick your nose into other people's affairs."

Springer observed with surprise the prestige that Quentin enjoyed among that class of people. Pacheco and his friend, who was a toreador called Bocanegra, sat down. Quentin introduced them to the Swiss, and they all fell into an animated conversation.

Carrahola remained some distance away, in an attitude of suspicion.

"Come, Carrahola," said Pacheco, "it was your fault."

"Then excuse me, if I was wrong," said Carrahola.

"Nothing has happened at all," said Quentin, holding out his hand. "Take a glass, and let's be friends."

Bocanegra, the toreador, said ironically:

"Come now, Carrahola, this isn't the first beating you ever had."

"Nor will it be the last," replied the other very seriously.

Springer watched the people with great curiosity. He was surprised at Pacheco's courtesy: one could see that he was cultured; a man of natural superiority, neat, and with well-kept hands. The toreador was a strong-looking fellow with bright eyes and white teeth.

"One moment," said Quentin. "Pacheco, please come here."

The bandit got up, and the two men went to one end of the table and conversed.

"Have you seen the Count?" asked Quentin.

"Yes."

"What does he say?"

"That the woman is mad; that he has only been married once, like every one else."

"All we have to do is to go to the town and get hold of the wedding certificate. Send one of your men."

"I'll need money for that, comrade."

"I have some. I'm going to give you all I have left. If you have time, pay El Cuervo what I owe him."

"Very well."

Quentin emptied his pocket upon the table.

"There's more than enough here," said the bandit. "You'd better keep some."

Quentin put away a few bills, and they rejoined the group.

The conversation again turned upon revolutionary ideas, about which Pacheco and Bocanegra were most enthusiastic. The bandit spoke very devotedly of General Prim.

"I don't think there is a man like him in the world, and you needn't laugh, comrade," said Pacheco to Quentin, "you are not as patriotic as I am."

"Every person admires his own likeness," replied Quentin coldly.

"Do you think I am like Prim?" asked the bandit.

"No. It is Prim who is like Pacheco."

"I think I ought to be angry with you...."

Suddenly El Sardino's voice interrupted the conversation, shouting:

"Look here, leave me alone; you're making my head hot."

El Manano, in the midst of the confusion, at that moment doubtless remembered his business of charcoal-burning, for he examined closely his interlocutor's head, which was huge, and murmured in a thick voice:

"Why, it would take a whole cartload of wood even to soften it a little!"

Everybody laughed when they saw El Sardino's expression of indignation, and went on talking.

"One can do nothing here," said Pacheco to Springer.

"We talk a lot, but words are as far as we get. We Andalusians are very like the colts from this part of the country: a great deal of hoof with very little sole."

"Don't say that, Señor José," Cornejo ejaculated indignantly.

"I say it because it is true. What do all those men on the committee do? Will you tell me? What good is that Lodge?"

"Even God's interpreter don't know that," said El Manano, who had joined the group in the last stages of alcoholic intoxication. "But here," and he struck his chest, "is a man, Señor José... a man among men... willing to die on a barricade. Sí, Señor... and whenever you or Don Quentin give the signal, we'll get after the *Oscurantistas*.... Long live the *Constipation*, and death to Isabella II!"

"That will do, that will do. Get out," said the bandit.

"But I'm always liberal, Señor José... here, and everywhere else...."

"Let's go," said Quentin. "He'll be giving us a great drubbing."

They got up, and the innkeeper lighted their way to the street door with a small lamp. They walked together as far as El Gran Capitán; Cornejo, Bocanegra and Pacheco turned in the direction of Los Tejares; Quentin and the Swiss went down the Calle de Gondomar.

"But what do you expect of those people?" Springer asked presently.

"I! I don't know, my boy; now—to be strong,... later—we shall see."

"Do you read Machiavelli?"

"I read nothing. Why?"

"You are an extraordinary man, Quentin."

"Bah!"

"Really. A type worth studying."

"Well, look here, if you wish to study me, go to the Café del Recreo some night. There you'll meet the girl that's living with me."

"I shall go."

They had reached Las Tendillas; it was very late, and the two friends took leave of each other with a warm handshake.

# CHAPTER XIX

## THE PLEASANT IRONIES OF REALITY

A FEW days later, on a Sunday afternoon, Quentin went out for a horseback ride. Before turning toward the mountain, he drew rein in the Paseo de la Victoria to watch the people as they went by.

His reputation as a gambler, a dare-devil, and a rude and powerful man, made it possible for him to have his little successes with the ladies, and more than one of them looked at him with the long, staring, and penetrating glance of a woman not altogether understood by her husband.

As was customary on fiesta days, the carriages were driven to and fro along the Paseo, and among them rode several horsemen on spirited mounts. In one of his turns, Quentin saw Rafaela and Remedios alone in a carriage. Neither of the two girls noticed his presence, and in order that this should not happen again, Quentin placed himself in such a position that they would have to see him as they came back.

Remedios was the first to recognize him, and she told her sister. Quentin bowed to them very ceremoniously. When they reached the extreme end of the drive, Rafaela must have told her coachman to leave the Paseo. Remedios looked back several times. Quentin rode up to the carriage and entered into conversation with the two sisters. Rafaela was pale and had dark rings under her eyes; she was in the last month of pregnancy; her eyes were sunken and her ears transparent.

Remedios was prettier than ever; she was just reaching that intermediate stage when the child becomes the woman.

"Are you two girls well?" Quentin asked them with real interest.

"I am well," answered Rafaela a trifle weakly. "Just waiting from day to day... and you can see for yourself that Remedios is prettier and healthier than ever."

Remedios burst into one of her silent laughs.

"Yes," replied Quentin, "one can see that the country is good for Remedios."

"Don't you believe it!" exclaimed the child. "I would rather live in our house on the Calle del Sol."

"They say you have become a terrible person," said Rafaela. "I believe you write for the papers,... that you keep bad company...."

"Nothing to it—just gossip."

"And you don't go to the house any more, either. You have deserted poor grandfather."

"That's true. I'm always thinking about going, but I never do."

"Well, he asks after you all the time. The poor dear is very ill, and so lonely.... Since we have been in town, we have been to see him every day."

"Well, I'll go, too, don't you worry."

"Go tomorrow," said Remedios.

"Very well, tomorrow it is. But did you two leave the Paseo on my account?"

"No," replied Rafaela, "I don't like to drive in that line for very long at a time. It makes my head swim. We are on our way home, now. Adiós, Quentin."

"Adiós!"

Quentin took the mountain road, and trotted his horse as far as the Brillante lunch-room.

The encounter had given rise to a mixture of sadness and irony within him, which seemed as distressing as it did grotesque to him.

"Is there anything of special significance about it?" he asked himself.

No, there was nothing of special significance about it. It was the logical thing. She had married; her husband was young; she was going to have a child. It was the natural course of events; and yet, Quentin wondered at her.

We often see strange birds flying in the heavens. They are like men's illusions. Sometimes these birds fall, wounded by some hunter, and when one sees them upon the ground with their sad eyes, their white feathers,—they are a surprise to whomsoever contemplates them…. It is because man idealizes all distant objects.

Quentin, dominated by his half-dolorous, half-grotesque impressions, returned slowly to the town.

When he reached the Paseo de la Victoria, night had already fallen. The line of carriages was still filing past. The mountain was wrapped in a mist; the sun was sinking over the distant meadows, its great, red disk hiding itself behind the yellow fields; a bluish hill surmounted by a castle stood out in silhouette against the rosy-tinted horizon.

Few carriages were passing now; above the old wall and gateway of Almodóvar, the yellowish tower of the cathedral showed against the azure sky, which was now beginning to be decorated with stars.

All of the carriages left the Victoria to drive up and down the Paseo del Gran Capitán.

Quentin entered a café.

"I must get out of this city," he thought. "I ought to go to London."

Then he remembered the frequent rain, the wooden coachmen in their cabs, the blue mist in the fields near Windsor, and the ships that glided down the Thames in the fog.

He left the café. The carriages continued to pass up and down El Gran Capitán, enveloped in an atmosphere of dust.

Quentin went home. María Lucena was getting ready to go to the theatre.

"What's the matter with you?" she said.

"Nothing."

Quentin stretched out upon a sofa and spent hour after hour recalling the fog, the dampness, and the cool atmosphere of England, until he fell asleep.

# CHAPTER XX

## PHILOSOPHERS WITHOUT REALIZING THE FACT

THE next evening, Quentin, whose nebulous and Anglo-maniacal fever had already quieted down, went to sup at the Café del Recreo.

María Lucena, with her mother and a chorus girl friend were waiting for him.

"Well, you're pretty late," said María Lucena as she saw him enter the café.

Quentin shrugged his shoulders, sat down and called the waiter.

María Lucena was the daughter of a farm operator near Cordova. She had little voice, but a great deal of grace in her singing and dancing; a strong pair of hips that oscillated with a quivering motion as she walked, a pale, vague-looking face; and a pair of black, shining eyes. María Lucena married a prompter, who after three or four months of wedded life, considered it natural and logical that he should live on his wife; but she broke up the combination by throwing him out of the house.

The girl who accompanied María Lucena in the café was a chorus girl of the type that soon stand out from their sisters and begin to take small parts. She was a small woman, with very lively black eyes, a thin nose, a mouth with a mocking smile that lifted the commissures of her lips upward, and black hair adorned with two red carnations.

The old woman with them was María's mother; fat, wrinkled, and covered with moles, with a lively but suspicious look in her eyes.

Quentin began to eat supper with the women. His melancholy fit of blues of the day before had left him, but he looked sad for dignity's sake, and because it was consistent with his character.

María Lucena, who had noticed Quentin's abstraction, glanced at him from time to time attentively.

"Well, let's be going." said María.

The two girls and the old woman arose, as it was time for the entertainment to begin, and Quentin was left alone, distracted by his efforts to convince himself as well as others, that he was very sad.

Then Springer, the Swiss, came in and sat by Quentin's side.

"What's the matter?" he said, taking his friend's funereal look seriously.

"I feel sad today. Yesterday I saw a girl I used to like. The granddaughter of a marquis. She who married Juan de Dios."

"What then? What happened to you?"

"She looks badly. She won't last long."

"The poor little thing!"

In a lugubrious voice Quentin told all about his love affair, heaping on insignificant details, and wearying excuses.

Springer listened to him with a smile. His fine, spiritual countenance changed expression sympathetically with everything his friend said. Then he himself spoke confusedly. Yes, he too had had a romantic love affair,… a very romantic one,… with a young lady; but he was only a poor Swiss plebeian.

Any one who heard them would have said that Quentin's affair had lasted years, and the Swiss's only days. It was exactly the opposite. Quentin's fidelity lasted just about two or three months, at the end of which time he began his affair with María Lucena. On the other hand, the Swiss had been faithful for years and years to an impossible love.

As they chatted, Don Gil Sabadía, the archæologist, appeared in the café. After shaking hands with the Swiss and with Quentin, he sat down at their table.

"It's a long time since I have seen you," he said to Quentin. "How about it—are we gaining ground?"

"Psh! If I could get out...."

"Don't pay any attention to him today," said Springer. "He's full of spleen."

"Why, what's the matter?" asked the archæologist.

"Women."

"The females in this city are very attractive, comrade; they are good to look at."

"They seem insignificant to me," said Quentin.

"Man alive, don't say that," exclaimed the Swiss.

"Pale-faced, rings under their eyes, weak, badly nourished...."

"Will you deny their wit, too?" asked Springer.

"Yes," answered Quentin. "They make a lot of gestures, and have a fantastic manner of speech that is overloaded with imagery. It's a sort of negro talk. I always notice that when María Lucena tells something, she compares everything, whether material or not, with something material: 'it's better than bread,' or 'it has less taste than a squash'... everything must be materialized; if not, I don't believe she would understand it.... She is like a child... like an impertinent child."

"What a portrait!" exclaimed the Swiss, laughing.

"Then she makes divisions and subdivisions of everything; every object has twenty names. There is a little bottle of cherry brandy in the house—of that cherry brandy that I hold as something sacred; well, sometimes María calls it 'the parrot,' sometimes 'the greenfinch,' and sometimes, 'the green bird.'... And that isn't all. The other day, pointing to the bottle, she called to her mother from her bed: 'Mother, bring me that what's-its-name.'... So you see, for that class of people, language is not language—it is nothing."

"Doesn't that indicate inventive genius?" asked the Swiss.

"But what do I want of inventive genius, Springer?" exclaimed Quentin loudly. "Why, a woman doesn't need inventive genius! All she needs is to be pretty and submissive, and nothing else...."

"You are tremendous," said the Swiss. "So that for you, a woman's intelligence is of no account?"

"But that isn't intelligence! That is to intelligence what the movement of those men who go hopping about nodding to one and talking to another, is to real activity. The former is not intelligence nor is the latter activity. The thing is to have a nucleus of big, strong ideas that direct your life.... As the English have."

"I have an antipathy for the English," said the Swiss. "As for Andalusia, I believe that if this country had more culture, it would constitute one of the most comprehensive and enthusiastic of peoples. Other Spaniards are constantly bargaining with their appreciation and admiration; the national vice of Spain is envy. Not so with the Andalusians. They are ready to admire anything."

"It's a racial weakness," exclaimed Quentin. "They are all liars."

"You, who are an Andalusian, must not say that."

"I? Never. I am a Northerner. From London, Windsor…. Why did I ever come here?"

María Lucena, her little friend, and her mother came in. The Swiss and Don Gil bowed to them.

"You must defend the Andalusians," said Springer to the actress; "for Quentin is turning them inside out."

"What's he here for, then?" inquired María bitterly.

"That's just what I was saying," added Quentin. "What did I come to this city for?"

"I know what all this sadness comes from," said María Lucena in Quentin's ear.

"Do you? Well, I'm glad."

"You saw your cousin yesterday; the one with a face that looks as if she had a sour stomach. They say that she can't yet console herself for her former sweetheart's leaving her. That's why she is so sad."

Quentin shrugged his shoulders.

"Has she had the baby yet, or is it just dropsy?"

Again Quentin did not deign to answer. She indignantly turned her head away.

"So, because you saw her changed into a worm, you came in so sad and downhearted yesterday, eh?"

"Possibly," said Quentin coldly.

"If you had seen me in the same condition, you would have felt it less."

"What intelligence!"

"Well, son, it's time we quit," replied the actress angrily. "If you think nothing of me, I feel the same way toward you."

Quentin shrugged his shoulders. The others, seeing the prelude to a tempest, were silent.

María Lucena's voice grew shrill and disagreeable.

"Do you know what her stepmother, the Countess, said? Well, she said: 'For all her prudishness, that hussy has married Juan de Dios for his money!'"

"What that female said is not important."

"All women are just females to you...."

"And it's true."

"Well, if you say that about me...."

"Come, come, this is no place for a scene, and don't shout so."

"Are you going to strike me? Tell me, are you going to strike me?"

"No; I shall prudently withdraw first," answered Quentin, rising and getting ready to go.

At this moment Cornejo, the poet, entered the café accompanied by a tall, thin gentleman with an aquiline nose, and a very black and very long beard cut in Moorish fashion. The two came up to the table and sat down.

The poet and the other gentleman had just left the last performance, and were discussing it. Cornejo thought that the musical comedy they had just seen was not altogether bad, the tall man with the black beard insisted that as far as he was concerned it had been superbly wearisome. This gloomy fellow then asserted that for him, life held little promise, and that of all disagreeable and irritating lives, the most irritating and disagreeable was that in a provincial capital; and of all the lives in provincial capitals, the worst was that of Cordova.

In absolute contradiction to Leibnitz and his disciple, Doctor Pangloss, the man with the black beard would have asserted, with veritable conviction, that he lived the worst life in the worst town, in the worst possible of worlds.

"You are right," said Quentin, with the honest intention of molesting his hearers. "There is nothing so antipathetic as these provincial capitals."

Don Gil, the archæologist, made a gesture of one who does not wish to heed what he hears, and turning to Springer, said:

"You are like me, are you not? A partisan of the antique."

"In many ways, yes," replied the Swiss.

"Theirs was a much better life. How wise were our ancestors! Everything classified, everything in order. In the Calle de la Zapatería were the boot-makers; in the Calle de Librerías, the book-sellers; in the Calle de la Plata, the silversmiths. Each line of business had its street; lawyers, bankers, advocates.... Today, everything is reversed. A tremendous medley! There are scarcely any boot-makers in the Calle de la Zapatería, nor are there any book-sellers in the Calle de Librerías. These ædiles change the name of everything.... The Calle de Mucho Trigo, where there used to be warehouses for wheat, today specializes in making taffy. How absurd, Señor! How absurd! And they call that progress! Nowadays men are endeavouring to wipe out the memory of a whole civilization, of a whole history."

"What good does that memory do you?" asked the man with the black beard.

"What good does it do me!" cried Don Gil in astonishment.

"Yes, what good does it do you?"

"Merely to show us that we are decadent. Not comparing the Cordova of today with that of the Arabian epoch, but comparing it with that of the eighteenth century, one sees an enormous difference. There were hundreds of looms here then, and factories where they made paper, and buttons, and swords, and leather, and guitars. Today... nothing. Factories, shops, even mansions have been closed."

"That may be true; but, Don Gil, why do you want to know these calamities?"

"Why do I want to know them, Escobedo?" cried Don Gil, who was stupefied by the questions of the man with the black beard.

"Yes; I cannot see what good that knowledge does. If Cordova disappears, why, another city will appear. It's all the same!" Escobedo continued—"Would that we could wipe out history, and with it all the memories that sadden and wither the lives of men and multitudes! One generation should accept from the preceding one that which is useful, that is,—mere knowledge; for example: sugar is refined in this manner,... potatoes are fried thusly.... Forget the rest. Why should we need them to say: 'this love you feel, this pain you suffer, this heroic deed you have witnessed, is nothing new at all; five or six thousand other men, exactly like you, felt it, suffered it, and witnessed it.' What do we gain by that? Will you tell me?"

The archæologist shrugged his shoulders.

"I believe you are right," said Quentin.

"History, like everything else we have to learn, ages us," Escobedo proceeded. "Knowledge is the enemy of felicity. This state of peace, of tranquillity, which the Greeks called with relation to the organism, *euphoria,* and with relation to the soul, *ataraxia*, cannot be attained in any other way than by ignorance. Thus at the beginning of life, at the age of twenty, when one sees the world superficially and falsely, things appear brilliant and worth coveting. The theatre is relatively fine, the music agreeable, the play amusing; but the evil instinct of learning will make one some day peer from the wings and commence to make discoveries and become disillusioned. One sees that the actresses are ugly...."

"Thanks!" interrupted María Lucena, dryly.

"He doesn't mean you," Springer assured her.

"And that besides being ugly, they are sad, and daubed with paint," continued Escobedo, heedless of the interruption. "The comedians are stupid, dull, coarse; the scenery, seen near to, is badly painted. One sees that all is shabby, rickety.... Women seem angels at first, then one thinks them demons, and little by little one begins to understand that they are females, like mares, and cows.... A little worse, perhaps, on account of the human element in them."

"That's true," agreed Quentin.

"You are very indecent," said María Lucena, rising with an expression of contempt and anger upon her lips. "Adiós! We're going."

The three women left the café.

"And the worst of it is," continued Escobedo, "that they deceive us miserably. They speak to us of the efficacy of strength; they tell us that we must struggle with will and tenacity, in order to attain triumph; and then we find that there are no struggles, nor triumphs, nor anything; that Fate shuffles our destinies, and that the essence of felicity is in our own natures."

"You see everything very black," said the Swiss, smiling.

"I think he sees it all as it is," replied Quentin.

"Then one would find out," said Escobedo, "that some of the exalted, beautiful things are not as sublime as the poets say they are—love, for instance; and that other humbler and more modest things, which ought to be profoundly real, are not so at all.

"Friendship! There is no such thing as friendship except when two friends sacrifice themselves for each other. Sincerity! That, too, is impossible. I do not believe that one can be sincere even in solitude. Great and small, illustrious and humble, every individual who gazes into a mirror will always see in the glass the reflection of a pretender."

"I'm with you," said Quentin.

"I believe," declared the Swiss, "that you only look upon the dark side of things."

"I force myself to see both sides," responded Escobedo—"the bright as well as the dark. I believe that in every deed, in every man, there is both light and darkness; also that there is almost always one side that is serious and tragic, and another that is mocking and grotesque."

"And what good does that do you?" asked Don Gil.

"A whole lot. From a funereal and lachrymose individual, I am metamorphosing myself into a jolly misanthrope. By the time I reach old age, I expect to be as jolly as a pair of castanets."

"Greek philosophy!" said Don Gil contemptuously.

"Señor Sabadía," replied Escobedo, "you have the right to bother us all with your talk about the signs on the streets of Cordova, and about the customs of our respectable ancestors. Kindly grant us permission to comment upon life in our own fashion."

*"Risum teneatis,"* said Don Gil.

"Do you see?" continued Escobedo—"That's another thing that bothers me. Why does Don Gil have to thrust at us a quotation so common that even the waiters in the café know it?"

The archæologist, not deigning to notice this remark,

commenced to recite an ancient Cordovese *romance* that went:

*Jueves, era jueves,*
*día de mercado,*
*y en Santa Marina*
*tocaban rebato.*

(Thursday, it was Thursday, Market Day, and in the Church of Santa Marina they rang the call to arms.)

Escobedo went on philosophising; a waiter in the café began to pile the chairs upon the tables; another put out the gas, and the customers went out into the street.

# CHAPTER XXI

## JUAN TALKS

THE afternoon of the following day, Quentin went to the Calle del Sol to see his grandfather, according to his promise to Rafaela. There was a carriage at the door. Juan, with his hat in his hand, was talking to an elegant lady with black eyes.

"Do you mean to say I cannot go in?" said she unpleasantly.

"The Señoritas have told me that they were not at home to any one."

"Not even to me?"

"Those are my orders."

"Very well. I shall wait until my husband comes."

"It will be useless," said Juan emphatically.

"Why?" asked she haughtily.

"Because the Señor Marqués told me that he does not wish to see you."

The woman made no reply.

"Home!" she said to the coachman angrily.

Quentin went up to Juan.

"What's up? May I not come in?" he asked.

"You may, of course," replied the gardener, "but not that designing hussy."

"Who is she?"

"The Countess. After saying all sorts of monstrous things about Rafaela and her grandfather, the hussy comes here to boast of her charity."

"How is the Señor Marqués?"

"Very bad."

"Has his illness been aggravated, or is it following its natural course?"

"It has been aggravated.... And meanwhile, the Count—do you know what he's doing? Well, he's selling everything he can lay his hands on. He's even sold the lead pipes and the paving stones in the stable, which he tore up with his own hands. I tell you it's a shame...."

"Why don't they stop him?"

"Who is there to do it? It's very sad. While the master is in bed, the second-hand men come and cart everything away. They've removed tapestries, bronzes, the gilt writing-desks that were in the hall, the sideboard, the dressing tables... and that shrewd female, who knows all about the business, wants to come and take part in the robbery. One can say nothing to the Count; but to that wicked woman, it's different. If you could see her! I don't see how she dares look at me after what has happened between us."

"Between whom? You and her?"

"Sí, Señor. Have they never told you?"

"No."

"Well, you know I have a son, who, though not so much to look at now, was several years ago a very beautiful child, whiter than snow, and with a pair of cheeks just bursting with blood. Moreover, he was strong, healthy, and very innocent. Well, pretty soon the lad began to get pale, and thin, and black circles appeared under his eyes. His mother and I wondered what was the matter with him, and what his trouble was. But it was useless; we were unable to understand what was going on, until one night the coachman saw him climbing about the roof. The man hid himself and found out everything. At that time the Countess lived here with her husband, and my son was on his way to her. When I told the Marquis what was happening, he went and loaded a pistol, and was for shooting his daughter-in-law. But she, the shrewd thing, came to me and said: 'If you need anything for your son, let me know.'—'Señora,' I answered, 'you are a very vicious woman, and my son shall never see you again.'"

"Whom is she living with now?"

"With Periquito Gálvez."

"Who is he?"

"A rich farmer."

"Young?"

"No; he's over fifty. But she would take to any one. When he came to an understanding with her, they say that one day he found one of the Countess' garters, which had a little sign on it that read:

*Intrépido es amor;*
*de todo sale vencedor.*

(Love is fearless; it conquers all obstacles.)

"Periquito had a pair of garters made just like it, with letters of diamonds and pearls, which he gave to her."

"How magnificent!"

"It certainly was."

Quentin left Juan, and went up to see the sick man.

In a drawing-room near the bedroom, Rafaela and Remedios were talking to a thin, graceful, very polished-looking gentleman. It was El Pollo Real, brother of the Marquis and of Señora Patrocinio. From time to time Colmenares, the hunchback, came out of the bedroom red-eyed, only to go back again immediately.

"I am going to pray at the hermitage of La Fuensanta," said Remedios to Quentin. "Do you wish to come with me?"

Remedios, her young maid-servant, and Quentin left the house as evening fell.

The two women said their prayers, and then Remedios and Quentin returned chatting from the hermitage. Remedios told Quentin that some of her stepmother's invectives had reached Rafaela's ears, and Quentin promised the girl that he would silence the Countess. He thought of dedicating a few stings to her in *La Víbora* which might mortify her. Then Remedios spoke of her brother-in-law. She felt a strong antipathy for him, and, while realizing that he was good and amiable, she could not bear him.

To prolong the conversation, they took the longest way home.

It was an autumn day with a deep blue sky.

In the west, long, narrow clouds tinged with red, floated one above the other in several strata. They walked by the Church of San Lorenzo. The square tower rose before them with its angel figure on the point of the roof; the great rose-window, lit by the rosy hue of late afternoon, seemed some ethereal, incorporeal thing, and above the rosette, a white figure of a saint stood out against a vaulted niche.

They returned by the Calle de Santa María de Gracia. Remedios read the signs on the stores as she passed them, and the names of the streets. One of these was called Puchinelas, another, Juan Palo, another El Verdugo....

A lot of questions suggested themselves to the child, to which Quentin did not know how to reply.

They went along the Calle de Santa María. Overhead, the rosy sky showed between the two broken lines of roofs; the water pipes stuck into the air from the eaves like the gargoyles and cantilevers of a Gothic church; the houses were bathed in a mysterious light....

Against the white walls of an ancient convent with tall Venetian blinds, the scarlet splendour of the sky quivered gently; and in the distance, at the end of the street, the hoary tower of a church, as it received the last rays of the sun, shone like a red-hot coal.

When they reached the house, the sky was already beginning to lose its blood-red colour; a veil of pale yellow opal invaded the whole celestial vault; toward the west it was green, to the east, it was blue, an intense blue, with great, purple bands....

# CHAPTER XXII

## STICKS, SHOTS, AND STONES

THAT night, Quentin went to look for Cornejo at the print-shop where *La Víbora* was published.

The shop was situated in a cellar, and contained a very antique press, which took a whole day to print its fifteen hundred copies.

"For the next number," said Quentin to the poet, "you've got to make up a poisonous poem in the same style as those that have been published against the Alguacil Ventosilla, Padre Tumbón, and La Garduña."

"Good. Against whom is it to be?"

"La Aceitunera."

"The Countess?"

"Yes."

"The devil! Isn't she a relative of yours?"

"Yes, on the left hand side."

"Let's have it. What must I say?"

"You already know that they call her La Aceitunera?"

"Yes."

"And you also know that she has no morals to boast of?"

"Yes."

"Well, with that you've got it all made. As a sort of refrain to your poem, you may use the quotation she wears on her garters; it goes like this:

*Intrépido es amor;*
*de todo sale vencedor."*

"Very good; but give me an idea."

"Do you need still more? You can begin with a poetic invocation, asking every crib in Cordova who the lady of such and such a description is; then give hers; including the fact that she wears garters with this motto engraved upon them:

*Intrépido es amor;*
*de todo sale vencedor."*

"Good! For example: I'll say that she has black eyes, and a wonderful pair of hips, and—"

"An olive complexion."

"And an olive complexion... and I'll finish up with:

*Y ésta leyenda escrita en la ancha liga,*
*que tantos vieron con igual fatiga:*
*Intrépido es amor;*
*de todo sale vencedor.*

(And this legend written upon her broad garter, which so many men have seen with the same feeling of fatigue: etc.)

"Eh? How's that?"

"Very good."

"All right, it won't take a minute to finish it. What shall I call the poem?"

*"To La Aceitunera."*

"It's done. How would you like me to begin like this?:

*Casas de la Morería;*
*Trascastillo y Murallón,*
*ninfas, dueñas, y tarascas,*
*baratilleras de amor.*

(Houses of La Morería, Trascastillo and Murallón; nymphs, mistresses, and lewd women, second-hand dealers in love.)"

"You may begin as you wish. The idea is that the thing must hurt."

"It'll hurt, all right; never fear."

Cornejo finished the poem; two days later the paper came out, and in cafés and casinos, the only subject of conversation was the Countess' garters, and everybody maliciously repeated the refrain:

*Intrépido es amor;*
*de todo sale vencedor.*

The following night, Quentin was waiting for the poet in the Café del Recreo. He had made an appointment with him for ten o'clock, but Cornejo had failed to appear.

Quentin waited for him for over two hours, and finally, tired out, he started to go home. As he left the café, a little man wrapped in a cloak came up to him at the very door.

"Listen to me a second," he said.

"Eh!"

"Be very careful, Don Quentin, they are following you."

"Me?"

"Sí, Señor."

"Who are you? Let's hear first who you are."

"I am Carrahola."

"Aren't you angry at me for what I did to you the other night?"

"No, Señor, you're a brave fellow."

"Thanks."

"Well, Señor José has sent Cantarote, the gipsy, and me to go home with you."

"Bah! No one interferes with me."

"Don't say what you know nothing about. Take this club"—and he gave him one which he had concealed under his cloak—"and walk on."

"Aren't you armed, Carrahola?"

"I?—Look!"—and lifting aside his cloak, he showed his sash, which was filled with stones.

Quentin took the club, wrapped himself up to his eyes in his cloak, and began to walk slowly along the middle of the street, looking carefully before passing cross-streets and corners. When he reached one corner, he saw two men standing in the doorway of a convent, and two others directly opposite. No sooner had he perceived them, than he stopped, went to a doorway, took off his cloak and wrapped it about his left arm, and grasped the club with his right hand.

When the four men saw a man hiding himself, they supposed that it was Quentin, and rushed toward him. Quentin parried two or three blows with his left arm.

"Evohé! Evohé!" he cried; and an instant later began to rain blow after blow about him with his club, with such vigour, that he forced his attackers to retreat. In one of his flourishes, he struck an adversary on the head, and his club flew to pieces  The man turned and fell headlong to the ground, like a grain-sack.

Carrahola and Cantarote came running to the scene of the fray; one throwing stones, the other waving a knife as long as a bayonet.

Carrahola hit one of the men in the face with a stone, and left him bleeding profusely. Of the three who were left comparatively sound, two took to their heels, while the strongest, the one who seemed to be the leader of the gang, was engaged in a fist fight with Quentin. The latter, who was an adept in the art of boxing, of which the other was totally ignorant, thrust his fist between his adversary's arms, and gave him such a blow upon the chin, that he fell backward and would have broken his neck, had he not stumbled against a wall. As the man fell, he drew a pistol from his pocket and fired.

"Gentlemen," said Quentin to Carrahola and Cantarote; "to your homes, and let him save himself who can!"

Each began to run, and the three men escaped through the narrow alleyways.

The next afternoon Quentin went to the Casino. The newspapers spoke of the battle of the day before as an epic; a ruffian known as El Mochuelo, had been found in the street with concussion of the brain, and a contusion on his head; besides this, there were pools of blood in the street. According to the newspaper reports, passions had been at a white heat. Immediately after the description of the fight, followed the news that the notable poet Cornejo had been a victim of an attack by persons unknown.

"They must have beaten him badly," thought Quentin.

He went to Cornejo's house and found him in bed, his head covered with bandages, and smelling of arnica.

"What's the matter?" asked Quentin.

"Can't you see? They gave me the devil of a beating!"

"They tried to do it to me yesterday, but I knocked a few of them down."

"Well, don't be overconfident."

"No, I'm not; I carry a pistol in each pocket, and I can't tell you what would happen to the man who comes near me."

"It's a bad situation."

"*Ca,* man! There's nothing to be frightened about."

"You can do as you like, but I'm not going out until I'm well; nor will I write for *La Víbora* any more."

"Very well. Do as you wish."

"I've got to live."

"Psh! I don't see why," replied Quentin contemptuously. Then he added, "See here, my lad, if this business scares you, take up sewing on a machine. Perhaps you'll earn more."... And leaving the poet, Quentin returned to the Casino. He was the man of the hour; he related his adventure again and again, and in order that the same thing might not be repeated that night, a group of eight or ten of his friends accompanied him to his house.

# CHAPTER XXIII

## PURSUIT AND ESCAPE

QUENTIN was worried, and in spite of his two pistols and the sword-cane that he carried, he feared that the first chance they got, they would set a trap for him and leave him in the same condition as they had left Cornejo.

He was very mistrustful of María Lucena, because she was beginning to hate him and was capable of doing him almost any ill turn.

Some two weeks after the nocturnal attack, Quentin went to the Café del Recreo. As he was learning to be very cautious, before entering he looked through a window and saw María Lucena talking to an elegant-ly-dressed gentleman. He waited a moment, and when a waiter went by, he said to him:

"See here, who is that gentleman there?"

"The clean-shaven one dressed in black?"

"Yes."

"Señor Gálvez."

"Periquito Gálvez?"

"Sí, Señor."

Quentin entered the café and pretended not to see the fellow. He noticed that María Lucena was more pleasant to him than ever before.

"There's something up," he said to himself. "They are getting something ready for me."

Quentin was not jealous, he was already very tired of

María Lucena, and if any one had made off with her, he would have thanked him rather than otherwise.

"Between the two of them," thought Quentin, referring to Gálvez and María, "they are plotting something against me."

Presently, Quentin got up, and left the café without even nodding to María.

"I'm going to see Pacheco," he murmured.

He was going along the Calle del Arco Real, when he looked back and saw two men following him.

"Devil take you," he remarked, seizing a pistol.

He raised the muffler of his cloak, and began to walk very rapidly. It was a cold, disagreeable night; the crescent moon shone fitfully from behind the huge clouds that were passing over it. Quentin tried to shake off his pursuers by gliding rapidly through tortuous alleyways, but the two men were doubtless well acquainted with the twists and turns of the city, for if he happened to lose them for an instant, he soon saw them behind him again.

After a half-hour's chase, Quentin noticed that there were no longer only two pursuers, but four of them, and that with them was a watchman. Presently there were six of them.

He sought safety in his legs, and began to run like a deer. He came out opposite the Mosque, went down by the Triunfo Column, through the Puerta Romana, and along the bridge until he reached the foot of the tower of La Calahorra. Everywhere he heard the whistles of the watchmen.

At the exit of the bridge, there were a couple of *guardias civiles*. Perhaps they were not warned of his flight; but suppose they were?

Quentin retreated. From the bridge he could see the Cathedral, and the black wall of the Mosque, whose battlements were outlined against the sky.

A vapour arose from the river; below him the dark water was boiling against the arches of the bridge; in the distance it looked like quicksilver, and the houses on the Calle de la Ribera were reflected trembling on its surface.

As he turned toward the city, Quentin saw his pursuers at the bridge entrance.

"They've trapped me!" he exclaimed in a rage.

They were evidently reconnoitering the bridge on both sides, for the watchman's lantern oscillated from left to right, and from right to left.

Quentin crept toward one of the vaulted niches in the middle of the bridge.

"Shall I get in there? They will find that easier than anything else. What shall I do?"

To throw himself into the river was too dangerous. To attack his pursuers was absurd.

As if to add to his misfortunes, the moon was coming from behind the cloud that had hidden it, and was shedding its light over the bridge. Quentin climbed into the niche.

What irritated him most was being made prisoner in such a stupid way. He did not fear prison, but rather the loss of prestige with the people. Those who had been enthusiastic over his deeds, when they learned that he had been made prisoner, would begin to look upon him as a common, everyday person, and that did not suit him in the least.

"I must do something… anything. What can I do?"

To face his pursuers with his pistol from the niche

would be gallant, but it would mean exposing himself to death, or going to prison.

Turning about in the niche, Quentin stumbled over a huge rock.

"Let me see. We'll try a little fake."

He removed his cloak and wrapped the stone in it, making a sort of dummy. Then he took the bundle in his arms and stepped to the railing of the bridge.

"There he is! There he is!" shouted his pursuers.

Quentin tipped the dummy toward the river.

"He's going to jump!"

Quentin gave a loud shout, and pushed the stone wrapped in the cloak into the water, where it splashed noisily. This done, he jumped back; and then, on hands and knees, returned quickly to his niche, climbed into it, and pressed himself against the inside wall.

His pursuers ran by the niches without looking into either of them.

"How awful!" said one of the men.

"I can't see him."

"I think I can."

"Let's go to the mill at El Medio," said one who appeared to be the leader. "There ought to be a boat there. Watchman, you stay here."

Quentin heard this conversation, trembling in his hole; he listened to their footsteps, and when they grew fainter in the distance, he got up and looked through a narrow loophole that was cut in the niche. The watchman had placed his lamp upon the railing of the bridge, and was looking into the river.

"I have no time to lose," murmured Quentin.

Quickly he took off his tie and his kerchief, jumped to the bridge without making the slightest noise, and crept toward the watchman. Simultaneously one hand fell upon the watcher's neck, and the other upon his mouth.

"If you call out, I'll throw you into the river," said Quentin in a low voice.

The man scarcely breathed from fright. Quentin gagged him with the handkerchief, then tied his hands behind him, took off his cap, placed his own hat upon the watchman's head, and carrying him like a baby, thrust him into the niche.

"If you try to get out of there, you're a dead man," said Quentin.

This done, he put on the watchman's hat, seized his pike and lantern, and walked slowly toward the bridge gate.

There were two men there, members of the *guardia civil.*

"There! There he goes," Quentin said to them, pointing toward the meadow of El Corregidor.

The two men began to run in the indicated direction. Quentin went through the bridge gate, threw the lantern and the pike to the ground, and began to run desperately. He kept hearing the whistles of the watchmen; when he saw a lantern, he slipped through some alley and fairly flew along. At last he was able to reach El Cuervo's tavern, where he knocked frantically upon the door.

"Who is it?" came from within.

"I, Quentin. They're chasing me."

El Cuervo opened the door, and lifted his lantern to Quentin's face to make sure of his identity.

"All right. Come in. Take the light."

Quentin took the lantern, and the innkeeper slid a couple of formidable-looking bolts into place.

"Now give me the lantern, and follow me."

El Cuervo crossed the tavern, came out into a dirty courtyard, opened a little door, and, followed by Quentin, began to climb a narrow stairway which was decorated with cobwebs. They must have reached the height of the second story when the innkeeper stopped, fastened the lantern to a beam on the wall, and holding on to some beam ends that were sticking from the wall, climbed up to a high garret.

"Let me have the lantern," said El Cuervo.

"Here it is."

"Now, *you* come up."

The garret was littered with laths and rubbish. El Cuervo, crouching low, went to one end of it, where he put out the light, slid between two beams that scarcely looked as if they would permit the passage of a man, and disappeared. Quentin, not without a great effort, did the same, and found himself upon the ridge of a roof.

"Do you see that garret?" said El Cuervo.

"Yes."

"Well, go over to it, keeping always on this side; push the window, which will give way, and enter; go down four or five steps; find a door; open it with this key, and you will be in your room—safer than the King of Spain."

"How about getting cut?"

"You will be notified."

"And eating?"

"Your meals will be sent to you. When Señor José gets back, he'll come to see you."

"Good; give me the key."

"Here it is. Adiós, and good luck."

The innkeeper disappeared whence he had come. Quentin, following the example of a cat, went tearing across the tiles.

From that height he could see the city, caressed by the silver light of the moon. Through the silence of the night came the murmuring of the river. In the background, far above the roofs of the town, he could make out the dark shadow of Sierra Morena, with its white orchards bathed in the bluish light, its great bulk silhouetted against the sky, and veiled by a light mist.

Quentin reached the attic, pushed open the window, descended the stairs as he had been told, opened the door, lit a match, and had scarcely done so when he heard a shriek of terror. Quentin dropped the match in his fright. There was some one in the garret!

"Who's there?" he asked.

"Oh, sir," replied a cracked voice, "for God's sake don't harm me."

When Quentin saw that he was being begged for help, he realized that there was no danger, so he lit another match, and with it, a lamp. By the light of this, he saw a woman sitting up in a bed, her head covered with curlpapers.

"Have no fear, Señora," said Quentin; "I must have made a mistake and entered the wrong room."

"Well, if that is the case, why don't you go?"

"The fact is, I'm surprised that it should be so. This was the only garret in the roof. Would you like an explanation? El Cuervo, the landlord of yonder corner tavern, told me to come here; that this was his garret."

"Well, I came here because José Pacheco brought me."

"Pacheco?"

"Yes."

"Then, this is the right garret."

"Do you know Pacheco?" asked the woman.

"He is a good friend of mine. Do you know him too?"

"Yes, sir. He is my lover," sighed the woman. Quentin felt an overpowering desire to laugh.

"Then, my lady," he said, "I am very sorry, but I am pursued by the police, and cannot leave this place."

"Nor can I, my good sir, permit you to remain in my bedroom."

"What do you want me to do?"

"Go and sleep outside."

"Where? Upon the roof? You don't know what kind of a night it is."

"You are not very gallant, Señor."

"Pneumonia would be less gallant with me, Señora."

"Do you think that I am going to allow you to remain in this room all night?"

"See here, Señora, I'm not by any means trying to violate you. Allow me to take a mattress, and stretch out upon the floor."

"Impossible."

"If you are afraid, leave the lamp lit. Furthermore, for your better tranquillity, and as a means of defence for your honour, I hand you these two pistols. They are loaded," said Quentin, as he cautiously unloaded them.

"Very well, then; I agree," replied the woman.

Quentin took a mattress, spread it upon the floor, and threw himself upon it.

"Woe unto you, Señor," said the woman in a terrible voice, "if you dare to take any undue liberties."

Quentin, who was tired, began in a very few minutes to snore like a water-carrier. The woman sat up in bed and scrutinized him closely.

"Oh! What an unpoetic person!" she murmured.

When Quentin awoke and found himself in the room, where a ray of light poured in through a high, closed window, he got up to open it. The poetic woman at that moment was snoring, with a pistol clasped in her fingers.

Quentin opened the window, and as he did so, he discovered that a cord was attached to the window lock. He jerked it, found that it was heavy, and pulled it toward him until a covered basket appeared.

"Here's breakfast," announced Quentin.

And sure enough; inside was a roast chicken, bread, a bottle of wine, and rolled in the napkin, a paper upon which was written in huge letters:

"Do not come out; they are still hanging around the street."

Quentin threw the basket out of the window, and lowered it the full length of the string. He was preparing to eat his breakfast with a good appetite, when the woman opened her eyes.

"Good morning, Señora," said Quentin. "They have sent me my breakfast. I'll treat if you wish. I'll go out for a stroll on the roof, and meanwhile, you can be dressing yourself. Then, if you would like to heat the food...."

"Oh, no. No cooking," replied she. "I feel very ill."

"Well, then; we'll eat the chicken cold."

Quentin went out on the roof. He took out his pencil

and notebook, and busied himself writing an article for *La Víbora.*

When he had finished, he went back to the garret.

"I'm not dressed yet," said the woman.

Quentin returned to the roof; wrote two selections for the paper, one insulting the Government and the other the Mayor; then he crawled about the roof. On an azotea some distance away, a girl was arranging some flower pots. Probably she was pretty.... Quentin drew near to watch her.

He was surprised in this espionage by Pacheco, who came on all fours along the ridge pole.

"Good day, comrade," said Pacheco.

"Hello, my friend."

"I must congratulate you, comrade; what you did yesterday is one of the funniest things I ever heard of."

"Who told you about it?"

"Why, they talk of nothing else in the whole town! This morning, some were still betting that your corpse was at the bottom of the river, and they went out in boats; but instead of the fish they expected to catch, they pulled out a rock wrapped in a cloak. All Cordova is laughing at the affair. You certainly were a good one."

"But listen, comrade," said Quentin, pointing to the garret, "what kind of a lark have you in that cage?"

"Ah! That's true! It's a crazy woman. She says she's in love with me, and in order to get rid of her, I brought her to this place, where she can't bother me."

"How did she get here? Along the roofs, too?"

"Yes; disguised as a man. In her pantaloons she had a look about her that was enough to make you want to kick her in the stomach and throw her into the court-yard."

"Very well, then; let's go to the garret, where breakfast is waiting. The thing I hate about this, comrade, is not being able to get out."

"Well, it's impossible now; the police have their eyes peeled."

"And haven't they tried to arrest you, my friend?"

"Me? They can't do it.... I have a pack of bloodhounds that can smell from here everything that goes on in the other end of Cordova. Just give one of them a message, and he tears through the atmosphere faster than a greyhound."

They knocked at the garret.

"I'm not dressed yet," came from within.

"Come, Señora," exclaimed Quentin. "You are abusing my appetite. If you don't want to open the door, give me the basket. I warn you, Pacheco is here."

When she heard this, the woman opened the door and threw herself into the arms of the bandit. She had her hair crimped, covered with little bow knots, and was wearing a white wrapper.

Quentin took the basket.

"Well," he said, "I'll leave you two alone if you wish."

"No!" exclaimed Pacheco in terror; then turning to the woman, he added: "This gentleman and I have some important matters to discuss. We are gambling with life."

"First we'll eat a little," said Quentin. "That's an idea for you."

"An alimentary one."

They divided the chicken.

"And do they say in town who it was that ordered them to pursue me?" asked Quentin.

"Everybody knows that it was La Aceitunera," answered Pacheco. "You insisted upon discrediting her, but she grew strong under the punishment, and wants no more stings from *La Víbora*. Then, so they say, as she seemed no mere stack of straw to the Governor, she allowed herself to be flirted with, and begged him to throw you into jail, and to stop your paper."

"We'll see about that."

"It will be done. He does what he wants here," replied the bandit. "You already know what they say in Cordova: 'Charity in El Potro, Health in the cemetery, and Truth in the fields.'"

"Then we'll go into the fields to look for it," said Quentin.

"Not that"—answered Pacheco. "I won't allow you to lose out; but if you want to give that woman a good scare...."

"Have you thought of some way?"

"Not yet; are you capable of doing something on a large scale?"

"I am capable of anything, comrade."

"Good. Wait for me until tonight."

"Very well," said Quentin. "Will you take these papers to the printer for me?"

"What are they?"

"Poison for *La Víbora*, or articles, if you like that better."

"Give them to me. I'll be here at seven." Then the bandit, turning to the woman, said: "Adiós, my soul!"

"Won't you stay a little while, José?" she asked.

"No. Life is too short," he answered gruffly, and went out through the attic window.

# CHAPTER XXIV

## THE VICTIM OF A FEUILLETON

THE woman and Quentin were left alone.

"If you don't want me to stay here," said Quentin—"tell me so."

"Do you hate me so much for last night?" she said.

"I? No, Señora; but since this chamber is so narrow that one can scarcely move in it, you must let me know if I'm in your way."

"No; you're not in my way."

Quentin seated himself upon a chair, took out his note book and pencil, and made up his mind to attempt one of the most disagreeable and difficult things in the world for him—making verses. Not by any chance did a consonance occur to him, nor did a single verse come out with the right number of feet, unless he counted them upon his fingers.

The good woman, with her crimped hair covered with little bow-knots, and her white wrapper, was contemplating the roof of the garret with desperate weariness.

Thus they remained for a long time. Suddenly the woman exclaimed in a choked voice:

"Señor!"

"What is it, Señora?"

"I seem very ridiculous in your eyes, do I not?"

"No, Señora,—why?" asked Quentin, and mumbled to himself: "nude, crude, stewed, conclude—No, they don't seem to come very easily."

"I am very unhappy, Señor."

"Why, what's the matter, Señora?" and Quentin went on mumbling: "rude, gratitude, fortitude.... No, they do not come easily."

"Will you listen to me, my good sir? At present you alone can advise me."

"Speak, Señora, I am all ears," answered Quentin, shutting his note book, and putting away his pencil.

The woman heaved a deep sigh, and began as follows:

"I, my good sir, am called Gumersinda Monleón. My father was a soldier, and I spent my childhood in Seville. I was an only child, and very much spoiled. My parents satisfied every caprice of mine that was within their means. It was 'Sinda' here, and 'Sinda' there—as they had abbreviated my name.... As I imagined myself at that time to be a somewhat exceptional person, and believed that I was out of my proper sphere in the modest home of my parents, I took up reading romantic novels, and I think I was by way of having my head turned by them.

"I lived with all the personages of my books; it seemed to me that all I had to do was to reach Paris and ask the first gendarme for Guillaboara, and he would immediately give me her address, or at least, that of her father, Prince Rudolf of Gerolstein.

"With my head full of mysteries, bandits, and black doctors, a suitor came to me—a rich young man who was owner of a fan-making establishment. I dismissed him several times, but he came back, and, with the influence of my parents, he succeeded in getting me to marry him. He was a saint, a veritable saint; I know it now; but I considered him a commonplace person, incapable of lifting himself to higher spheres above the prosaic details of the store.

"After we had been married two years, he died, and

I became a widow of some thirty-odd years and a considerable fortune; not to mention the fan-making establishment which I inherited from my husband. A young widow with money, and not at all bad looking, I had many suitors, from among whom I chose an army captain, because he wrote me such charming letters. Later I found out that he had copied them from a novel by Alfonso Karr that was appearing in the feuilleton of *Las Novedades*. Handsome, with a fine appearance, my second husband's name was Miguel Estirado. But, my God, what a life he led me! Then I learned to realize what my poor Monleón had been to me.

"Estirado had a perfectly devilish humor. If we made a call upon any one, and the maid asked us who we were, he would say: 'Señor Estirado and his wife,' and if the girl smiled, he would insult her in the coarsest way.

"After six months of married life, my husband quit the active service and retired to take care of the store. Estirado had no military spirit; he sold the gold braid from his uniform, and put his sword away in a corner. One day the servant girl used it to clean out the closet, and after doing so, left it there. When I saw it, I felt like weeping. I grasped the sword by the hilt, which was the only place I *could* take hold of it, and showing it to my husband, said: 'Look at the condition your sword is in that you used in defence of your country.' He insulted me, clutching his nose cynically, and told me to get out; that he cared nothing for his sword, nor for his country, and for me to leave him in peace. From that day I realized that all was over between us.

"Shortly after that Estirado dismissed an old clerk who used to work in the store, and hired two sisters in his place: Asunción and Natividad.

"Six months later, Asunción had to leave and spend a few months at a small village. She came back with a little baby. Not long after her return the trip was repeated.

"They talked of nothing else in the whole neighbourhood. On account of the attitude of the two sisters toward me, I dared not go down to the store, and they did just about as they pleased.

"One day, after six years, my husband disappeared, taking Natividad, the younger sister, with him. The other girl, Asunción, brought this news to me with her four children hanging on her arm; and she told me a romantic tale about her mother, who was a drunkard, and about her sweetheart. She reminded me of Fleur de Marie, in 'The Mysteries of Paris,' and of Fantine, in 'Les Miserables;' so I comforted her as best I could—what else was I to do? Time passed, and Estirado began to write and ask me for money; then the letters ceased, and after half a year my husband wrote a letter saying that Natividad had run away from him, that he was seriously ill in a boarding house in Madrid, and for Asunción and me to come to take care of him. I realized that it was not honourable, nor Christian, nor right, but at the same time I gave in, and we, his wife and sweetheart, went and took care of him until he died. At his death I granted a pension to the girl, left Seville, and came to live in Cordova. That is the story of my life."

"Señora, I think you were a saint," said Quentin. "What astounds me is how, after such an apprenticeship, you managed to get mixed up in *this* adventure."

"Well, you see I did not learn by experience. I met Pacheco one day in the country, when he entered my farm. He reminded me of a novel by Fernández y Gonzáles. We spoke together; his life fascinated me; I wrote to him; he answered my letter, assuredly through civility; my head was filled with madness, even to the point of disguising myself as a man and following him."

"Fortunately, Señora, you have encountered extremely trustworthy persons," said Quentin, "who will not abuse your faith."

"What advice do you give me?"

"Why something very simple. Tonight Pacheco and I shall probably leave here. You must come with us; we'll leave you at your house; and that will be an end to the adventure."

"That's true. It's the best thing."

"Now let's see," said Quentin, "if El Cuervo has put any ballast in the basket."

He climbed upon a chair and opened the window.

"It's heavy," said he, jerking the cord; *"ergo*, there are provisions. Cheer up, Doña Sinda," he added, "and get the table ready."

# CHAPTER XXV

## AN ABDUCTION IS PREPARED

AT nightfall Quentin went out on the roof, stretched his spine along the ridge, and waited for Pacheco. The Cathedral clock was striking eight, when the bandit appeared, making his way toward the garret on all fours.

"Hey!" called Quentin.

"What is it? Is it you?"

"Yes."

"Why are you waiting outside for me?"

"So we can talk without that woman hearing what we say. I have persuaded her to go home peaceably."

"Very good. But listen. comrade; I've got a plan ready for something worth while."

"I'm with you in everything. What have you thought of?"

"Of kidnapping La Aceitunera tonight."

"But can it be done?"

"Absolutely. The Countess is going to the theatre. She will go in her carriage as usual, and if Cabra Periquito Gálvez doesn't show up to accompany her, she will go home alone in her carriage. If Periquito does show up, and does go with her, we won't do a thing; if she is alone, why, we'll steal her away."

"That's all very well; but how?"

"First of all, I'll see to it that the coachman gets drunk so I can take his place; meanwhile, you go to the theatre, make sure that she is alone, then station yourself on the sidewalk opposite the lobby, and stay there quietly; if she comes out escorted, you light a match as if you were about to smoke—understand?"

"Where will you be then?"

"On the box. If the Countess is escorted, why, I'll take her home, and we'll leave the matter for another day. If she is alone, I'll trot the horses as far as the Campo de la Merced, where I'll stop; you get on—and away we go!"

"Very good. You're a wonder, comrade! But let's look coldly at the inconveniences."

"Out with them."

"First of all, the departure from this place. They are still hanging around the street, according to El Cuervo."

"Ah, but do you think I am such an idiot as to go out through El Cuervo's tavern? Ca, man!"

"No?"

"Of course not."

"Well, where, then?"

"You'll see."

"Good. That solves the first problem: second, I have to go to the theatre to see if the Countess is alone, and people know me; if one of the police...."

"Nothing will happen. Take this ticket. Steal in when the performance has begun, and go upstairs, open one of the top boxes which are usually empty, and if the usher comes in, give him a peseta. He's a friend of mine."

"Good. Now we'll tell the woman, and be on our way. Shall we have supper first?" asked Quentin.

"No; we must have clear heads. We'll have supper at the El Pino farm, or—in jail."

"You've spoken like a man. Let's go."

They entered the garret.

"Doña Sinda," said Quentin, "we are going to crawl about the roof a bit."

"Wait a moment, comrade," said Pacheco. "They won't do anything to me; but if they see you, they'll tie you up," and as he spoke, he opened a wardrobe, took out a grey cloak, a kerchief, and a broad-brimmed hat.

"Who's that for?"

"For you."

Pacheco made a bundle of the things, and said:

"Hurry! I'll go first, then the Señora, and then you, Quentin."

They formed themselves in single file and began to move. The night was dark, threatening a storm; distant flashes of lightning illuminated the heavens from time to time.

Doña Sinda moved slowly and painfully.

"Come, Señora, come," said Quentin; "we are near you."

"My hands and knees hurt me," she murmured. "If I could only walk on my feet."

"You can't do it," said Pacheco. "You would fall into a courtyard."

"Ay, dear me! I'm not going a step farther."

"We're going as far as that azotea."

Doña Sinda yielded; they crawled along the ridge of a long roof, and came out upon the azotea. They leaped the balustrade.

"Oh, dear! I'm going to stay here!" exclaimed Doña Sinda.

"But my dear woman, it's only a little farther," said Quentin.

"Well, I won't budge."

"Very well then, we'll go on alone," said Pacheco.

"Are we going to leave her here?" asked Quentin.

The bandit shrugged his shoulders, and without more ado, leaped over the balustrade again. Quentin followed him, and the two men rapidly covered a great distance.

"Now be careful," warned Pacheco. "We've got to go around this cornice until we reach that window."

It was a stone border about half a metre wide. At the end of it they could see a little illuminated balcony window, which as it threw the light against the wall, made the cornice look as if it were on the brink of a deep abyss. They went along very carefully on all fours, one behind the other. As they reached the balcony, Pacheco seized the balustrade and jumped upon the stairway. Quentin followed his example.

"Do you know, comrade," remarked Quentin, "that this is scary business?"

"Then too, that light is enough to drive you crazy. In the daytime it doesn't scare you at all to come over it. Now then, put on your cloak and the other tackle."

Quentin tied his kerchief about his head, put on the hat, wrapped himself in the cloak and the two men descended the stairs into a garden. Crossing this, they came out upon the street.

"What is this building?" asked Quentin.

"It is a convent," replied the bandit. "Now, we mustn't go together any more. You come along about twenty or thirty paces behind me."

Quentin followed him at a distance, and after traversing several intricate alleys, they came out upon the Plaza de Séneca, and from there upon the Calle de Ambrosio de Morales, where the theatre was. A gas light illuminated the door, scarcely lessening the shadows of the street. The play had not yet begun. Pacheco entered a near-by shop, and Quentin followed him.

"You stay here," said the bandit, "and when everybody has gone in, you follow. I'm going to the Countess' house."

People were crowding into the theatre; two or three carriages drove up; several whole families came along, with a sprinkling of artisans. When he no longer saw anyone in the lobby, Quentin left the little shop, entered the theatre, relinquished his ticket, climbed the stairs with long strides until he reached the top floor and when he saw the usher, handed him a peseta.

The usher opened the door of a box.

"How is Señor José?" he asked.

"Well."

"He's a fine fellow."

"Yes, he is."

"I've known him for a long time; not that I am from Ecija exactly, for I come from a little village near Montilla; I don't know if you've heard its name...."

"See here," said Quentin, "I came here because I am a relative of the actor who takes old men's parts, and I am interested in hearing the performance and seeing how he acts; if you talk to me, I won't be able to hear anything."

"Gonzáles? Are you a relative of Gonzáles?"

"Of Gonzáles, or Martínez, or the devil! Take another peseta, and leave me alone, for I'm going to see what kind of an actor my relative makes."

"He's a good comedian."

"Very well, very well," said Quentin, and pushing the garrulous usher into the aisle, he closed the door.

As there was scarcely any light up there, no one could recognize Quentin. The theatre was almost empty; they were giving a lachrymose melodrama in which appeared an angelic priest, a colonel who kept shouting "By a thousand bombs!" a traitor money-lender with crooked eyes who confessed his evil intentions in asides, a heroine, a hero, and a company of sailors and sailoresses, policemen, magistrates, and others of the proletariat....

While Quentin was being bored in his heights, Pacheco, leaning against the wall of La Aceitunera's house, was awaiting the return of her carriage from the theatre.

He did not have long to wait. The horses stopped before the gate, and before it could be opened, the bandit approached the coachman and said:

"Hello, Señor Antonio!"

"Hello, Señor José!"

"I want to talk with you a moment."

"What about?"

"About some horses I am ordered to buy, and as you know so much...."

"I'll be right out."

The house gate opened, the coachman drove his carriage inside, and in a few moments rejoined Pacheco.

He was a talkative and gay little man.

"Let's go somewhere and have a little wine with our talk," suggested the bandit. "You've got time?"

"I'm free until eleven-thirty."

"It's nine, now."

They went into a tavern where Pacheco explained to his friend how the horses must be. The matter must have been arduous and difficult, for the coachman lost himself in a labyrinth of endless equinal considerations. The bandit kept filling and refilling his glass for him as he drank.

"Man," said Pacheco, "today I was taken to a tavern where there was a superior wine that you can't find anywhere else."

"Really?"

"I should say so. Would you like to go and see if we can find it?"

"Well, you see I've got to go at eleven-thirty."

"There's more than time enough."

"All right; let me know when it's eleven o'clock."

"Certainly, don't you worry. Do you have to go back and get the Señora?"

"Yes."

"And harness up the horses again?"

"No. I left them harnessed. When I get back from the theatre, I go through the gate, turn the carriage around in the patio, and leave it in the entryway facing the street,—see? Then I go, open the gate, and I'm off."

Pacheco conducted the coachman through side streets to El Cuervo's tavern.

"But where is that tavern, my friend?" asked the little old man.

"Right here."

They went into the tavern.

"Bring me wine—the best you have," said Pacheco, winking at El Cuervo.

The innkeeper brought a large jar and filled the glasses. The coachman smelled the wine, tasted it slowly, relished it; then he smacked his lips, and emptied the glass in one gulp.

"What wine!" he murmured.

"Don't you think it's a little bit strong?"

"Well, that's a good kind of a fault to have, comrade!"

Pacheco got up and said to El Cuervo:

"You've got to keep this fellow interested."

El Mochuelo and Cantarote, the gipsy, came over to Pacheco's table with the pretext that there was no light where they had been sitting, and began to play cards.

"Would you like to play?" said Cantarote to Pacheco.

"No, thanks."

"And you?" the gipsy asked of the coachman.

"I? To tell the truth, I've got something to do. What time is it?"

"A quarter past ten," said El Cuervo.

"All right, I'll play a hand."

"After all, what have you got to do?" asked Pacheco. "Just knock till they open the gate, and then climb up on the box...."

"No, I've got the key to the gate here," remarked the coachman, patting his vest pocket.

Pacheco looked at Cantarote, and made a gesture with his hand as if he were picking up something. Cantarote lowered his eyelids as a sign that he had understood, and with the utmost neatness put his hand into the old man's vest, took out the key, and, holding his cards in his left hand, handed it to Pacheco behind the coachman's back.

The bandit got up.

"Let me have a cap," he said to El Cuervo.

The innkeeper brought one.

"Keep him busy for an hour."

This said, Pacheco hurried to the Countess' house, opened wide the gate, climbed to the box, and drove the carriage outside; then he closed the gate, climbed back again, and took his place near the theatre.

From his hiding-place, Quentin had discovered something curious and worthy of note. In one of the boxes near the curtain was the Countess, alone, with her back to the stage, and gazing at some one through her glasses. Quentin followed her look, and by bending low and leaning his body over the box, he discovered that the box at which she was directing her glances was occupied by the Governor and two other persons; but the Countess also looked elsewhere: toward a parquette where there were a toreador and several young gentlemen.

"Which is she looking at?" Quentin asked himself. "Is it the Governor, or the toreador?"

The Countess rested her opera glasses absently upon the railing of the box.

"Perhaps she isn't looking at any one," thought Quentin.

On the stage, they were spilling an ocean of tears: the priest, with his snow-white hair, saying, "My children" everywhere he went, was busy making his fellows happy.

The Countess cast an absent-minded glance at the stage, picked up her glasses, and took aim.

"It's the Governor," said Quentin.

The woman's glasses were lowered a bit, and he had to correct himself.

"It's the toreador," he remarked.

After many vacillations, Quentin realized that the Countess was playing with two stacks of cards, and was dividing her glances between the First Authority of the province, and the young toreador, so recently arrived in cultured society from a butcher shop in the district of El Matadero.

The Governor, very serious, very much be-gloved, looked at the woman; the little toreador, with his foot on the parquette rail, preened himself and smiled, showing the white teeth of a healthy animal.

At the beginning of the last act, the toreador, who had been concealed behind the curtains of the parquette, appeared with a square piece of paper that looked like a note in his hand; he showed it cautiously, and twisted it about his fingers.

Presently the woman, looking at the stage, nodded her head in the affirmative.

The play was about to come to an end; every one on the stage, from the priest and the two turtle-doves to the colonel—by a thousand bombs!—was happy; only, he of the crooked eyes had been seized by the police at the height of his evil machinations. Quentin opened his box, descended the stairs by leaps and bounds, and took up his post opposite the entrance to the theatre. Fat drops of rain commenced to fall, and the thunder kept grumbling overhead. There were two carriages at the door of the theatre. Pacheco was not in the first, and Quentin could not tell whether he was in the second one or not.

The audience began to come out of the theatre; when they saw the heavy rain drops that spattered the sidewalk, some hesitated to leave, then they made up their minds and began to hurry along, pressing close to the walls of the houses.

A fat lady with her escort entered the first carriage, and drove off toward the Plaza de Séneca. The second carriage drew up. Pacheco was on the box. He and Quentin glanced at each other. Everything was going splendidly.

Just then the Countess appeared in the lobby of the theatre wrapped in a white cape; she opened the door of the carriage and climbed rapidly into it. Behind her appeared the toreador, and as the carriage was about to move off, he held out his hand and threw a note through the window.

Pacheco clucked to the horses, and the carriage started up the street toward the confluence of the Calle del Arco Real and the Cuesta de Luján. Quentin started off rapidly in the direction of the Campo de la Merced; he ran as fast as his legs could carry him, fearing all the while that he might meet some watchman who would recognize him. When he reached the appointed place he was played out. He waited, soaked in a torrential downpour. Before long, a carriage came in sight and stopped before him. Quentin opened the door and stood upon the step. A woman screamed shrilly. Quentin closed the carriage door; there came two tremendous cracks of a whip; and the coach moved off through the rain and obscurity, drawn by the horses at a full gallop....

# CHAPTER XXVI

## EXPLANATIONS

"BUT good heavens! What is it?—Who are you?—" cried the Countess, trembling.

"Don't be alarmed, Señora," said Quentin. "We have no idea of harming you."

"What do you want of me? I have no money with me."

"We are not looking for money."

"Then what do you want?"

"We'll tell you that later. Have a little patience."

Several moments passed in the carriage without the woman saying a word. She was huddled motionless against a window.

After some time had elapsed, the horses moderated their pace, one could hear the rain on the cover of the carriage. Suddenly Quentin heard the door-fastening rattle.

"Don't be foolish, my lady," he said rudely. "And don't try to escape. It will be dangerous."

"This violence may cost you dear," murmured the Countess.

"Most assuredly. We men are prepared for anything."

"But if you don't want my money, what do you want? Tell me, and let us bring this affair to a close at once."

"That is a secret that does not belong to me."

"But, sir," exclaimed the woman—"I'll give you anything you want if you will only take me home."

At this moment a flash of lightning violently illumined the night, and the Countess and Quentin were enabled to see each other's faces in the spectral light. Then came a thunderclap as loud as a cannon shot.

"Oh, my God!" gasped the Countess as she devoutly crossed herself.

Quentin felt a tremor run through him at the sight of the woman's terror, and said to her:

"My dear lady, do not let us cause you any alarm. Please rest assured that we have no intention of harming you. I rather think that the man on the box is some gentleman who is in love with you, and not being able in any other way to attain good fortune, is abducting you in this manner."

Quentin's accent, his gallant meaning in those circumstances must have surprised the Countess, as she made no answer.

"Don't you think so?" said Quentin. "Don't you believe that this is a matter of some one courting you?"

"It's a fine way to court," she replied.

"All ways are good if they come out right."

"Do you believe that this method of treating a lady can come out right?"

"Why not? Other more difficult things have been seen in the world, and they do say that women like the novel."

"Well, I don't like it a bit."

"Are you so prosaic that you are not enchanted by the thought of meeting soon a young, good-looking, respectful abductor who offers you his heart and life?"

"No, I am not enchanted. What is more, if I could send that abductor to prison I would do so with much pleasure."

"You know that love is intrepid and...."

Quentin was silent. He thought of the poem written by Cornejo for *La Víbora*.

"I don't know why," said the woman at length, "but it seems to me that I am beginning to realize who my abductor is. It strikes me that he is a half-relative of mine who dislikes me very much. A waif...."

"I think you are getting warm, my lady."

"Who writes insults and calumnies about a woman who has never offended him."

"You are not quite so near the point, there. Listen: The day before yesterday, that relative of yours was rushing madly about these God-forsaken streets, hounded by a dozen men; on a night that was as cold as the devil, he was on the point of throwing himself into the river and scraping an acquaintance with the shad that live in it."

"So you are Quentin?"

"I am the lady's most humble servant."

"How you frightened me! I shall never forgive you for this night."

"Nor will I forgive you for the one I spent the day before yesterday."

"Where is my coachman? Is he on the box?"

"No, my lady."

"Where is he?"

"He is conveniently drunk in a tavern on the Calle del Potro."

"Then who is driving the carriage?"

"Pacheco."

"Pacheco! The bandit?"

"In person. In all ways a gentleman, and whom I shall have the pleasure of presenting to you tonight as soon as we reach the farm where we are to stop."

"What are you two going to do with me there?"

"We shall think it over."

"I believe you intend to kill me...."

"Kill you?—Nothing of the sort. We shall entertain you; you will take rides over the mountain; you'll get a trifle brown—Besides, we are doing you a great favour."

"Doing me a favour? What is it?"

"Keeping you from answering that little toreador who had the presumption to send you a note."

"To send *me* a note?"

"Yes, my lady; you. As you came out of the theatre. I saw it with my own eyes."

"It must be true if you saw it."

"Of course it is! In the first place, that toreador is a stupid good-for-nothing who would go about boasting that you looked upon him with sympathy, and that...."

"Enough, or I'll even have to thank you for bringing me here."

"And it's true."

The Countess was growing calmer and less timid with every minute.

"How many days are you going to keep me kidnapped?" she asked rather jovially.

"As many as you wish. When you get too bored, we'll take you back to Cordova. Then, if you still bear us a grudge, you may denounce us."

"And if I don't?"

"If you don't, then you will permit us to come to call some day."

"We'll see how you act."

Just then the carriage stopped. Quentin prepared to get down, and said to the woman:

"I don't know what Pacheco wants. Perhaps he's tired of riding on the box."

"Don't leave me alone with him," murmured the Countess.

"Never fear; Pacheco is absolutely a gentleman, and will take no undue liberties...."

"That makes no difference."

"Then I shall tell him of your wish. If you want to be alone, tell me, and I'll ride on the box."

"No, no: I prefer you to ride with me."

Pacheco jumped down from the box, and coming up to Quentin, said:

"It seems to me that I have done my duty like a man, and that it's your turn to take my place on the box."

"That's what I think. Come, I'm going to present you to the Countess."

Quentin opened the carriage door and said:

"Countess, this is my friend."

"Good evening, Pacheco."

"A very good evening to you, my lady."

"How tired you are making yourselves on my account!"

"Señora Condesa!" stammered the bandit in confusion.

"You are very nice," she added graciously.

"You are most flattering," replied Pacheco.

"No; you two are the flatterers!"

"But are you sorry, my lady?" asked Pacheco gravely.

"I!—On the contrary; I am having a very good time."

"That's better, my lady. You mustn't be afraid; if you order me to, we'll go back this minute."

The Countess considered for a moment, and then cried gayly:

"No; let us go on. We'll go wherever you wish. You stay with me, Quentin, for I want to talk to you."

Again Pacheco climbed to the box, clucked to the horses, and the carriage went on its way. It was beginning to clear up; here and there a patch of star-sprinkled sky appeared between the great, black clouds.

"He seems like a fine fellow," said the Countess, who was now completely at her ease, when she and Quentin were alone.

"Do not deceive yourself; there are only two places where true gentlemen can be found: in the mountains, or in prison."

"How awful!" she cried.

"That is the way the two extremes meet," he went on. "When a man is a great, a very great rascal, and utterly disregards the ideas of the people and everything else, he has reached the point where the bandit is joining hands with the gentleman."

"See here, Sir Bandit," said the Countess easily, "why did you take this dislike to me, and put me in the papers? Because I said that Rafaela was a hussy, and that she had married Juan de Dios for his money?"

"Yes, my lady."

"Did I not speak the truth?"

"It is true that she married; but it was not because she wished it, nor because she was ambitious to be rich, but because the family made her."

"You should laugh at that idea, my friend!" replied the Countess. "Not that the girl isn't docile! When a woman does not care to marry a man, she simply doesn't marry him.... Of course, you were after her cash."

"I?—*Ca!*"

"I don't know why, but I think I see through you. You are very ambitious, and with all those foolish deeds of yours, you are only trying to fish for something. You cannot deceive me."

"Well, you are wrong," said Quentin. "I, ambitious? I covet nothing."

"Tell that to your grandfather, not to me. You are very ambitious, and she is a very romantic damsel, but very close with her money. If you two had married, a fine disappointment you would have had!... And she liked you, believe me; but as you were not a marquis, or a duke, but a poor son of a shop-keeper, she would have nothing to do with you."

Quentin felt deeply mortified by the phrase, and fell silent. Presently she burst into gracious laughter.

"What are you laughing at?" said Quentin, piqued.

"With all your boasting, you are worth less than I am: all your cravings are for things that are not worth while. I don't mind it in the least when they call me La Aceitunera, but you, on the other hand, are utterly cast down because I called you the son of a shop-keeper."

"Yes, that's true," assented Quentin ingenuously.

"And why is it true, my friend?" asked the Countess. "Why, we of the proletariat are worth more than dukes and marquises, with all their ceremonies and fripperies. Where is the salt of the earth? Among the masses...."

Why am I what I am? Because I married that bell-ox of an uncle of yours. The ambitions of my family annoyed me; they filled my head with titles and grandeurs; it's one and the same thing whether you are a duke's son, or the daughter of an olive merchant like me, or the son of an importer, like you."

The Countess was growing in Quentin's eyes. The sincere contempt that she felt for aristocratic things, seemed to him to be a stroke of superiority. As far as the question of birth, and family, and social position was concerned, Quentin was peevishly susceptible; and though he concealed these sentiments as best he could, they were often clearly apparent in him.

The Countess realized that this was one of Quentin's vulnerable spots, and took delight in wounding him.

"They must sell a great many things in that store. It is a beautiful shop, very large and...."

"My dear lady," said Quentin comically, when the annoyance that the woman's words cost him commenced to take on an ironical and gay character—"You are very sarcastic, but I realize that you have a right to be."

"So, you realize it?"

"Yes, my lady; and if you keep it up, I shall beg Pacheco to take my place in this delicate mission."

"I will not allow you to leave me," said the Countess mockingly.

"Well, if this turns out to be a long journey, I shall be found dead on the bottom of the coach."

"Dead! From what, Quentin?"

"From the pin pricks you are giving me right square in the heart. You are about to remind me for the fifth time that the chocolate we make in the store is adulterated.... I know you are."

"No, I've said nothing about it."

"Then you are going to talk to me about the coffee which is mixed with chicory, and then, eventually, and in order to complete the offence, you will bring my step-father's nickname before my eyes."

"El Pende—that's it, isn't it?"

"Yes, my lady that is what they call him."

"Well, to show you that I am more generous than you think me, I shall not mention it again. Henceforth you shall guard the secret of my olives, as I will guard the secret of your spices. Tell me: Is it true that you have a good voice?"

"For Heaven's sake! What are you trying to do, my lady? Have pity and compassion on a poor little chap like me."

"Go on, please sing."

Quentin hummed the swaggering song from *"Rigo-letto"*:

*"Questa o quella per me pari sono."*

"But sing out loud," said the Countess.

Quentin sang with his full voice:

*"La costanza tiranna del core*
*detestiamo qual morbo crudele*
*sol chi vuole si servi fedele*
*non v'ha amor se non v'é libertá."*

And this last phrase, which Quentin launched forth with real enthusiasm, echoed in the damp and tepid night air....

"Is that a song of circumstances?" said the Countess with a laugh.

"Yes, my lady," answered Quentin, without fully understanding what she meant.

"Listen... another thing. Why don't you make love to Remedios?"

"To Remedios! She is only a child."

"She's fourteen. How old are you?"

"Twenty-four."

"That's just right."

"Yes, but how about the groceries?"

"She would overlook that. Believe me, that child has a soul. My husband's older daughter is good, I won't deny it, but she is a cold thing. Just as she married Juan de Dios, she would have married any one, and she will be faithful to him, as she would to any one else, because she hasn't the courage to do otherwise; but not so with the little one, she's full of it."

Quentin recalled the two sisters and thought that perhaps the Countess was right. With the memory, he fell silent for a long time.

"Well," said the Countess, "if you continue this silence, it will seem as if I were the one who is abducting you, and that doesn't suit me. Why, just think if one of those verse-scribbling penny-a-liners should find out about this! They would paint me green."

"I'll not say another thing against you, my lady, because...."

"Because why, my friend? What were you going to say?"

"Nothing; I'll say that you are one of the most...."

"One of the most what?"

"One of the most—but here we are at the farm."

And Quentin opened the carriage door.

"I thought you were a braver man than that," said the Countess.

The carriage stopped and Quentin jumped to the muddy road. It was beginning to rain again.

"Can't you get the carriage closer to the house?" Quentin asked Pacheco.

"Take hold of the bridle of one of the horses. That's it."

"Shall I knock here?"

"Knock away."

Quentin gave two resounding knocks.

Several minutes passed, and no one appeared at the door.

"Knock again," said Pacheco.

Quentin did so, adorning his blows with a noisy tattoo.

"Coming! Coming!" came a voice from within.

They saw a beam of light in the door jamb; then the wicket opened and a man appeared with a lantern in his hand.

"It's I, Tío Frasquito," said Pacheco. "I have some friends with me."

"Good evening, Señor José and company," said the man.

"Is the ground impossible?" inquired the Countess from the inside of the carriage.

"Yes, it's very muddy," replied Quentin.

"How can I get out in these white slippers? I'm done for."

"Would you like me to carry you in my arms?" said Quentin.

"No, sir."

Then Pacheco, who had climbed down from the box,

removed his cloak, seized it as if he were about to tease a bull with it, and with a flourish spread it out upon the damp earth from the step of the carriage to the door of the house.

"There! Now you can get out."

The Countess, smiling and holding up her silk dress, walked across the cloak in her white shoes, and quickly entered the vestibule.

"Long live my Queen!" cried Pacheco, carried away by his enthusiasm. "And hurrah for all valiant women!"

It began to pour.

"What will poor Doña Sinda do?" said Quentin.

"Who is Doña Sinda?" asked Pacheco.

"The woman we left out on the roof. She must be soup by this time."

# CHAPTER XXVII

## IN WHICH A COUNTESS, A PROFESSIONAL BANDIT, AND A MAN OF ACTION HAVE A TALK

ONE afternoon a few days later, Quentin knocked at the Countess' door.

"May I come in?"

"Come!"

Quentin opened the door and entered. The room was large, whitewashed, with a very small window divided into four panes, the floor paved with red bricks, and blue rafters in the ceiling. Everything was as clean as silver; in the centre was a table covered with white oil-cloth, upon which was a glass bottle converted by the Countess into a flower stand full of wild flowers.

"My lady," announced Quentin, "I came to find out if you wanted anything in Cordova."

"Are you going there?"

"Yes, my lady. If you are bored, we'll take you in the carriage whenever you wish."

"No, I'm not bored. To the contrary."

"Then, why don't you stay here?"

"No, I cannot.—When do you go?"

"I was thinking of going today, but if you want me to go with you, I'll wait until tomorrow."

"Very well, we'll wait until tomorrow."

The Countess had made friends at the farm. Late in the afternoon she would take her sewing to the door, and, sitting in the shade, would work among the women of the house. They told her about their lives and their troubles, and she listened with great interest. Quentin and Pacheco used to join the group and chat until the farm bell signalled the labourers, and night fell, and the flocks of goats returned with a great tinkling of bells.

The labourers' children used to play in front of the doorway; three of them had made friends with the Countess. They were three children who had been left motherless; Miguel, the eldest, was seven, Dolores, the second, was five, and Carmen, the third, was three.

The eldest was very lively, already a little rascal; the second had a tangled mass of blond hair, sad, blue eyes, and a sun-burned face; she wore one of her father's vests, a dirty apron, stockings around her ankles, and a pair of huge shoes. The littlest one spent hour after hour with her finger thrust into her mouth.

These three children, accustomed to being alone, were content to play with each other; they played around, striking and throwing each other about the ground, and never cried.

"She bosses 'em all," said one of the old wives to the Countess, pointing to the second child.

"Poor girl. What is your name?"

"Dolores."

The Countess looked at the child, who lowered her eyes.

"Would you like to come with me, Dolores?" she asked.

"No."

"I'll give you pretty dresses, dolls—Will you come?"

"No."

The Countess kissed the girl, and every afternoon the

three children came, waiting for her to give them some money....

"Look there," said the Countess to Quentin, pointing to a hen that was strutting along the barnyard with her still featherless chicks—"I envy her."

"Do you?" asked Quentin. "You are more romantic than I thought you were."

"Romantic, my friend? Why? That is Truth, Nature."

"Ah! But do you believe in the goodness of Nature?"

"Don't you?"

"No, I do not. Nature is a farce."

"*You* are the farce!" said the Countess. "I could never live with a man like you, Quentin."

"Couldn't you?"

"No. If I had married you, we would have ended badly."

"Would we have beaten each other?"

"Probably."

"Look here; two things would have pleased me," replied Quentin. "To allow myself to be struck by you would have been magnificent, but to give you a drubbing would also have been good."

"Would you have dared?" said the Countess with a slight flush in her cheeks, and her eyes shining.

"Yes, if I were your husband," answered Quentin calmly.

"Don't pay any attention to this fellow," said Pacheco, "for all that is just idle fancy."

Pacheco manifested a respectful enthusiasm toward the Countess, but at times he wondered if Quentin, with his wild ideas and outbursts, might not interest the Countess more....

... And as they chatted, the afternoon advanced; the sun poured down, its reflected rays were blinding as they fell on stones and bushes; and the air, quivering in the heat, made the outlines of the mountain and the distant landscape tremble.

"Would you like to take a ride, my lady?" said Pacheco.

"Yes, indeed."

"Shall I saddle your horse?"

"Fine!"

The Countess mounted, followed by Pacheco and Quentin, and the three made their way toward the top of the mountain by a broad path that ran between stout evergreens.

It was late Autumn; the days were sweltering, but as soon as the sun set, the air became very refreshing.

The mountain was splendid that afternoon. The dry, clean air was so transparent that it made even the most distant objects seem near; the trees were turning yellow and shedding their dried leaves; the harvested meadows had not yet begun to turn green. In the highways and byways, brambles displayed their black fruit, and the dog-rose bushes their carmine berries among their thorny branches.

"What are you thinking of doing, Quentin? What have you up your sleeve?" asked the Countess suddenly.

"Everybody knows," replied Pacheco—"that he's a lively fish."

"Ca, man," answered Quentin. "Why, I'm an unhappy wretch. Just now, I admit, I am capable of doing anything to get money and live well."

"He contradicts himself at every turn!" exclaimed the Countess, somewhat irritated. "I'm beginning to disbelieve everything he says; whether he tells me that he is bad, or whether he assures me that he is unhappy."

"You see I'm not to be classified by common standards. One half of me is good, and the other half bad. Sometimes it seems as if I were a demagogue, and I turn out to be a reactionary. I have all sorts of humility and all sorts of arrogance within me. For example, if you were to say to me tomorrow: 'By selling all the inhabitants of Cordova into slavery, you can make a fortune,' I would sell them."

"A lie!" replied the Countess. "You would not sell them."

"No, I would not sell them if you told me not to."

"Really, now!"

"Do you know what I used to think of doing when I was in England?" said Quentin.

"What?" asked Pacheco.

"Of putting up a money box. You must have seen one of them in Madrid, I think in the Calle del Fuencarral; people throw lots of money into it. Well, I saw it on my way through the city, and in school I was always thinking: 'When I get to Spain, I'm going to set up four or five money boxes, and take all the money that's thrown into them.'"

"What ideas you do have!" said the Countess.

"I have always thought that the first thing to do was to get rich."

"Why not work?"

"One can never make one's self rich by working. I have two aphorisms that rule my life; they are: first, be it yours or another's, you will never get on without money;

second, laziness has always its reward, and work its punishment."

"You are a faker, and one cannot talk to you," said the Countess. "What about you, Pacheco?"

"He? Why, he's another romanticist," replied Quentin.

"Really?" asked the woman.

"Yes, somewhat," replied the bandit with a sigh.

"Some fine day," added Quentin, "you will hear that Pacheco has done something either very foolish, or very heroic."

"May God hear you," murmured the bandit.

"Do you see?"

"Isn't it better to do something famous, than to live in a hole like a toad all your life?"

"What would you like to do?" asked the Countess with curiosity.

"I?—Take part in a battle; lead it if possible."

"Then you want to be a soldier."

"You mean a general," interrupted Quentin with a laugh.

"And why not, if he has good luck?"

"What does one need to be a general?" asked Pacheco. "To have a soul, to be valiant, and to be ready to give up your life every minute."

"And furthermore, to have a career," replied Quentin ironically... "to have good recommendations."

"But you always look upon everything as small and niggardly!" exclaimed the bandit hotly.

"And you, my friend, hope to encounter great and strong things in a mean society. You are deceived."

269

Pacheco and Quentin fell silent, and the Countess contemplated the two men as they rode quietly along....

It was late afternoon. The dry earth, warmed by the sun, exhaled the aroma of rosemary and thyme and dried grass. Upon the round summit of the mountain, trees, bushes, rocks, stood out in minutest detail in the diaphanous air.

The sun was sinking. The naked rocks, the thickets of heather and furze, were reddened as if on the point of bursting into flame. Here and there among the yellow foliage of the trees, appeared the white and smiling walls of farmhouses....

Soon night began to fall; bands of deep violet crept along the hillsides; one could hear in the distance the crowing of cocks and the tinkling of bells, which sounded louder than usual in that peaceful twilight; the air was tranquil, the sky azure.... Herds of cattle spread over the fields, which were covered with dry bushes; and along the damp pathways, bordered by huge, grey century-plants, a torrent of sheep and goats flowed, followed by their shepherd and his great, gentle-eyed, white mastiff.

When they returned to the farmhouse, Tío Frasquito said to Pacheco:

"We have been waiting for you."

"Why, what's up?"

"They just baptized a baby in the farm next to ours, and are having a little dance. If you people would like to go...."

"Shall we go?" Pacheco asked the Countess.

"Why not?"

"Then we'll have supper right away, and be there in a moment."

They ate their supper; and on foot and well cloaked, as it was rather cool, they walked along paths and across fields to the neighbouring farm.

As they drew near, they could hear the murmur of conversation and the strumming of a guitar. The entry-way in which the fiesta was being celebrated was large and very much whitewashed. It had a wide, open space in the centre, with two columns; suspended from the beams of the ceiling, were two big lamps, each with three wicks. Seated upon benches and rope chairs were several young girls, old women, sun-blackened men, and children who had come to witness the baptism.

In the centre was a space left free for the dancers. Seated near a small table, which held a jug and a glass, an old man was strumming a guitar, a man with a face and side-whiskers that just begged for a gun.

The entrance of the Countess and her escorts was greeted with loud acclaim; one of the farm hands asked, and it was not easy to tell whether in jest or in all seriousness, if that lady was the Queen of Spain.

The caretaker of the farm, after installing the three guests in the most conspicuous place, brought them some macaroons and glasses of white wine.

Boleras and fandangos alternated, and between times they drank all the brandy and wine they wanted. The Countess went to see the mother of the baptized child.

"Aren't you going to dance, Pacheco?" asked Quentin.

"Are you?"

"Man alive, I'm not graceful enough. I'll play the guitar. You ask the Countess to dance with you."

"She won't do it."

"Do you want me to ask her for you?"

"Good idea."

Quentin did so when she returned. She burst out laughing.

"Well, will you do it?"

"Of course, man."

"Hurrah for all valiant women. Ladies and gentlemen," said Quentin, turning to the bystanders, "the Señora is going to dance with Pacheco; I shall play the guitar, and I want the best singer here to stand by me."

Quentin sat in the chair where the old man had been, and near him stood a little dark-haired girl with large eyes. He tuned the guitar, turning one key and then another, and then began a devilish preparatory flourish. Little by little this uncouth flourish grew smoother, changing into a handling of the strings that was finesse itself.

"Go ahead," cried Quentin. "Now for the little highlander!"

The Countess arose laughing heartily, with her arms held high; Pacheco, very serious, also arose and stood before her. An old woman, a mistress of the art, began to click her castanets with a slow rhythm.

"Girlie," said Quentin to the singer, "let's hear what you can do."

In almost a whisper, the girl sang:

*"Con abalorios, cariño,*
*con abalorios."*

(With glass beads, love, with glass beads.)

The dancers made their start rather languidly.

The girl went on:

*"Con abalorios,*
*tengo yo una chapona,*
*tengo yo una chapona,*
*cariño! con abalorios."*

(With glass beads, I have a dressing sack, I have a dressing sack, love! with glass beads.)

The dancers were a little more lively in the "parade," the castanets clicked louder, and the high, treble voice of the girl increased in volume:

*"Están bailando*
*el clavel y la rosa,*
*están bailando*
*el clavel y la rosa,*
*ay! están bailando!"*

(They are dancing, the pink and the rose, they are dancing, the pink and the rose; Ah! they are dancing!)

This last phrase, which was somewhat sad, was accompanied by a ferocious sound of castanets, as if the player wished to make the dancers forget the melancholy of the song.

The girl went on:

*"Porque la rosa*
*entre más encarnada,*
*Porque la rosa*
*entre más encarnada*
*ay! es más hermosa!"*

(For the rose, the more she blushes, for the rose, the more she blushes, Ah! the more beautiful she becomes.)

Then the castanets clicked wildly, while all the bystanders cheered the dancers on. Pacheco pursued his partner with open arms, and she seemed to provoke him and to flee from him, keeping out of his reach when he was about to conquer her. In these changes and movements, the Countess' skirts swished back and forth and folded about her thighs, outlining her powerful hips. The whole room seemed filled with an effluvia of life.

Quentin enthusiastically continued to strum the guitar.

The singer had offered him a glass of white wine, and without ceasing to play, he had stretched out his lips and drained it.

The dance was repeated several times, until the dancers, worn out, sat down.

"Splendid! Magnificent!" exclaimed Quentin with tears in his eyes.

Suddenly the little girl who had sung told him she was going.

"Why?"

"Because some joker is going to put out the lights."

Quentin put down the guitar and went over to the Countess.

"You'd better go," he told her, "they are going to put out the lights."

She got up, but did not have time to go out. Two big youths put out the lamps with one blow, and the entryway was left in darkness. Quentin led the Countess to a corner, and stood ready to protect her in case there was need. There was a bedlam of shrill shrieks from the women, and laughter, and voices, and all started for the door which was purposely barred. Quentin felt the Countess by his side, palpitant.

"That'll do," said the landlord, "that's enough of the joke," and he relit the lamps.

The fiesta became normal once more, and soon after, all began to file out.

The following was the day fixed upon for the departure. Pacheco had, as he said, reasons for not going to Cordova, so he did not go. Quentin sat upon the box and drove off with the Countess. At nightfall, they were on the Cuesta de Villaviciosa. From that height, by the light of the half-hidden sun, they could see Cordova;

very flat, very extensive, among fields of yellow stubble and dark olive orchards. A slight mist rose from the river bed. In the distance, very far away, rose the high and sharp-peaked Sierra of Granada.

Carts were returning along the road, jolting and shaking; they could hear the Moorish song of the carters who were stretched out upon sacks, or skins of olive oil; riders on proud horses passed them, seated upon cowboy saddles, their shawls across their saddle bows, and their guns at their sides....

When they entered Cordova, night had already fallen; the sky was sprinkled with stars; on either side of the road, which now ran between the houses, great, many-armed century plants shone in the darkness.

Quentin drove the carriage to the Countess' palace, and jumped from the box, much to the astonishment of the porter.

"Goodbye, my lady." said he, holding out his hand and assisting her from the carriage.

"Goodbye, Quentin," she said rather sadly.

# CHAPTER XXVIII

## THE MASON'S MESSAGE

"SO you know nothing about him?" asked the Swiss.

"Not a thing," replied María Lucena. "He left here the very night they tried to arrest him, and he hasn't showed up yet. They say that he and Pacheco kidnapped the Countess."

"The devil! An abduction!"

"Yes. Let me tell you, that man disgusts me, and I wish I hadn't met him."

Paul Springer contemplated the pale face of the actress sympathetically.

"He'll show up," he said.

"I hope he never does!" she replied.

The Swiss was disturbed.

"How did you meet Quentin? Through the fracas he started here?"

"Yes. They told me that there had been a dispute between a young chap and a vile man who had insulted me. I asked Cornejo, the fellow who writes topical songs for the musical comedies, who my defender was, and he said: 'I'll show him to you.' Every night I asked him: 'Who is he? Who is he?'—but he never showed up. After awhile I got impatient and said to Cornejo: 'Look here; you tell your friend that I want to meet him, that if he doesn't come to the theatre, to go to my house, and that I live near here in a boarding house called Mariquita's House.' Would you believe it? There I was, waiting day after day, and he never showed up!"

"You must have been indignant," said Springer.

"Naturally! I said: 'If he doesn't know me, why did he defend me? And if he does know me, why doesn't he come to see me?'"

"How did you get to meet him finally?"

"You'll see; one day Cornejo came in here with Quentin, and introduced him to me as the man who had insulted me and had been struck by my defender. I said a lot of outrageous and insulting things to him, and just then a friend of his came in and greeted him with a 'Hello, Quentin!' Then I realized that *he* was my defender and we made friends."

"Yes, he's very fond of those farces."

"Why did he do it? I can't understand that man."

"Nor does he understand himself, probably; but he's a good fellow."

At the very second that the Swiss was saying these words, Quentin entered the café, looked about him indifferently and came up to the table at which María Lucena and Springer were seated.

When she saw him, María suddenly turned red.

"Ah! So you've come at last!" she cried angrily. "Where have you been?"

"If you had had your way, my dear, I would have been in prison."

"That's where you ought to be always. Thief! May a nasty viper sting you! Tell me, what have you been doing all these days?"

"Why, I've been on a farm, hiding from the police."

"I'm likely to believe that! You've been with a woman."

The procedure of extracting the truth with a lie produced results, for Quentin said candidly:

"Where did you find that out?"

"You see, it's the truth! And now you are tired of her and have come back here. Well, son, you can clear out; for there's no more meat on the hook for lack of a cat, and I want nothing more to do with you. I have more than enough men who are better than you are, who have more money than you have, and more heart."

"I don't deny it," replied Quentin coldly.

"Ah! You don't deny it? You don't deny it?" she shouted, raising her voice in her fury. "But what do you think I am? What do *you* think?"

"Come, don't shriek so," said Quentin gently.

"I'll shriek if I want to. Tell me, you evil-blooded scoundrel; what did you take me for? Do you think you can laugh at me like this?"

"That is admirable logic!" replied Quentin. "One believes here that his life is the axle of the universe; other people's lives have no importance."

"Why—"

"Please; I am talking. I left the café the other night, and thanks to the influence of Señor Gálvez, with whom you were…."

"I!" said María. "That's not true."

"I myself saw you."

"Where could you see me from?"

"From the door, my dear."

"But you don't know Gálvez!" she replied, believing that Quentin must have had the news at second-hand.

"True; but I know the waiter, and I asked him: 'Who is the gentleman talking with María Lucena?' And he answered: 'Señor Gálvez.' So don't lie about it. Very well; thanks to the beneficent influence of that gentleman friend of yours, I was on the point of being carried off to prison, or of throwing myself into the river... yet, I do not go screeching about the place—because I do not believe that my life can be the axle of the universe."

"Fool, *more* than fool!"—she shouted. "I'll pound your brains out this very minute!"

"You'll pound nothing; and listen, if you will."

"What for? You're going to lie."

"Very well then: don't listen."

"I wish they'd take you to prison and keep you there all your life with your head stuck through a pillory."

"If you care to listen, I'll tell you whom I was with."

"I'm listening."

"Well, I was with the Countess."

"Then you haven't the least bit of shame," said María furiously.

"The Countess," Quentin continued, "was upset by the verses in *La Víbora*, and wished to avenge herself, and had asked the Governor to have me thrown into prison."

"Then what?"

"Well, Pacheco and I joined forces, and instead of her arresting us, we arrested her, and carried her off in her carriage to a farm."

"What happened there?" asked the actress.

"Nothing; we became good friends."

"Bah!"

"What ideas women have of each other!—" said Quentin sarcastically. "For them, all other women are prostitutes."

"Not all: just *some*."

"Do you believe that the Countess is a chorus girl?" said Quentin acridly.

María paled and looked at Quentin with concentrated fury.

"What did the Countess do there?" asked the Swiss.

"Nothing—rode and walked. She acted like what she is: a fine lady. Pacheco was crazy about her."

"Weren't you?"

"You know, Springer, that I am marble as far as women are concerned."

"What a faker!" exclaimed the Swiss.

"What a liar!" added María Lucena.

"May they pluck my wings, as the gipsies say, if I'm not telling the truth. You know, María, that I'm like a box of mixed candy that has neither cover nor flap."

"I don't believe you."

"Then I say you're a St. Thomas in skirts."

María was gradually calming down and speaking more pleasantly, as she prepared to leave for the theatre, when a man, tall, thin, with a black beard, kangaroo arms, and ferocious-looking hands, came up to Quentin. After making some mysterious grimaces, and winking his eyes, he whispered something in Quentin's ear.

"What did that man say to you?" asked María.

"That man is a hardware dealer and a Freemason; he told me that I must go to the Patrician Lodge tonight."

"There you go again with your humbugs. I've lost all patience with you. So he's a Fleemason, eh? Do you think I'm a fool?"

"Hey!" called Quentin to the hardware dealer, who had already reached the door.

"What is it?" asked the Mason.

"Will you kindly tell this woman what you wanted of me?"

"Ah! I cannot," replied the man, smiling and placing one of his paws—which were worthy of long-handed Artaxerxes—upon his breast. "No, I cannot."

He then raised his hand to his forehead, then to his shoulder, making several strange gestures.

"Do you believe he is a *Fleemason?*" said María to the Swiss in a whisper.

"Yes; assuredly."

"All right, Diagasio, that will do," said Quentin.

"Ha...ha...!" laughed the actress. "That poor man really has a peculiar look."

The hardware merchant bowed, a smile appeared within his black beard, like a ray of sunlight in a thicket, and moving his huge hands lazily, he thoughtfully retired, not without having knocked a bottle off a table and stepping on a dog.

"Poor fellow," said Quentin, "he has become unbalanced with all this Masonry."

"What did you call him?" asked the Swiss.

"Diagasio. His real name is Diego, but Diagasio seems more euphonious to me. In the Lodge we have baptized him Marat."

The Swiss smiled, and Quentin left the café. He traversed several alleys, and was walking along the Calle de los Dolores Chicos toward the Calle del Cister, when a man wrapped in a cloak approached him.

"Wait a moment, Quentin," said a voice.

"Hello, Don Paco."

"Where are you going?"

"To the Lodge, as I have just received notice to do."

"I sent the notice to you."

"You did? What's up?"

"We must speak alone, Quentin."

"Whenever you wish."

"Things are moving rapidly, my friend. The Revolution is gaining ground; but in this city, the Revolutionary Committee does nothing—or almost nothing. Inter nos, its members haven't enough patriotism; understand? We must stir them up; and you, who know many strong-minded people, can help a lot."

"Pacheco has more influence than I have, in that respect."

"But to ally oneself with a bandit!"

"As to that, you chaps will find out whether he suits you or not."

"What do you think of him?"

"I'll talk to him."

"Is he in Cordova?"

"He is near Cordova."

"Good: I shall speak here in the Lodge, and in the Junta: if they are agreed, you make an appointment with Pacheco, and we shall meet later."

"Very well. Will you know tomorrow if they are agreed?"

"Yes. I'll let you know; and when you get an answer from Pacheco, we'll go to see him."

"Very well. Until another time."

"Until very soon."

The two conspirators shook hands by way of a farewell, and wrapping themselves to their eyes in their cloaks, they glided along the narrow alleyways.

# CHAPTER XXIX

A FEW days later, at nine-thirty in the evening, Quentin climbed the stairs of a house on the Calle del Cister.

He entered the second floor, traversed the lay-brother's school—a large room with tables in rows and placards on the walls—and passed into the Lodge, which was a garret with a table at one end and an oil lamp that provided the only light.

Quentin could not tell whether the honourable Masons there assembled were in a white meeting or coloured meeting; the session must have been over, for the President, Don Paco, was perorating—though now deprived of his presidential dignity—among the rabble of the Aventine Hill.

Don Paco was a veritable river of words. All of the stock revolutionary phrases came fluently to his lips. "The rights of a citizen,"—"the ominous yoke of reaction"… "the heroic efforts of our fathers"…, "a just punishment for his perversity"….

Don Paco pronounced all these phrases as though by the mere act of saying them, they were realized.

If they charged one of the Masonic brothers with a dangerous mission, and he made the excuse of having a family, Don Paco said, as Cato would have remarked:

"Country before family."

But if the dangerous mission were for *him,* Don Paco would argue that he did not wish to compromise the sacred cause of liberty by a rash act.

Sometimes, instead of saying sacred, he said venerable, which, for Don Paco, had its own value and distinctive meaning.

If some Progressist leader in Madrid was supposed to have been a traitor against either the sacred, or the venerable cause, Don Paco cried out in the Lodge:

"*A la barra* with the citizen! *A la barra!*"

He himself did not know what *la barra* was; but it was a matter of a cry that would sound well, and that sounded admirably: *A la barra!*

When he was too excited, Don Paco admired English parliamentarism above everything else. Quentin had once told him that he looked like Sir Robert Peel.

Quentin had seen the figure of that orator on an advertisement for shoe-blacking; he had nothing but the vaguest ideas of Sir Robert's existence; but it was all the same to Don Paco, and the comparison made him swell with pride.

Aside from these political farces, Don Paco Sánchez Olmillo, Master Surgeon and Master Mason, was a good sort of person, without an evil trait; he was a small, bald-headed old man, pimply and apopleptic. He had a thick neck, eyes that bulged so far from his head that they looked as if they had been stuck into his skin. At the slightest effort, with the most insignificant of his phrases, he blushed to the roots of his hair; if he turned loose one of his cries, his blush changed from red to violet, and even to blue.

Don Paco had great admirers among the members of the Lodge; they considered him a tremendous personage.

Quentin called to Diagasio, the long-handed hardware merchant, and said:

"Tell Don Paco I'm waiting for him."

"He's speaking."

"Well, I'm in a hurry."

Diagasio left him, and presently Don Paco came over, still orating, and surrounded by several friends.

"No," he was saying, "I claim it, and I shall always claim it. We Spaniards are not yet ready to accept the republican form of government. Ah, gentlemen! If we were in England! In that freest of all lands, the cradle of liberties,... of sacred liberties."

"Very well,"—said Quentin quickly, "that discourse does not concern me. I came to tell you that I have received an answer to the letter I sent, and that he has made an appointment."

Don Paco returned to his friends, and now and then a phrase reached Quentin: "A dangerous mission," "mysteries," "the police," "the result will be known later." Then the worthy President came over to Quentin.

"Will some one accompany us?"

"No; why should they? The more people that go, the worse it will be."

"That's true. They will mistrust us."

Don Paco took leave of his friends as Sir Robert Peel might have done had they taken that gentleman to the gallows: they descended the stairs, and came out upon the street.

They made their way to the Gran Capitán, from there to the Victoria, and then, passing the Puerta de Gallegos, they travelled toward the Puerta de Almodóvar.

Quentin felt a great sense of satisfaction when he observed the fact that the old man was frightened. At every step Don Paco said to him:

"Some one is following us."

"Don't be idiotic. Who is going to follow us?"

"Ah! You don't know what a terrible police force those men have!"

To Don Paco, life was all mystery, darkness, espionage, conspiracy. To sum up: it was fear, and the fear in this instance was neutralized by speaking aloud, and humming selections from comic operas.

This mixture of petulance and fright amused Quentin greatly. When he saw that the old man was very animated, humming an air from "Marina," or from "El Domino Azúl," he said to him:

"Hush, Don Paco, I think I saw a man spying on us from among those trees."

Immediately the animation of the worthy President changed into an evil-omened silence.

As the two men followed the wall, the enormous, red moon rose over the town like a dying sun; the Cathedral tower looked very white against the dark blue sky.... They passed a tile-kiln, and Quentin, seeing that Don Paco was dispirited, said:

"I think we can be at ease now, for from here on there are no guards nor watchmen to spy on us."

These words heartened the old man; a moment later, he was humming a piece from "El Domino Azúl," which contained words to the effect that he did not want his dove so near the hawk.

Then, absolutely at ease, he commenced to say in a pompous voice:

"There are moments in the lives of cities as there are in those of individuals...."

"A speech! Don Paco, for Heaven's sake! At a time like this!" exclaimed Quentin....

The old man, seeing that he could not continue his discourse, said familiarly:

"The things that have been accomplished in our lifetime, Quentin! When we first met, there in the Café de Pepon, on the Calle de Antonio de Morales, we were a mere handful of men with advanced ideas.... Today, you see how different it is. And all through my efforts, Quentin. I inaugurated the Reading Centre for workmen, and the Patrician Lodge...; I was one of the Hatchet Club, and one of the founders of the Committee. I was always conspiring."

"You are very brave," said Quentin slyly.

"No; all I am is patriotic; really, Quentin. How many times at night have I ventured out in disguise, sometimes along the Gran Capitán, or through any of the sally-ports on the left, and reached the bridge by encircling the wall! There I used to glide along the fosses of the Calahorra castle, climb down to the other bank of the Guadalquivir, and continue down stream until I struck the Montilla turnpike. At other times I crossed the river by the Adalid ford, to come out later behind the Campo de la Verdad in a bit of land called Los Barreros, where a guard received me most informally."

"Why all these masquerades, Don Paco?"

"You may believe that they were all necessary."

Don Paco and Quentin were walking toward the river, when suddenly, between the Puerta de Seville, and the Cementerio de la Salud, they heard a loud, harsh voice that rang out powerfully in the silence of the night.

"Halt! Who goes there?"

"Two men," answered Quentin sarcastically, "at least that's what we look like."

"For God's sake don't!" exclaimed Don Paco. "They might shoot."

The voice, louder and more threatening than before, shouted again:

"Halt, in the name of the *guardia civil!*"

"We are halted," stammered Don Paco, trembling.

"Advance."

They approached the spot where they had heard the voices; one of the guards, after looking at them closely, said:

"What are you doing here at this time of night?"

"This gentleman," said Quentin, "has been called to a farmhouse to bleed a sick man."

"Is he a blood-letter?"

"I'm a doctor," said Don Paco.

"What are you?"

"I'm his assistant."

"Why didn't you answer us immediately?"

"On account of the effect you had on us," said Quentin slyly.

"Well, you're lucky to be let off," remarked the guard.

"Why, what's the matter?" asked Quentin.

"Pacheco has been about these nights."

Don Paco began to tremble like a leaf.

"Well, we must go and bleed that sick man," said Quentin. "Adiós, Señores."

"Good night."

They went around the wall, and suddenly Don Paco came to a determined halt.

"No; I'm not going!" he exclaimed.

"What's the matter with you?"

"It is very imprudent for us to go and see Pacheco," the old man stammered. "We shall discredit the cause."

"You might have thought of that before."

"Well, I'm not going."

"Very well; I shall go alone."

"No, no.... Ah, my God!"

"Are you ill, Don Paco?"

"Yes; I believe I've taken cold—" replied the terrible revolutionist in a trembling voice. "Furthermore, I do not see the necessity of visiting Pacheco at this time of night."

"Then I'll go if you wish."

"What's the use?" added the old man insinuatingly. "Everybody will think that we went to see Pacheco. Neither of us need deny the fact; so why should we go now and expose ourselves to a serious danger? Besides, it's a cold night, and cold is not healthy."

"But we have an appointment with Pacheco."

"What difference does that make?"

"Then there is still another reason," continued Quentin.

"What is it?"

"If we go back now, and the guards see us, they'll get suspicious."

"Then what shall we do?"

"I think the best thing to do is to go ahead."

Don Paco sighed, and very reluctantly followed after Quentin. The moon was climbing higher in the sky. The old man walked along profoundly disheartened. After half an hour had elapsed, he said:

"Now we can go back."

"What for? We've only a little farther to go."

A moment later they left the road and approached the house. Quentin thrust his fingers into his mouth and whistled shrilly.

"They're coming," said Don Paco, trembling.

In a few seconds, they heard another whistle. Quentin went to the door of the house; at the same time, a small window was opened, and Pacheco said in a low voice:

"Is that you, Quentin?"

"Yes."

"I'll be right down."

The door opened noiselessly, and Don Paco and Quentin entered a dark vestibule.

"This way," said Pacheco's voice.

"Why don't you light a lamp?" asked Don Paco.

"Light can be seen at a distance."

They crossed the vestibule and entered a kitchen illuminated by a lamp.

"Be seated, gentlemen," said the bandit. He closed the kitchen door, and threw an armful of dried branches upon the fire. "It's a cold night," he added.

Don Paco and Quentin sat down, and the latter began to speak:

"This gentleman," he said, "is Don Paco Sánchez Olmillo, who, as you know, is one of the members of the Revolutionary Junta and Chief of the Patrician Lodge."

"No, not Chief," Don Paco interrupted. "The Masons have no chiefs."

"We won't discuss the use of words now; the idea is

to come to an understanding. This gentleman, and other members of the Junta, have thought that you, comrade, could help them start a movement, and wish to get into touch with you."

"The fact is," said Don Paco, who believed that Quentin was compromising him a bit too much, "that I have no power—"

"It's not a question of legal power, nor of lawyers," replied Quentin. "With us, one's word is sufficient."

"It's absolute, comrade," added Pacheco.

"Don Paco, you wished to know if Pacheco could organize the movement, did you not?"

"Yes; that is it essentially."

"Very well; now you know, Pacheco. Kindly tell us if you can undertake the work, and under what conditions."

"See here, Quentin," said the bandit, "you already know my ideas, and that I am more liberal than Riego. I don't want a thing for helping along the Revolution: no money, nor any kind of a reward; I'm not going to haggle over that. What I do want is, that they will not do me a bad turn. Because those Junta fellows, and I don't mean this gentleman, are capable of 'most any thing. I'll go to Cordova and see what people I can count on, and I'll do all the work there is to do; but under one condition; and that is, that all those gentlemen of the Junta will guarantee that the police will not interfere with me. That is to say, I don't mind exposing myself to being shot, but I don't want to get shot in the belt for nothing."

"I have no authority—" said Don Paco, "nor the attributes...."

"You will have to take that up with the Junta," said Quentin. "Why don't you go, comrade?"

"No; I'm not going to Cordova."

"Why not?"

"Because I'm afraid that they have sold me, and it wouldn't go well with the man who did it."

"A couple of guards stopped us yonder, and told us that they were waiting for you," said Quentin.

"Where?"

"Near the Cementerio de la Salud."

"Well, let 'em squat," said Pacheco, "but let us get at what we are going to do. Comrade, if you will do me the favour of seeing those Junta fellows and speaking to them, you can tell them exactly what I want. If they accept, tell El Cuervo; he'll see to it that I receive the answer, and the next day I'll be in Cordova."

"Then, there's nothing more to say."

The three men rose to their feet.

"Well, let's be going, Don Paco," said Quentin.

"Man alive, wouldn't it be better for us to stay here all night?"

"As you wish."

"Are there any beds here?"

"I should say not!"

"I sleep in the strawloft," said Pacheco. "I'll go with you, if you wish."

Don Paco hesitated between going over the road again, and passing a bad night, and chose the latter.

"Let us go to the strawloft."

Pacheco took a lantern, opened the kitchen door, traversed a patio, then another, and mounting a staircase, came to a hole; it was the strawloft.

"Stretch out," said Pacheco; "tomorrow, day will break, and the one-eyed man will see his asparagus. Good night!"

Quentin removed his boots, and in a little while was fast asleep.

In the morning a loud voice awoke him.

"Muleteers! Day's dawning!"

Quentin sat up; the sun was pouring through the cracks in the loft; cocks were crowing. Pacheco had gone. Don Paco, seated on the straw, with a coloured handkerchief on his head, was groaning.

"What a night! My God, what a night!" Quentin heard him say.

"What! Didn't you sleep, Don Paco?"

"Not a minute. But you slept like a log."

"Well, let's be going."

They got up, and picked the straw off their clothes, like feathers from a goose.

They left the farm. It was a superb day. When they drew near the Cementerio de la Salud, they descended to the river, and traversing the Alameda del Corregidor, between the Seminary and the Arabian mill, they came out at the bridge gate.

"This afternoon at the Casino," said Don Paco, who once within the city was beginning to regain his presence of mind.

"At what time?"

"At dusk."

"I'll be there."

"Now you see what one does for one's ideas," said Don Paco in the Casino. "One sacrifices one's self for the

Revolution, and for the Country; one faces the odium of the Moderates for years and years; one exposes one's self to all the dangers imaginable; and even then they do not count one among the founders. They speak of Olózaga, of Sagasta.... I tell you it is an outrage."

"Hello, Don Paco," greeted Quentin. "Are you all rested from your bad night?"

"Yes. Let us interview those men."

"Whenever you wish."

"Let us go now."

"Where do we have to go?"

"To the house of the Count of Doña Mencia. The Junta is meeting there."

The Count lived in one of the central streets of Cordova. They entered the vestibule and rang. A servant opened the gate and accompanied them to the main floor, to a large hall with a panelled ceiling, and illuminated by two wax candles. On the walls were highly polished portraits, in enormous, heavily carved frames. A young man with a black beard greeted Don Paco and Quentin, and conducted them into an office where eight or ten persons were seated.

These men did not interrupt their conversation at the entrance of the new comers, but went on talking: the Revolution was spreading throughout all Andalusia; the Revolutionary troops were marching on Cordova....

Don Paco heard this news, and then spoke to one of the gentlemen about his conversation with Pacheco. This gentleman came up to Quentin and said:

"Tell Pacheco that he can rest easy as far as I am concerned. I shall do all in my power to keep them from apprehending him."

"Do you hear what the Count of Doña Mencia says?"

Don Paco asked Quentin.

"Yes, but it is not enough," replied Quentin, who felt profoundly irritated upon hearing that name. "I went to see Pacheco because Don Paco told me that he could be useful to you in organizing the people. Whether or not my friend has power, I do not know; what I do know is this, that Pacheco, in order to come to Cordova, makes the condition that you gentlemen must give your word that he will not be arrested, and that they will play no tricks on him. Now you may find out whether that suits you or not."

The violent tone employed by Quentin surprised the gentlemen of the Junta; some of them protested, but the Count went over to the protestants and spoke to them in a low voice. They discussed Pacheco's proposition; some said that such complicity with a bandit was dishonourable; others were merely concerned with whether he would be useful or not. Finally they made up their minds, and one of them came up to Quentin and said:

"You may tell your friend," and the man emphasized the word, "that he will not be molested in Cordova."

"Do you all hold yourselves responsible for him?"

"Yes."

"Very well. Good afternoon."

Quentin inclined his head slightly, left the office, crossed the hall, and went into the street. He made his way to El Cuervo's tavern, where he told the landlord to let Señor José know that he could come to Cordova with absolute safety.

# CHAPTER XXX

## PROJECTS

IT was very convenient for Quentin to have Pacheco in Cordova. The latter carried on the conspiracy as smoothly as silk; he had come to an understanding with the secretary of the Count of Doña Mencia, who was expecting to contribute the money realized from a sale of some Government bonds in Madrid. It was also convenient for Quentin to have Pacheco agitate the people; if the agitation was successful, he would profit by it; if not, he would peacefully retire.

Some days later, Quentin had not yet arisen when Pacheco presented himself at his house. María Lucena's mother opened the door and conducted him into the bedroom.

"Don't get up," said Pacheco. "Stay right in bed."

"What's doing? What brings you here?"

"I came this early because I did not want to meet any one in the streets; it might prove to be a provocation. I talked with one of the members of the Junta, and he assured me again that I have no need to be afraid, that they will not arrest me; then he asked me if I had any plan, any project, and I told him that I couldn't explain as yet. Understand? Now the result is that some of them think that I have the Revolution all prepared."

"That's funny," said Quentin.

"What shall I do?"

"The first thing you ought to do, is to get that money from the Count."

"They are going to give it to me this week."

"Good; then go on buying arms and organizing a following."

"Right in Cordova?"

"Yes; but without showing yourself in the streets; let every man stay in his house. We must figure out our strength, and wait for the proper opportunity."

"And then—"

"Then, circumstances will tell us what to do. If it suits us to start a row now, why we'll start it; if we have to shoot a few guns in the streets tomorrow, why, we'll shoot them. Nobody knows what may happen. The troops are out there on the bridge, and messages and letters and packages come and go. The idea in the city is to be strong, and to keep hidden."

"So I must go ahead and recruit?"

"Of course."

"All right. I'm living outside of the town now, in a hut on the Campo de la Verdad; you see I don't like to stay in the city."

"You have done well."

"The house faces the river, and has a horseshoe over the vestibule. Come and see me tomorrow."

"At what time?"

"In the afternoon."

"I'll be there."

During the subsequent days, Quentin went every afternoon to Pacheco's house in the Campo de la Verdad; sat down in a cloth-bottomed rocking-chair; put his feet on the window sill, and smoked his pipe.

He listened to the conversation, and gazed indifferently at the town.

Through his half-closed eyes he saw the half-ruined gate of the bridge; beyond, and above it, rose the grey walls of the Mosque, with their serrated battlements; above these walls hung the dark cupola of the cathedral, and the graceful tower rose glistening in the sun, with the angel on its peak inlayed in the huge sapphire of the sky.

On one side of the bridge, the Alcázar garden displayed its tall, dark cypresses, and its short shrub-like orange trees; then the Roman Wall, grey, spotted with the dusty green of parasite weeds, continued toward the left, and stretched on, cut here and there by cubes of rock, as far as the Cementerio de la Salud.

On the other side, the houses of the Calle de la Ribera formed a semi-circle, following the horseshoe bend of the river, which flowed on as though trying to undermine the town.

These houses, which were reflected in the surface of the river—a serpent of ever changing colour—were small, grey, and crooked. Upon their walls, which were continuously calcined by the sun, grew dark-coloured ivy; between their garden walls blossomed prickly pears with huge intertwined and pulpy leaves; and from their patios and corrals peeped the cup-shaped tops of cypress trees and the branches of silver-leafed fig trees.

Their roofs were grey, dirty, heaped one above the other; with azoteas, look-outs, and little towers; a growth of hedge mustard converted some of them into green meadows.

Beyond these houses the broken line of the roofs of the town was silhouetted against the crystal blue sky. This line was interrupted here and there by a tower, and reached as far as the river, where it ended in a few blue and rose houses near the Martos mill.

Some bell or other was clanging almost continuously.

Quentin listened to them sleepily and drowsily, watching the hazy sky, and the river of ever-changing colour.

Pacheco's house had a room with a window that looked out on the other side: upon a little square where a few tramps peacefully sunned themselves.

Among them was one who interested Quentin. This fellow wore a red kerchief on his head, side-burns that reached the tips of his ears, and a large, ragged sash. He used to sit on a stone bench, and, his face resting in his hand, would study the actions and movements of a cock with flame-coloured plumage.

This observer of the cock was at the same time the pedagogue of the feathered biped, which must have had its serious difficulties, to judge by the reflective attitude which the man struck at times.

Quentin listened to what they said in the meetings that went on about him.

How far away his thoughts were in some instances! From time to time, Pacheco, or one of the conspirators put a question to him which he answered mechanically. His silence was taken for reflection.

Quentin excited the bandit's self-esteem. He was waiting for the time when they would get the Count's money so that he could take his share and skip off to Madrid. He did not wish this intention of his to become known, so he gave the bandit to understand that he wanted the money for revolutionary purposes only.

Every day Quentin played at the Casino and lost. He had bad luck. He had become tied up with money-lenders and was signing I. O. U.'s at eighty percent, with the healthy intention of never paying them.

After conferring with all the rowdies that came to see him, Pacheco consulted with Quentin. The bandit had romantic aspirations; at night he read books which narrated the stories of great battles; this stirred him up, and made him believe that he was a man born for a great purpose.

"Do you know what I've been thinking?" Pacheco said one afternoon to Quentin.

"What?"

"That if I have my people organized beforehand in order to win the battle of Alcolea, I shall become master of the town."

"Don't be foolish,' Quentin told him. "You aren't strong enough for that."

"No? You'll see. I have more followers in the city than you think I have."

"But you have no arms."

"Wait until the Count's money comes—it won't be long now."

"Are you going to oppose the troops?"

"The troops will join us."

"Then what? What are you going to do then?"

"If I win,—proclaim the Republic."

Quentin looked closely at Pacheco.

"The poor man,' he thought, "he has gone mad with the idea of greatness."

At this moment El Taco, a corrupt individual who had been made Pacheco's lieutenant, came in to say that some men were waiting for him below.

"I'll be back," said the bandit.

Quentin was left alone.

"That chap is going to do something foolish," he murmured, "and the worst of it is, he's going to break up my combination. I mustn't leave him alone for a minute until I get hold of that money. Suppose he keeps it here, and then they shoot him in the street? Goodbye cash! How does one prove that money belongs to one? I could ask him for a key to this room, but he might get suspicious, and I don't want him to do that. Let's have a look at that key."

Quentin went to the door; the key was small, and the lock new; doubtless Pacheco himself had put it on.

"I've got to take an impression of it," said Quentin to himself.

The next day he presented himself at Pacheco's house with two pieces of white wax in his pocket. He listened to the discussions and intrigues of the conspirators as usual, stretched out in his armchair. When he noticed that they were about to go, he said to the bandit:

"By the way, comrade, let me have a little paper and ink, I want to do a little writing."

"All right; here you are. We're going to El Cuervo's tavern. We'll wait for you there."

Quentin sat down and made a pretence at writing, but noticed that some one had stayed behind. It was El Taco. He went on writing meaningless words, but El Taco still remained in the room. Annoyed and impatient, Quentin got up.

"I've forgotten my tobacco," he said; "is there a shop near here?"

"Yes, right near."

"I'm going to buy a box."

"I'll bring you one."

"Good." Quentin produced a peseta and gave it to El Taco. The moment the man had left the room, he kneaded the wax between his fingers until he had softened it, took out the key, and made the impression. He was softening the other piece of wax, in case the first had come out badly, when he heard El Taco's footsteps skipping up the stairs. Quentin quickly inserted the key in the lock and sat down at the table. He went on pretending to write, thrust the paper in the envelope, and left the house. El Taco locked the door.

"Let's go to El Cuervo's tavern," said Quentin.

They crossed the bridge and entered the tavern.

There they found, seated in a group, Cornejo, now recovered from his beating, Currito Martín, Carrahola, El Rano, two or three unknown men, and a ferocious individual whom they called El Ahorcado (The Hanged Man), because, strange as it may seem, he had been officially hung by an executioner. This man had a terrible history. Years ago, he had been the proprietor of a store near Despeñaperros. One night a man, apparently wealthy, came into the store. El Ahorcado and his wife murdered the traveller to rob him, only to discover that their victim was their own son, who had gone to America in his childhood, and there enriched himself. Condemned to death, El Ahorcado went to the gallows; but the apparatus of the executioner failed to work in the orthodox manner, and he was pardoned. He was sent to Ceuta where he completed his sentence, and then returned to Cordova.

El Ahorcado had the names of those in his district who were affiliated with Pacheco, and he read them by placing one hand on his throat—the only way in which he could emit sounds.

"Now then, let's have the list," said Pacheco.

El Ahorcado began to read.

"Argote."

"He's a good one: a man with hair on his chest," commented Currito.

"Matute, El Mochuelo, Pata al Hombro," continued El Ahorcado, "El Mocarro."

"He's got the biggest nose in Cordova," interrupted Currito, "and has to wipe it on his muffler, because handkerchiefs aren't big enough."

Thus the list of names went on, with Currito's responding commentary.

"El Penducho."

"Good fellow."

"Cuco Pavo, El Cimborrio."

"There's a man who cleans his face with a used stocking, and dirties the stocking by doing it."

"Malpicones, Ojancos."

"He's a money-lender who loans at a thousand percent."

"Muñequitas, La Madamita."

"They're from Benamejí."

"They just got out of the Carraca prison," said El Rano.

"El Poyato."

"Now we're coming to the sweepings," interrupted Currito.

"Don't you believe it," replied El Ahorcado, "El Poyato is no frog; and even if the wheat does hit him in the chest when he walks through the fields, he is a very brave man."

"That's right," said Carrahola, defending a small man from a sense of comradeship.

"Boca Muerta," continued El Ahorcado. "El Zurrio, Cantarote, Once Dedos."

"That chap has one arm longer than the other, and an extra finger on it," said Currito.

"Ramos Léchuga."

"He's a great big good-for-nothing," said one.

"And very soft mouthed," replied another.

"What about women?" asked Pacheco.

"They are put down on this other paper," answered El Ahorcado. "La Canasta, La Bardesa, La Cachumba...."

"There's a fine bunch of old aunties for you," said Currito with a laugh.

"La Cometa, La Saltacharcos, La Chirivicha...."

"That's very good," said Pacheco. "Within three days you may come here and get your money."

Quentin understood by this that the bandit was sure of getting hold of the money by that time. He left the tavern, and inquired at the Lodge for Diagasio's hardware shop. It was in a street near La Corredera. He called on the long-handed individual, and, taking him into a corner very mysteriously, told him what he wanted.

"I'll give you the key tomorrow in the Lodge."

Quentin pressed the hardware merchant's hand, and went home.

# CHAPTER XXXI

## NIGHT AND DAY

TWO evenings later, Quentin was in the Café del Recreo. His streak of bad luck at the Casino continued. María Lucena was talking to Springer: Quentin was smoking, and thoughtfully contemplating the ceiling. Very much bored, he rose to his feet, with the intention of going to bed.

In the street he met the clerk, Diego Palomares, who was going in the same direction.

"What's doing, Palomares?" he said.

"Nothing. I'm living a dull and stupid life."

"I too."

"You? What you have done is to understand life as few people can. While I...."

"Why, what's the matter with you?"

"You are a revolutionist, aren't you?" said Palomares. "Well, if you ever take up arms against the rich, call on me. I'll go with all my heart, even to the extent of making them cough up their livers. There are nothing but rich men and poor men in this world, say what you will of your Progressists and Moderates. Ah! The black-guards!"

"Have they done anything to you at the store?"

"Not just now; but they have been for many years. Twenty years working as if it were my own business, and helping them to get rich; they in opulence, and me with thirty dollars a month. And that man, just because he saw me take home a chicken to my sick girl, said to me: 'I see that you are living like a prince.' Curse him! Would to God he had sunk in the ocean!"

Palomares had been drinking, and with the excitement of the alcohol, he exposed the very depths of his soul.

"You are terrible," said Quentin.

"You think I'm a coward! No; I have a wife and three small children… and I'm already decrepit…. Believe me, we should unite against them, and wish them death. Yes sir! Here's what I say: the coachman should overturn his master's carriage, the labourer should burn the crops, the shepherd should drive his flock over a precipice, the clerk should rob his employer—even the wet nurses should poison their milk."

"You're all twisted, Palomares."

"Why do you say that?"

"Because I thought you were a sheep, and you are almost, almost a wolf."

"Why, there are some days when I would like to set fire to the whole town. Then I'd stay outside with a gun and shoot anybody who tried to escape."

"The tortoise will get there," remarked Quentin.

He said goodbye to Palomares, and went home. As he opened the door and stepped into the entryway, he heard some one weeping sadly. Attracted by the wails, he went through the corridor, crossed a patio, and asked in a loud voice:

"What's the matter?"

A door opened, and a weeping woman with disheveled hair came out with a lamp in her hand. In a voice choked with sobs, she told Quentin that her two-year-old son had died, that her husband was not in town, and that she had no money with which to buy a casket.

"Would you like to see the boy, Señorito?"

Quentin entered a small whitewashed room; the boy's body lay on a mattress across the table.

"How much do you need to bury him?" asked Quentin.

"A couple of dollars."

"I'll see if I have them. If not, we'll pawn something from my house."

Quentin went back through the patio followed by the woman; and the two climbed up to the main floor. Quentin lit the lamp, and went through all the drawers. He found four dollars in María Lucena's bureau, and gave them to the woman. This done, he closed the door and got into bed…. The voices of María Lucena and her mother awakened him.

"There were four dollars here," cried the actress. "Who took them?"

"I took them," said Quentin calmly.

"Eh?"

"Yes. One of our neighbours was crying because her baby boy had died and she could not buy him a casket; so I gave them to her. I'll return them to you tomorrow."

"That's it. That's fine," said the actress. "Give that woman the money I earn."

"Am I not telling you that I will return them to you?"

"Little that woman cares for her baby," screamed María.

"She's probably buying drinks with the money by this time," added her mother.

"Señoras," said Quentin, sitting up in bed, "I find you absolutely repulsive."

"You are the one who is repulsive," screeched the old woman.

"Very well; the thing to do now is to get out of this den of harpies; they are beginning to smell."

"Well, son; get out, and never come back," cried María.

Quentin dressed rapidly, and put on his boots and his hat.

"Well; give me the key."

"I give the key to no one," rejoined the actress.

"See here, don't you exhaust my patience, or I'll give you a thumping."

When the old woman heard this, thrusting her face close to Quentin's, she began to insult him, shaking her hands in his face.

"Rowdy!" she said, "you're an indecent rowdy. A fan-dango-dancing rowdy!"

"Hush, ancient Canidia," said Quentin, pushing the old woman away from him, "and get you gone to your lab-oratory."

"Don't you call my mother names; do you hear?"

"Nobody can call me names."

"Well: will you give me the key or won't you?" asked Quentin.

"No."

Quentin went to the balcony window and opened it wide. He jumped to the other side of the railing, hung by his wrists, felt for the grated window of the floor below, and dropped to the sidewalk.

"Until—never!" he called from the street.

He had blood on his cheek from one of the old woman's scratches. He washed at a fountain, dried himself on his handkerchief, and went to the Casino. He went through a door on the right, and entered a large salon which was lined with enormous mirrors.

A sleepy waiter approached him.

"Do you wish something, Don Quentin?" he asked.

"Yes; put out that light as if there were no one here."

"Are you going to stay here?"

"Yes."

"But that is not allowed."

"Bah! What's the difference?"

The lights were put out, and, after a little, Quentin fell asleep on the divan.

Two waiters in coarse, white aprons awoke Quentin. One was placing the chairs upon the tables, and the other was cleaning the divans with a mop and brush.

"Have you been asleep, Señorito?" said one of them with a laugh.

"Yes; what time is it?"

"Very early. Do you know that there is a great hub-bub in the streets?"

"What is happening?"

"Pacheco has entered Cordova with a gang of toughs, and they are all running through these God-forsaken streets yelling and rioting."

Quentin jumped up. There was a bucket of water on the floor.

"Is it clean?" he asked the waiters.

"Yes."

Quentin kneeled on the floor and ducked himself twice. The waiters laughed, thinking that it was all from the effects of a convivial evening.

"Now my head is clear," said Quentin.

"I'll bring you a towel," announced one of the boys. Quentin dried himself, and went into the street.

He walked rapidly toward Las Tendillas, where he found great excitement, and heard all sorts of comments and gossip. He asked a man where Pacheco was.

"He's near the Plaza de la Trinidad now."

Quentin ran on, opening a path through the crowd with his elbows.

"The man is an idiot," he thought. "Could he have imagined that he was really going to head the Revolution?"

After a hard struggle, Quentin could see two horsemen riding at the head of the rabble. One of them was Pacheco; the other was his brother.

"Long live Liberty! Long live the Revolution!" shouted the bandit, waving his arm.

The crowd echoed his cry with enthusiasm, and added:

"Long live the second Prim! Long live General Pacheco!"

"Why, the man is crazy," murmured Quentin. "I wonder if he's got the money yet?" Then he thought—"Suppose he has it with him? He's fixed me if he has."

Quentin continued to advance, digging right and left with his elbows, in order to get near enough to speak with Pacheco. Suddenly he heard the sound of a shot, and immediately after, almost instantaneously, another; a bit of smoke came from one of the screened windows of the Trinidad barracks.

The crowd drew back, terrified; people began to run pell-mell, and in the alleyways the noise made by the heels of those who fled sounded like a squadron of horses at a gallop. Quentin was forced to take refuge in a doorway in order to keep from being trampled.

Several other persons also pushed their way into the same place.

"What happened?" they asked one another.

"They are beginning to shoot, and there's a great rumpus yonder."

Another who had just arrived, said:

"They've killed Pacheco."

"Did you see it?" asked Quentin.

"Sí, Señor. I was going by without knowing what was up, when I saw Pacheco fall. His brother jumped from his horse, leaned over the corpse, and said, weeping: 'He is dead.'"

Quentin went into the street.

"If that fellow had the money in his pocket, there is no way of getting it. I'll have to explain where it came from.... But if it is still at his house?—*Cristo!* I mustn't waste any time."

He reached the Gran Capitán in a hurry, and took a carriage. "To the Mosque," he said, "and hurry." The coachman left him at one of the doors of the cathedral.

"Wait for me," Quentin instructed him, "I shall be some time." He jumped from the carriage, went through the church, rushed like a cannon ball through the Patio de los Naranjos, went down by the Triunfo Column, crossed the bridge, and entered Pacheco's house. He took out the key which Diagasio, the Mason, had made for him, and opened the door.

The bed was untouched; he looked through the little night stand, and found nothing; then he went to the table, took out his penknife and removed the lock from the drawer. Upon some books lay a Russian leather pocketbook, tied with a ribbon. He opened it; there were the bills. He did not count them.

"I am the favourite of Chance," said he, smiling.

He closed the door, crossed the bridge, and threw the key into the river. The news evidently had not reached that part of the city, for the people were quiet, and there were no gossiping groups. Quentin went up by the Triunfo, again traversed the Patio de los Naranjos, then the church, and got into the carriage.

"To the Gran Capitán," he said.

By this time the news was spread all over the city; the old wives were shouting it to each other from door to door, and from window to window.

"Where can I leave this money with safety?" Quentin asked himself.

Whomever he trusted would be apt to ask indiscreet questions. His stepfather? Impossible. Palomares, perhaps? But Palomares, in his indignation against the rich, would be likely to keep the money. Señora Patrocinio? She would probably be angry at him. Springer? He was the best.

"I'll go to his house," he thought; and he gave the coachman the address of the Swiss watch-maker.

# CHAPTER XXXII

## THE CITY OF THE DISCREET

SPRINGER was somewhat taken aback when he saw Quentin enter his store, and he rose to his feet and said, turning a trifle pale:

"I can imagine why you have come."

"You can? It would be rather hard. But first do me the favour of giving me a few pesetas with which to pay the coachman."

The Swiss opened a drawer and gave him two dollars. Quentin paid the coachman, and returned to the watch store.

"Boy," he said to his friend, "I came here because you are the only trustworthy person I know."

"Thanks," said Springer sourly.

"I would like you to keep a large amount of money for me," continued Quentin as he held out the pocketbook.

"How much is it?"

"I don't know, I'm going to see."

Quentin opened the purse and began counting the bills.

"Before you place this trust in me," said the Swiss with the air of a man making a violent decision, "I have something to tell you—as a loyal friend. Something that may annoy you."

"What is it?" asked Quentin, fearing that the low trick he had played on the Count of Doña Mencia had become known in the city.

"María Lucena and I have come to an understanding—I cannot deceive a true friend like you...."

Quentin gazed in astonishment at the Swiss, and seeing him so affected, felt like bursting into laughter; but laughter seemed improper under the circumstances.

"I'm glad you told me," he said gravely. "I was thinking of leaving Cordova, and now, knowing this, I shall go as soon as possible."

"And it will not cool your friendship?"

"Not in the least."

Springer affectionately pressed his friend's hand.

"Well, will you keep this money for me?"

"Yes; give it to me."

The Swiss placed the bills in an envelope.

"What must I do with it?"

"I'll let you know; I shall probably tell you to send it to me in Madrid in various quantities."

"Good; it shall be done."

The Swiss climbed the spiral staircase that went from the back room to the main floor, and returned presently, saying:

"I've put it away."

They were chatting together, when Springer's father entered hurriedly.

"There's a riot in the town," he announced from the door.

"Is there? What is going on?"

"They have killed a bandit... Pacheco, I think they told me his name was."

"Your friend. Did you know it?" the Swiss asked Quentin.

"No," he answered calmly. "He must have done something foolish."

"Let's ask about it in the streets."

The father and son and Quentin went out to Las Tendillas. They passed from group to group, listening to the comments, and at one of them where there seemed to be a well-informed gentleman, they stopped.

"How did his death occur?" asked Springer's father.

"Well, like this. Pacheco entered by the bridge, and crossed the city till he reached the barracks in the Plaza de la Trinidad, where it seems that the General, when he noticed the riot and uproar, and when he heard them shout 'Long live General Pacheco!' asked: 'Who is that fellow they call General? I'm the only General here. 'It's Pacheco,' a lieutenant answered. 'The people are calling him a General of Liberty.'—'The bandit?'—'Sí, Señor.' Then the General, seeing that the crowd was coming toward the barracks, ordered two soldiers to take their posts with their guns sticking through the cracks in the shutters. When Pacheco came opposite the barracks, he shouted several times: 'Long live Liberty! Long live the Revolution!' instantly two shots rang out, and the man fell from his horse, dead."

All listened to the story, and after it was finished there was a series of remarks.

"That was treachery," said one.

"A trap they set for him."

"They've wickedly deceived that man."

"Deceived him? Why?" Springer's father asked of a man in a blouse who had just made the assertion.

"Because they had promised him a pardon," replied he of the blouse. "Everybody knows that."

"But promising a pardon, and entering the city the

way he did—like a conqueror—are two very different things," rejoined the watch-maker.

"This is going to make a big noise," replied the man.

They returned to the watch-maker's shop, and as the other stores were closed, the Swiss closed his also.

"Would you like to dine with us?" said Springer to Quentin.

"Indeed I should!"

They climbed the spiral stairs to the floor above, and Springer presented Quentin to his mother; a pleasant woman, thin, smiling, very active and vivacious.

They dined; after dinner, the three men lit their pipes, and Springer's father spoke enthusiastically of his home town.

"My town is a great place," he said to Quentin with a smile.

"What is it?"

"Zurich. Ah! If you could see it!..."

"But father, he has seen Paris and London."

"Oh! That makes no difference. I've known many people from Paris and Vienna who were astounded when they saw Zurich."

Springer's father and mother, though they had been in Cordova for over thirty years, did not speak Spanish very well.

What a difference there was between that home, and the house where Quentin had lived with María Lucena and her mother! Here there was no talk of marquises, or counts, or actors, or toreadors, or ponies; their only subjects of conversation were work, improvements in industry, art, and music.

317

"So you are leaving us?" asked Springer's father.

"Yes. This place is dead," replied Quentin.

"No, no—not that," replied the younger Springer. "It isn't dead; Cordova is merely asleep. All the kings have punished it. Its natural, its own civilization has been suppressed, and they have endeavoured to substitute another for it. And even to think that a town can go on living prosperously with ideas contrary to its own, and under laws contrary to its customs and instincts, is an outrage."

"My dear lad," rejoined Quentin rather cynically, "I don't care about the cause for it all. What I know is that one cannot live here."

"That is the truth," asserted the older Springer. "One can attempt nothing new here, because it will turn out badly. No one does his part in throwing off this inertia. No one works."

"Don't say that, father."

"What your father says, is right," continued Quentin "and not only is that true, but the activity of the few who do work, annoys and often offends those who do nothing. For instance: I, who have done nothing so far but live like a rowdy, have friends and even admirers. If I had devoted myself to work, everybody would look upon me as a good-for-nothing, and from time to time, secretly, they would place a stone in my way for me to stumble over."

"No, it would not be a stone," said Springer, "it would be a grain of sand."

"Still more outrageous," rejoined Quentin.

"No," added his friend, "because it would not be done with malice. These people, like nearly all Spaniards, are living an archaic life. Every one here is surrounded by an enormous cloud of difficulties. The people are all dead, and their brains are not working. Spain is a body suffering from anchylosis of the joints; the slightest movement causes great pain; consequently, in order to progress, she will have to proceed slowly,—not by leaps."

"But among all this rabble of lawyers and soldiers and priests and pawn-brokers, do you believe there is one person who is the least bit sane?" asked Quentin.

"I think not," the father broke in. "There are no elements of progress here; there are no men who are pushing on, as there are in my country."

"I think there are," replied his son; "but those who are, and they stand alone, end by not seeing the reality of things, and even turn pernicious. It is as if in our shop here, we found the wheel of a tower clock among the wheels of pocket watches. It would be no good at all to us; it would not be able to fit in with any other wheel. Take the Marquis of Adarve, who was a good and intelligent man; well, now he passes for a half-wit, and he is, partly—because as a reaction against the others, he reached the other extreme. He carries an automatic umbrella, a mechanical cigar-case, and a lot of other rare trifles. The people call him a madman."

"All you have to be here," said the older Springer, "is either a farmer or a money-lender."

"The vocations in which you don't have to work," Quentin asserted. "The Spaniard's ideal is: to work like a Moor, and to earn money like a Jew. That is also my ideal," he said for his own benefit.

"As we were saying before," added the younger Springer; "it is an archaic life, directed by romantic, hidalguesque ideas...."

"Ah, no!" replied Quentin. "You are absolutely wrong there. There is none of your romance, nor of your hidalgos; it is prose, pure prose. There is more romance in the head of one Englishman, than in the heads of ten

Spaniards, especially if those Spaniards are Andalusians. They are very discreet, friend Springer; *we* are very discreet, if you like that better. A great deal of eloquence, a lot of enthusiastic and impetuous talk, a great deal of flourish; a superficial aspect of ingenuous and candid confusion; but back of it all, a sure, straight line. Men and women;—most discreet. Believe me! There is exaltation without, and coldness within."

It was time to work, and the two Springers went down to their shop.

"Do you see?" said the Swiss to Quentin, as he sat in his chair and fastened his lens to his eye, "perhaps you are right in what you say, but I like to think otherwise. I am romantic, and like to imagine that I am living among hidalgos and fine ladies.... There you have me—a poor Swiss plebeian. And I am so accustomed to it, that when I go away from Cordova, I immediately feel homesick for my shop, my books, and the little concerts my mother and I have in which we play Beethoven and Mozart."

Quentin gazed at Springer as at a strange and absurd being, and began to walk up and down the store. Suddenly he paused before his friend.

"Listen," he said. "Do you think that I could deceive you, give you disloyal advice through interest or evil passion?"

"No; what do you mean by that?"

"Don't compromise yourself with María Lucena."

"Why?"

"Because she is a perverse woman."

"That's because you hate her."

"No; I know her because I have lived with her without the slightest feeling of affection; and even so she was more selfish and cold than I was. She is a woman who thinks she has a heart because she has sex. She weeps, laughs, appears to be good, seems ingenuous: sex. Like some lascivious and cruel animal, in her heart she hates the male. If you approach her candidly, she will destroy your life, she will alienate you from your father and mother, she will play with you most cruelly."

"Do you really believe that?" asked the Swiss.

"Yes, it is the truth, the pure truth. Now," Quentin added, "if you are like a stone in a ravine, that can only fall, you will fall; but if you can defend yourself, do so. And now—farewell!"

"Farewell, Quentin; I shall think over what you have told me."

Quentin put up at one of the inns on the Paseo del Gran Capitán. He intended to leave the city as soon as he possibly could.

Accordingly, that night after supper, he left the house and walked toward the station; but as he crossed the Victoria, he noticed that four persons were following him. He returned quickly, as he did not care to enter any lonesome spots when followed by that gang, and took refuge in the inn.

Who could be following him? Perhaps it was Pacheco's brother. Perhaps one of his creditors. He must be on his guard. His room at the inn happened to be in an admirably strategic situation. It was on the lower floor, and had a grated window that looked out upon the Paseo.

The next day Quentin was able to prove that Pacheco's friends were constantly watching the inn. Their number was frequently augmented by the money-lenders who came to ask for Quentin.

In the daytime, he did not mind going into the street, but when night fell, he locked his room, and placed a wardrobe against the door. Quentin was afraid that his last adventure might result fatally for him.

"I've got to get out of here. There are no two ways about it; and I've got to get out quietly."

One day after the battle of Alcolea, Quentin was being followed and spied upon by Pacheco's men, when as he passed the City Hall, Diagasio the hardware dealer, who was standing in the doorway, said:

"Don Paco is upstairs."

Quentin climbed the stairs, slipped through an open door, and beheld the terrible Don Paco surrounded by several friends, up to his old tricks.

The revolutionist had ordered the head porter to take down a portrait of Isabella II, painted by Madrazo, which occupied the centre of one wall. After heaping improprieties and insults upon the portrayed lady, much to the astonishment and stupefaction of the poor porter, Don Paco had a ferocious idea; an idea worthy of a drinker of blood.

He produced a penknife from his vest pocket, and handing it to the porter and pointing to the portrait, said:

"Cut off her head."

"I?" stammered the porter.

"Yes."

The poor man trembled at the idea of committing such a profanation.

"But, for God's sake, Don Paco! I have children!"

"Cut off her head," repeated the bold revolutionist contumaciously.

"See here, Don Paco, they say that this portrait is very well painted."

"Impossible," replied Don Paco, with a gesture worthy of Saint-Just. "It was executed by a servile artist."

Then the porter, moaning and groaning, buried the penknife in the canvas, and split it with a trembling hand.

At that moment several persons entered the hall, among them Paul Springer.

"Are you playing surgeon, Don Paco?" asked the Swiss with a mocking smile.

"Sí, Señor; one must strike kings in the head."

After cutting the canvas, the porter took the piece in his hand, and hesitatingly asked Don Paco:

"Now what will I do with it?"

"Take that head," roared Don Paco in a harsh voice, "to the President of the Revolutionary Junta."

Quentin looked at the Swiss and saw him smile ironically.

"How do you like this execution in effigy of yonder chubby Marie Antoinette?"

"Magnificent."

"Just as I said. We are the City of the Discreet."

The two friends bid each other goodbye with a laugh, and Quentin went home.

# CHAPTER XXXIII

QUENTIN returned to the inn and shut himself up in his room. He wrote a farewell article for *La Víbora* entitled "And this is the End."

When night fell, he lit his lamp and sent for his supper. He ate in his room to avoid any unpleasant encounters in the dining-room.

With his supper, the waiter brought two letters. One, by the rudely scrawled envelope, he saw was from Pacheco's brother. It read as follows:

If you do not return the pocketbook you found in my brother's house, you will not leave Cordova alive. Don't fool yourself; you will not escape. Every exit is watched. You can leave the money in El Cuervo's tavern, where some one will go and get it.

A Friend.

"Very good," said Quentin, "let's see the other letter." He opened it, and it was still more laconic than the first.

We know that you have money, and do not wish to pay. Be careful.

Various Creditors.

"Well, sir," murmured Quentin, "a whole conspiracy of bandits and money-lenders is plotting against me."

It suited neither him nor the others to have the law mixed up in the affair. The cleverest, the strongest, or he who had the most cunning, would gain the day.

Quentin figured that he possessed those qualities to

a greater degree than his enemies; this thought calmed him a little, but in spite of it, he could not sleep that night.

When he got up, he looked, as was his daily habit, through the windows of his room. Directly opposite, seated upon a bench, there were several loathsome individuals spying on him. At that very moment others took their places. Evidently there was a relief.

After eating, Quentin left the inn. When he reached the corner of the Calle de Gondomar, he looked cautiously behind him. Three men were following him, though apparently unconcerned with his movements. Quentin went down the street to Las Tendillas, turned to the left, entered the Casino, and sat down to take his coffee near a window that looked out upon the street.

The three individuals continued their espionage.

Quentin pretended not to see them. He seized several newspapers; and while he appeared to be deeply engaged in reading them, he was thinking up plans of escape and turning them over and over in his mind. The important thing was to keep the law from interfering, that there might be no scandal.

Don Paco, who had come in to take coffee, surprised him in this caviling. The man was oozing joy. The Revolution was made, the most glorious, the most humane that the centuries had ever witnessed. The entire world, the French, the English, the Swiss, the Germans;—all envied the Spaniards. Spain was going to be a different sort of country. Now, now, the great conquests of Progress and Democracy would be realized: Universal Suffrage, Freedom of Worship, Freedom of Association.

"And do you believe that all that will make life any better?" asked Quentin coldly.

"Why, of course!" exclaimed Don Paco, astonished at the question. "I tell you that the whole Progressist program is to be realized!"

325

Quentin smiled mockingly.

Don Paco continued his oration. His eternal sorrow was to see that after what he had done for the Revolution, they did not appreciate his true worth.

While the old man discoursed, Quentin continued to ruminate on his plans, and to absently watch his pursuers. Suddenly an idea occurred to him.

"Well, good afternoon, Don Paco!" he said; and without another word, he rose from his chair and left the room. He crossed the patio of the Casino, went up a stairway, asked a waiter for the key to the terrace, waited for it a moment, and went out upon the azotea. He could escape in that way, but there was still the danger of his exit from the city....

"Suppose I go to El Cuervo's tavern and leave by the convent route?" he said to himself. "That would be admirable. Place myself in the wolf's mouth to make my escape! That's just what I'll do. I'll wait for it to get dark first."

He went down to the salon again and took his place by the window. The espionage still continued. Late in the afternoon, Carrahola and El Rano passed along the street.

Quentin went to the door of the Casino and called to Carrahola.

"Do you mind telling me what this persecution means?" he said.

"You know better than any one else, Don Quentin," answered Carrahola. "You are wrong not to return that money."

"Bah!"

"Sí, Señor; that's the truth. Everything is guarded; the station, the roads,—you won't leave Cordova unless you pay."

"Really?" asked Quentin apparently frightened.

"You hear me. So you'd better hand over that money and not expose yourself to a stab with a dagger."

"The devil! You very nearly convince me."

"Do it, Don Quentin."

"To whom shall I hand the money?"

"To Pacheco, Señor José's brother. He goes to El Cuervo's tavern every night about eight o'clock."

"I'll think it over."

"Don't stop to think, my friend! You ought to take that money back right away."

"Well, you have persuaded me. I'll go right away."

Quentin made his way to the inn, followed by Carrahola and El Rano. He entered his room, closed the window, and lit the lamp. He still had in his pocket the pocketbook that he had found in Pacheco's house. He took it out and placed it on the table.

He opened the wardrobe, searched the drawers, and in one of them found some copy paper written by a child, and in another a torn, and well-worn catechism by Father Ripalda

He took the copy paper and the catechism, tied them together with a pack-thread, and thrust the package into the pocketbook which he tied up with another bit of thread.

"Very good," he murmured with a smile.

This done, he put out the light, thrust the purse into his coat pocket, and left the inn. He began to walk rapidly, as one who has made a quick decision. He made his way to El Cuervo's tavern, escorted by Carrahola and El Rano.

He looked into the office, and when he saw El Cuervo, exclaimed sourly:

"Hello!"

"Hello, Don Quentin!"

"Is Pacheco's brother here?"

"No, Señor."

"What time will he come?"

"Oh, somewhere around eight o'clock."

"Good. I have come to have an understanding with him, and I can't make up my mind whether to give him the money or a stab with a dagger. Look here, here's the pocketbook he's looking for. Keep it. I'm going to wait in here for Pacheco, because I have some letters to write."

"Go right upstairs."

Quentin and El Cuervo went upstairs to a room with a balcony overlooking a patio.

"I'll bring you some paper and ink presently," said the landlord.

"Good. Until Pacheco comes, I do not wish to be disturbed by any one. Do you understand?"

"Very good."

"When he comes, call me, and he and I will come to an understanding. But he must agree not to open the pocketbook until I am with him."

"Never fear."

The innkeeper went out and left Quentin alone in the room. He listened for a moment and heard the gay voices of Carrahola and El Rano. Evidently they were already celebrating their victory.

"Come, there's no time to be lost," said Quentin. Climbing to the outside of the balcony, which was not very high, and clinging to a water pipe, he lowered himself to the patio. This he skirted, hugging close to the wall. He pushed open the little door, closed it noiselessly behind him, and began slowly to climb the stairs. The steps creaked beneath his weight.

When Quentin arrived at the top of the stairs, he saw that the door through which he had once passed with El Cuervo, was locked. It had a transom, which he opened, and with a superhuman effort, managed to squeeze himself through, not without injuring one of his feet. He made a slight noise as he jumped down.

He listened for a while to see if any one were following him. He heard nothing. He closed the transom.

"Any one could tell where I went out," he murmured.

He lit a match which he held in the hollow of his hand until he found the stairway made of beam ends sticking from the wall. When he had located it, he blew out the match, and climbed to the attic in the dark.

He lit another match and hunted for the aperture through which he and El Cuervo had passed, but he could not find it. Looking more carefully, he saw that it was fastened up by some boards held in place by bricks. He tore these aside with his nails one by one then he removed the boards, and the hole appeared.

Quentin went out on the roof. It was still light.

"Let's get oriented," he said to himself. "That's the garret, which is the first place to go."

Stooping on all fours, he slid along until he reached it. He paused to get his bearings again.

"Now I've got to cross that azotea where we abandoned Doña Sinda: it must be that one. Here goes."

He went on his way, jumped the balustrade on one side, then on the other, went a little further,—and turned the wrong way. He was confused, not knowing which way to go: whether to the right or to the left. It was beginning to get dark, and Quentin went around and around fruitlessly, unable to find the cornice along which he had passed with Pacheco.

Suddenly he heard the *ding dong* of a bell and supposing it to be that of the convent, he followed the direction of the sound, climbed a ridge pole, and saw beneath him the patio of a convent where several nuns were walking to and fro.

Quentin climbed down the whole side of a roof, found the cornice, and reached the balcony on all fours. The little window was open, and he jumped to the stairs.

There was a little passageway opposite, on one side of which was an open door that led into a kitchen. It was probably the gardener's house; in the middle of the kitchen, seated upon the floor, was a child playing. Upon the wall hung a dirty blouse and an old hat.

"At them!" cried Quentin.

He entered the kitchen, seized the blouse with one hand and the hat with the other, and beat a hasty retreat. The child was frightened and began to cry. Quentin descended the stairs into the garden, and as no one was looking, put on the blouse, stuck the hat on his head, and went out into the street.

He went through alley after alley in the direction of El Matadero and the Campo de San Antón. As night fell, he was already well on his way to Madrid.

Meanwhile in El Cuervo's tavern, everything was excitement and merry making. The news, divulged by Carrahola, that Quentin was there with the money, had attracted all the ruffians who had taken part in Pacheco's chimerical attempt. They thought they would get paid for their services, and El Cuervo trusted them for wine.

They awaited impatiently the arrival of Pacheco, who was later than usual that evening. At eight-thirty he appeared.

"Pacheco! He's come!" they all shouted at once when they saw him.

"Who?"

"Quentin. Here's the pocketbook."

"Did you let him go without following him?" asked the man, fearing a trick.

"Ca!" replied El Cuervo. "He's upstairs. He said not to open the pocketbook until he was with you."

"All right," and Pacheco turned pale. "Tell him I am here."

Pacheco knew from his brother what kind of a man Quentin was, and it irked him. He expected a surprise, and prepared himself accordingly.

El Cuervo went up to the room where he had left Quentin, and called several times:

"Don Quentin! Don Quentin!"

No one answered

"Don Quentin! Don Quentin!"

The same silence.

El Cuervo gently opened the door. The bird had flown. But where?

In response to El Cuervo's cries, Pacheco, Carrahola, and El Taco, came hurrying up the stairs.

"What's the matter?" they asked.

"He's not here."

"That's what I thought!" exclaimed Pacheco. "What can be in the pocketbook? Let's look at it."

They descended rapidly, Pacheco cut the threads, opened the pocketbook, and spilled upon the counter the child's copy papers and Father Ripalda's catechism, worn and shabby.

A cry of rage burst from every throat.

"We must look for him," said one, "and make him pay for this joke."

They ran through the whole house and looked into every corner. Nothing.

"Ah!... Now I know where he went," said the innkeeper, "that way,"—and he pointed to the door in the patio. He lit a lantern and examined the steps one by one to see if there were any tracks in the dust. There was some discussion as to whether the traces they found were Quentin's or not, but when they saw the closed door upstairs, nearly all of them were of the opinion that he could not have passed that way.

"Nevertheless," said El Cuervo, "we'll keep on going." He opened the door, climbed to the attic, and saw the boards which had been torn down to allow free passage to the roof.

"He escaped through here."

"What can we do?" asked Pacheco.

"A very simple thing," replied El Cuervo; "surround this whole block of houses. He is probably waiting for it to get dark before he leaves, so perhaps we can catch him yet."

"Good," said Pacheco; "let's go downstairs right away."

The idea seemed an admirable one to all those who were in the tavern. Pacheco placed them on guard, and told them to warn the watchmen.

With the hope of pay, the whole gang of ruffians firmly stood their posts. Now and then they returned to the tavern for a glass.

Day dawned, and Pacheco's men were still walking the streets, now hopeful, now with no hope at all.

The morning of the following day the rowdies were still on guard, when two lancers came up the street at a smart trot and drew rein before the tavern.

"Is this El Cuervo's tavern?" asked one of them.

"Sí, Señor."

"Good. Here's a letter."

The innkeeper, his face the picture of surprise, took the missive, and as he could not read, handed it to Pacheco, who opened it and read:

*Dear Friends:*

By the time you receive this letter, I shall be many leagues away. I have left Cordova alive, in spite of your warnings. I left no money in the pocketbook, but something better for the salvation of your souls. Regards to my dear friends.

Q.

Pacheco went white with anger.

"Now we can't do a thing," he murmured.

That night in the coterie at the Casino, they were talking about Quentin.

A gentleman was reading the farewell article that Quentin had published in *La Víbora* under the title, "And this is the End."

"Let's hear it; let's hear the end of it," said several.

The gentleman began to read the ending. It went like this:

Adiós, Cordova, City of the Discreet, Mirror of the Pru-

dent, Cross-roads of the Cunning, Nursery of the Sagacious, Encyclopedia of the Witty, Shelter of Those who
Sleep in Straw, Cave of the Cautious, Conclave of the
Ready-witted, Sanhedrim of the Moderate! Adiós, Cordova! And this is the end.

"Fine!" said some one with a laugh. "The fact is, Quentin is a very likable lad."

"He'll prosper."

"Rather!"

"Some day he'll be a deputy."

"Or a minister."

"He really is a most likable boy."

And Escobedo, he of the black beard, who was present, added:

"He who triumphs is always likable."

# CHAPTER XXXIV

## THE END

SIX years after, on the terrace of the Casino at Biarritz, Quentin was listlessly smoking a cigar. They were playing *La Fille de Madame Angot*, and the seducing music and the warm autumn air, made him sleepy.

Upon the table before him was the *liste rose* of an hotel; and among the names of dukes and marquises could be seen: "Quentin García Roelas, Deputy, Madrid." This made Quentin smile as at the memory of a childish vanity.

Quentin's face had changed, especially as to expression; he was no longer a boy; a few wrinkles furrowed his forehead, and crows' feet were beginning to appear at the corners of his eyes. For six years the quondam dare-devil had displayed a tireless activity. He went from triumph to triumph. During Amadeo's reign, he had made his father a marquis; he had amassed a considerable fortune by his operations in the Bourse; and if his political position was not greater, it was because he was keeping quiet, waiting for an Alphonsist or Carlist situation.

And yet, in spite of his successes and his triumphs, his heart was empty. He was thirty-two years old. He could continue the brilliant career he had won for himself, could become a minister, and enter aristocratic society; but all this held no enchantment for him. In the bottom of his heart he realized that he was growing ill-natured. Biarritz bored him frightfully.

"Perhaps the best thing for me to do would be to take an extended voyage," he thought.

With this idea in mind he got up from his chair, left the Casino, and went for a walk along the beach. He was standing near the Place Bellevue watching the sea, when he heard a voice that made him tremble.

It was Rafaela, Rafaela herself, with two children clinging to her hands, and another carried by a nurse and protected by a parasol. Quentin went over to her.

They greeted each other emotionally.

Rafaela was scarcely recognizable; she had taken on flesh and looked extremely healthy; she dressed very elegantly. The only thing that she retained of her former appearance was her sweet, gentle eyes, clear and blue. Her smile was now motherly.

Rafaela and Quentin talked for a long time. She told him of her great grief over the illness of her children. One had died; fortunately the other two children had become stronger, thanks to the open air; and the little girl, the baby at breast, promised to be very strong.

"And Remedios?" asked Quentin.

"Remedios!" exclaimed Rafaela. "You don't know how provoked I am with her."

"Why?"

"Because she has an impossible nature. She will not yield to anything."

"Yes, even as a child one could see that she had a will of her own."

"Well, she has a much greater one now. She has hated my husband and my mother-in-law from the very first; and they have done all in their power to please her and spoil her... but no."

"She is terrible," said Quentin with a smile.

"We wanted to bring her here, and then to Paris; but

at the last minute she refused to come. Then, you see, she is twenty-two years of age, and most attractive; she could marry very easily, for she has suitors,—rich boys with titles; but she will have none of them. She has too much heart. I tell her that one cannot be like that in life; one must conceal one's antipathies, and moderate one's affections, somewhat…. Doing as Remedios does exposes one to much suffering."

"And yet, isn't it almost better to deceive one's self than to find out the truth, at the cost of withering one's heart little by little?"

"I think it is better to know the truth, Quentin."

"I don't know about that. You are as discreet as ever, Rafaela."

"No, I am much more practical than I was. But you, too, have lost something."

"It's true," said Quentin with a sigh.

At this moment an elegantly dressed gentleman, with a white waistcoat and grey gloves, presented himself.

"Don't you know each other? My husband… Quentin, our relative."

The two men shook hands, and they and Rafaela sat down upon a rock while the children played in the sand. Quentin was astonished at the change in Juan de Dios. The rude, coarse lad had been metamorphosed into a correct and polished gentleman with Parisian manners. There was no reminder of the Cordovese gawk.

Juan de Dios spoke pleasantly; Quentin could see that he was dominated by his wife, because every minute or two he glanced at her as if begging her approval of what he was saying. She encouraged him with a gesture, with a look, and he continued. He spoke of the situation into which the Republicans had led Spain, of the factious parties that were organizing on the frontier….

Quentin did not listen to him, as he was thinking about Remedios; that little wilful child, so big-hearted, who despised her suitors. In the midst of their chat, he asked Rafaela:

"Where is Remedios now?"

"On one of our farms, near Montoro."

"I'm going to write to her."

"Yes, do," said Rafaela; "you don't know how happy she would be. She attaches great importance to those matters. She thinks of you very often. She has read every one of the speeches you made in the Cortes."

"Really?" asked Quentin with a laugh.

"Yes, really," replied Juan de Dios.

"What address shall I put on the letter?"

"Just Maillo Farm, Montoro."

Quentin waited a moment while he formulated a plan; then he exchanged a few phrases of farewell with Rafaela and her husband, and went to his hotel. He had decided to take the train and go in search of Remedios. Why not attempt it? Perhaps she had thought about him since childhood. Perhaps that was why she rejected her suitors.

Yes, he must try it. He ordered his baggage packed, boarded the train, and in a few moments got off at San Juan de Luz.

"There's no sure way of crossing to Burgos without getting into trouble," they told him at the station.

"What can I do?"

"Take ship to Santander, and go from there to Madrid by rail."

He did this, and the next day, without stopping, he took the train for Andalusia.

He descended at Montoro in the morning, hired a horse, asked the direction of the Maillo farm, and immediately left town.

It was a foggy October day. It began to sprinkle.

Eight years before Quentin had come to that country on his return from school, on a morning that was also drizzly and sad.

What a wealth of energy and life he had spent since then! True, he had conquered, and was on the road to being a somebody, but—what a difference between the triumph as he had looked forward to it, and the same triumph as he looked back upon it! It was best not to remember, nor to think—but just to hope.

Ahead of him, along the misty horizon, he could see a line of low convex hills. Quentin had been told that he must go toward them, and in that direction he went at the slow pace of his horse. The road wound in and out, tracing curves in the level country between fields of stubble.

Here and there yokes of huge oxen tilled the dark soil; magpies skimmed along the ground; and overhead, flocks of birds like triangles of black dots, flew screeching by.

At this point a man mounted on a horse appeared in the road. He carried a long pike, with the point up and the butt supported by his stirrup, like a lance. He signalled Quentin to get to one side of the road. As he did so, several bulls and bell-oxen rushed past. Behind them rode two *garrochistas* or bull-stickers on horseback, each with a pike held in the middle and balanced horizontally.

"The peace of God be with you, Señores," said Quentin.

"Good morning, *caballero*."

"Am I taking the right direction for the Maillo farm?"

"Sí, Señor; you are right."

"Thanks very much."

Quentin continued his way. Just before he reached the somewhat hilly country, a farmhouse appeared before his eyes. He went up to it, riding his horse across a red field which had been converted into a mud-hole by the rain.

"Hey!" he shouted.

An old man appeared in the doorway; he wore a pair of black leather overalls adorned with white bands, and fastened at the knee by clasps.

"Is this the Maillo farm?" asked Quentin.

"No, Señor. This is the Las Palomas farm, which is owned by the same man. Do you see that hill with the trees on it? When you pass that you can see the farm."

Quentin thanked him and urged on his horse. A drizzly rain was falling. Among the distant trees, which were yellow and nearly bare of leaves, flowed a bluish mist.

From the top of the hill he could see an enormous valley divided into rectangular fields; some still covered with stubble, others black with recently tilled soil, and some that were beginning to turn green. In the middle of it all, like dark and barren islands, were small hills covered with olive orchards; in the distance horses were grazing in huge pastures.

Quentin had stopped for a moment on the top of the hill, hesitating, not knowing which road to take, when he heard behind him a tinkling of bells, and then a voice shouting:

"*Arre*, Liviano! *Arre*, Remendao!"

It was a youth mounted on the haunches of a donkey,

with his feet nearly touching the ground, and leading an ass laden with a pannier by the halter.

"The Maillo farm?" asked Quentin.

"Are you going there? So am I."

The boy began to talk, and chatting like old friends, they reached the farm. It was a huge place, with a very large fence that enclosed all the departments and apparatus of the house. Inside was a chapel with a cross and weather-vane.

"Who can tell me where Señorita Remedios is?" asked Quentin.

"Call the manager."

The manager was not in, and he had to wait. At last a man of some forty years came toward him; he was powerfully built, and round-faced. Learning Quentin's wishes, he pointed to a garden with a little gate at one end of it. Quentin knocked, the gate was opened to him, and an old woman appeared on the threshold.

"Is Señorita Remedios in?"

"It's you!" exclaimed the old woman. "How glad the child will be! Come in, come in!"

"You are Rafaela's nurse, are you not?" asked Quentin.

"Sí, Señor."

They crossed a patio and entered an immense kitchen with a cooking-stove in one corner. Near the fire was a little old man with white hair.

"Don't you know him?" said she who had opened the door. "It is Juan, the gardener of the other house. Juan!" she cried, "Señorito Quentin has come!"

The old man arose and seizing Quentin's hand, held it between his for some time.

"I cannot see well. I'm getting blind and deaf." And Juan burst out laughing.

"You must be getting on in years, eh?"

"Seventy-five. Ha! ha! Sit down here and dry yourself a bit. The little girl will be here soon. It's a long time since you have seen her, isn't it?"

"Six years."

"Well, she's a beauty!... A lily! And then, so affectionate! If you could see her! She is teaching the children of all the farm hands to read and to sew."

"So you are here with her, Juan?"

"Sí, Señor, always with her. All my children are on the place. That's what you ought to do. Señorito: come and live here."

"If I only could," sighed Quentin.

As they were conversing, the door opened, and Remedios came running in.

Quentin rose to his feet and stared at her in surprise.

"It's Quentin!" she cried.

"That's who it is!"

"At last you have come," she added, and held out her hand. "What are you looking at me like that for? Have I changed so very much?"

"Yes, very much."

She was charming in her white dress, which clung to her graceful figure and well-rounded hips. There was a gracious smile on her lips, and her black eyes were shining.

"You are just the same," she said.

"Yes, the same—but older. I saw Rafaela and Juan de Dios in Biarritz. They told me you were here."

342

"And you came here immediately?"

"Yes."

"Very well done. Let's go to the dining-room. I am now the mistress of the house."

They went into the dining-room. It was a large white-washed room, with blue rafters in the ceiling, and a large, unpolished cabinet for the table-service. In the centre was a heavy table of oak, with a white oil-cloth cover, in the middle of which was a glass vase full of flowers. Near the window was an embroidery frame, and a small wicker basket full of balls of coloured yarn.

"Come, sit down," said she. "They'll set the table presently. Why do you look at me so much?"

"You are changed, child; but changed for the better."

"Really?"

"Yes, really; you no longer have that restless look."

A young girl set the table, and Remedios and Quentin sat down. Remedios talked of her life, a most simple one.

"I've already heard that you are giving lessons to the children," said Quentin. "Does that entertain you?"

"Very much. They are all such clever little creatures!"

After dinner, the old servant showed Quentin to a large room with an alcove. He sat down in an armchair, preoccupied. The presence of Remedios had produced a most unusual effect upon him. He felt attracted to her as he had never felt attracted to any other woman. At the same time he was restrained by a feeling of humility; not because she was an aristocrat and he wasn't, nor because she was young and pretty, and he was already growing old; but because he realized that she was good.

"If this visit turns out well," he thought, "how glad I

shall be that I came! But if it does not turn out well, my life will be ruined."

Quentin arose and paced the room for over an hour. He gazed at the Carmen Virgin, with her bead-work shawl, that stood upon the walnut dressing-table; he looked absent-mindedly at the coloured lithographs on the wall, of which some represented scenes from the novel "Matilde, o las Cruzadas," and others, scenes from "Paul et Virginie."

"I must speak to Remedios immediately," he thought.

Having made up his mind, with beating heart he went to look for her. She was sewing in the dining-room.

Quentin seated himself and began to talk on different subjects.

"When are you going to marry?" Quentin suddenly asked her.

"How do I know?" replied Remedios.

"Rafaela told me that you have refused many suitors."

"You see, they want me to marry a man," she replied, "because he has money or a title. But I don't wish to. It makes no difference to me whether he is rich or poor; what I want is for him to be good, for him to have a blind trust in me, as I shall have in him."

"And what do you call being good?" asked Quentin.

"Being worthy, sincere, incapable of treachery, incapable of deceit...."

Quentin fell silent, got up, and returned to his room. There he spent the entire afternoon pacing up and down like a wild beast in a cage.

At supper he said nothing; nor could he eat, no matter how hard he tried. As he rose from the table, he said in a voice choked with emotion:

"Listen, Remedios."

"What is it?" she asked, perceiving his emotion without knowing the cause for it.

"I am going away."

"You are going, Quentin? Why?"

"Because I am not sincere, nor am I capable of self-sacrifice and abnegation."

"Aren't you?"

"No. I am a deceiver, Remedios. I have lied so many times that now I do not know when I am lying, and when I am telling the truth."

"And I believed in you, Quentin," she said sadly.

"Now you know me. I have confessed this to no one but you. I cannot deceive you. No; I would deceive most any one—I'm so used to it!—but not you. Believe me, this is a great sacrifice on my part."

"Aren't you honest, Quentin?"

"Just enough so to keep out of jail."

"And no more?"

"No more. I have been interested in no one but myself. I have been an ingrate."

"Ungrateful too, Quentin?"

"Yes, that too. I am self-centred, a liar, a deceiver.... But even so, Remedios, there are men who have filthier souls than I."

"You hurt me, Quentin."

"What would you? I wished to be rich; and my heart, along with what few good qualities there were in it—if there were any—has gone on withering and being lacerated by the brambles along the road."

"How sad it must be to live like that!"

"Pst!—Not sad.... No. It is like a magic lantern, understand?—Things happen; just happen, and that's all."

"Without love or hate?"

"Without anything."

"Before—when you first met us, were you a deceiver then?"

"That is when I first began."

"Adiós, Remedios. Believe that I have made, with this confession, a very great sacrifice.—Goodbye!" And Quentin held out his hand to her.

She drew back.

"Do I frighten you still?"

"No."

"But won't you give me your hand?"

"No. Not until you are good."

"And then?"

"Then—perhaps."

Quentin left the room with lowered head.

He sat at his window for many hours, smoking.

The night was clear, cool, and soft. The moon silvered the distant hills; a nightingale sang softly in the darkness. A flood of thoughts crowded Quentin's brain.

"Conscience," he said to himself, "conscience is a weakness. What is honesty? Something mechanical. For a woman it is the certainty of living with the mate provided by the Church; for a man, the proof that the money he owns was won by methods not included in books. But another, a higher honesty, such as that girl wants; is it not madness in a world where no one concerns himself with it? This girl has completely upset me."

346

Quentin felt a strong desire to weep at the thought of having been so near happiness. He might have deceived Remedios.... No, he could not have deceived *her*.... Then he would not have been happy. As he thought, the full moon was climbing the heavens; its light, filtering through the leaves of a grape-vine, made beautiful little lace patterns on the ground. He could hear the continuous tinkling of the bells on the goats and cows; now and then there came to him the distant sound of footsteps and voices, the whispering of the wind in the foliage, the lowing of oxen, the neighing of horses and the knocking of the cows' horns against the corral fence.

Suddenly Quentin made up his mind. He must go. It was necessary. He left his room, descended the stairs noiselessly, and made his way to the stable. He lit a lantern, saddled his horse, put on the bridle, and taking the animal by the bit, led him into the patio. He opened the wooden gate and followed the fence until he came to the road.

Quentin mounted and remained for a long time contemplating the front of the farmhouse, which was bathed in the moonlight.

"Ah, poor Quentin," he murmured. "Your sophistry and cunning have been of no avail, here. Are you not good? Then you cannot enter paradise. You are not fighting brokers here, nor politicians, nor insincere folk. But a mere slip of a girl who knows not the world other than what her heart tells her. She has conquered you, you cannot enter paradise."

The horse walked slowly along; Quentin looked back. A great cloud covered the moon; the whole country lay in darkness.

Quentin's heart was heavy within him, and he sighed deeply. Then he had a surprise. He was weeping.

He continued on his way.

Pío Baroja

And the nightingales went on singing in the shadows, while the moon, high in the heavens, bathed the country in its silver light.

El Paular, June, 1905.

THE END